# THE NIGHT RANGERS

## SAVANNAH NIGHTS

# J.R. FROEMLING

The Night Rangers: Savannah Nights

Copyright © 2022 J. R. Froemling
All rights reserved.

Printed in the United States of America

This is a work of fiction.
Names, characters, places, and incidents are used fictitiously.
Any resemblance to actual events, locales, or persons, living or
dead, is entirely coincidental.



Published by The Great Yarn Dragon, LLC
Effingham, IL 62401

ISBN: 978-1-957393-17-9

First Edition: 2022

# OTHER BOOKS BY J.R. FROEMLING

<u>The Wolfe Legacy</u>
>Mistress Giselle - Book One of Hope-Marie
>A Devil's Hope - Book Two of Hope-Marie
>The Naughty List - Book One of Elijah Joseph

<u>Savannah Nights</u>
>The Triple Six
>The Night Rangers
>Poltergeist Girl

<u>Immortal Love Saga</u>
>My Viking Alpha
>My Celtic Luna

To my husband, who is my world.

You bring to life the characters with me in such a way that we will live forever.

I love you.


To my editor, Tirzah!

You did a great job making me step out of my comfort zone and to think about scenes in a way I would never have done before.

Thank you.

# TABLE OF CONTENTS

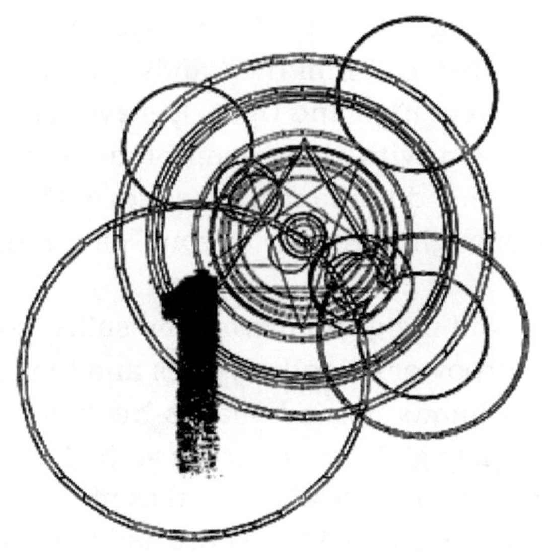



"No. You're crazier than Trevor thought if you think I'm going to let you do this." Jack's Southern drawl grumbles from across the war table. "There has to be another way to lure this fanged fuck out of his hole."

"We tried the other ways, Sir. What did it get us? Desecrated graves, a dead gravedigger, and us being no closer to catching him than we were three months ago, that's what. I can do this. It'll work." I thump my fist down on the table. After staring at Jack, I glance at the other two men present. I'm the only one who thinks this is the way to go. I sigh as I cross my arms and sulk.

"I'm not fucking using you as bait. There's no way I'm going to put my soldiers in that kind of danger." Jack's perfectly pouty lips jut out as he shifts into commander voice.

Jack Talbett is one of the prettiest men I have ever seen.

Trust me, I've seen a lot of soldiers. He's charming, too. It's no wonder they call him the Candyman. He wears his dirty blond hair cut high and tight. His eyes remind me of the Atlantic Ocean with their deep blue color and silver specs. Jack's quiet dominance, coupled with his perfect physique, is enough to make anyone pause in crossing him.

It's hard to hold my ground when he sulks like this. It's one of his superpowers. I roll my eyes and look at Trevor.

He holds his hands up and shakes his head. "Don't be lookin' at me, girly girl. You're crazy as fuck."

Trevor's brassy Chicago accent makes me smile. Tattoos cover him from head to toe. There isn't a trace of his natural black hair as his head is freshly buzzed, revealing the tattoos on his scalp. His mustache and goatee make me want to tug on it. Soul patch, he calls it. How does a man who misses nothing when shooting miss how terrible that patch of hair looks? His piercing brown eyes are sharp as he stares at me. I half expect him to start crossing himself. His superstitions can get out of hand. If he looks at a black cat he spends two days performing all the rituals he can think of to protect against the furry demon.

With a huff, I look to our demolitions expert and my favorite of the group, Buck. No one knows if that's his first name, last name, or nickname. His flirt game might be weak as hell, but he's a beast of a man. Clocking in at six foot six with shoulders twice as broad as mine, I can't believe he passed the size requirements for training. His soft green eyes remind me of moss growing over stone. I've seen a picture of his wavy, unruly hair when he grows it out; but, like the rest of the guys, the top of head is buzzed tight.

"Awe, c'mon." Buck shakes his head. "Don't drag me into

this. You two sort it out. I'll blow the shit up. That's the deal. I'm shit for making plans. You know that." He holds his hands up to say he's out.

That leaves me, Tabitha Murphy, Murphy for short. I'm the new guy. A demon possessed the last guy and drove him bat-shit crazy, leaving this team without their healer. Technically, I'm more the close-quarters, sneak attack, rune maker. I'm no Half Divine, but I learn fast and have an affinity for magic. With a snort, I cross my arms. "All in favor of the plan, raise your hand."

"I abstain," Buck and Trevor throw out faster than I had hoped.

"Great. That means we're doing it." I chirp.

"Hold up there, Murphy. They're out, so it's just you and me, and my vote counts twice. We're not doing it."

"That's not how democracy works."

"This ain't a democracy." Jack crosses his arms and shrugs.

"You would think someone called the Candyman would be sweeter than this."

All three men erupt into laughter at me pouting and sulking. Then I grin at the joke and laugh with them.

The tension breaks, and we relax.

Once the moment passes, I look down at the map, palming the table. Buck comes closer and presses against me while pretending to read the map.

"Do you have a better plan, Jack? We have been at this for months with nothing to show for it. I don't think there's any other way to get him to come out and play." I chew against my lip in thought, then smirk. "Unless you think he's into dudes?"

I look up to find Jack staring at me, frowning, fear swimming in his eyes like the tide rushing in.

I hate this macho, protect the girl, bullshit. I'm every bit a soldier he is. He isn't seeing me. He's seeing Kevin, the guy they found out after-the-fact was a descendant of an angel. When the demon got to Kevin, it caused his angelic side to fall, rendering him a threat to humanity. He turned on Jack, Buck, and Trevor, forcing them to murder him. He was responsible Kevin's safe return home, and he failed.

"I'm not him. I'll be smart. I'll get runed up and keep a weapon on me."

"You think he'll show up with you wearing tactical gear?" Jack's brow raises as he crosses his arms.

My eyes roll so hard it hurts. "Of course not. I said a weapon on me. It's not like I'm going out there in my Superman cape. If you don't want to do this plan, then we pack our shit and go home. Tell the Iscariot we can't help and that they can go play nice with the Van Helsings. You really want to let those English fucks crow about catching the big bad vampire the yanks are afraid of?"

"Fuck that noise." Buck butts in.

I bite my lip hard to keep from smirking. His ego is as big as the rest of him.

"I say we parade her ass right on out there and blow the fanged fucker to mist." He waves his hand in my general direction, but he's looking at jack and puffing like a bull about to attack the red cape.

Jack narrows his eyes and shakes his head. "Buck, stop thinkin' with your dick, man. You blow him up; you blow her up. Then who are you going to jack off to?" To Trevor, "Could you take the shot? In the dark? That's what three, three-twenty?"

Trevor twists the toothpick between his teeth, rolling it between two fingers as he eyes the map. "I need a few days to scope it out. We weren't planning on dealing with this part of the city. The holy rollers ain't gonna like it."

"You let me deal with the Iscariot. You have three days. Meanwhile, you two, keep your hands to yourselves. Buck, you prep for containment. You," he says as he points to me.

I bat my eyelashes to look as innocent as possible.

"You fucking wipe that grin off your face. If Trevor says he can't get a clean shot from any angle, we scrap the plan and come up with a new one. You're heading to the library to brush up on your runes. Talk to Rowena Harper." Jack glances at his watch and sighs. "I'll talk with Cardinal Renford in the morning."

Buck and Trevor give each other a look before they run. Cowards.

Jack rubs his hand over his face. "Murphy, you don't have to prove yourself. This is what, our third, or fourth, mission together?"

"It's not about proving myself, Jack. It's about being the right man for the job. We know he has an affinity for young, pretty girls who wander away from crowds. He won't mess with a girl who has a guy on her arm. And he knows the Iscariot. You saw him abandon his hunt and vanish the moment he got a whiff of one of those holy rollers."

"This isn't like Monaco. This beast is older. We have no idea what he can do and how fast he can do it. One thing goes wrong, and you're a sitting duck. Or worse."

I come around the table and rest my hand on Jack's shoulder. "No fear, Jack. That's what you said when I joined the team. I'm not afraid to face the bad guys. You can't be afraid, either. I need you on my six. We're in this together, and if Trevor says he can't take the shot, we'll find another way. I'm crazy, not stupid."

"That's the problem, Tabitha. You should be quaking in your boots. These monsters are dangerous. Just because we understand we have to fight them doesn't mean we're not afraid. Fear keeps you alert. Keeps you sharp."

"You're wrong, Jack. Fear makes you dumb. It paralyzes you. It makes you take the safe path, not the right one. We're all that stands between these monsters and humanity." All the jovial banter leaves my tone as I square up to face off with my commander. "You are so hung up on losing Kevin you can't think about how to use us right. You need to trust us to do our jobs when the time comes. You have to be willing to take the risk to get the reward, Sir."

He studies me in silence for several seconds. "Fine, we'll do it your way. But, if anything goes wrong, we are there to protect you. Not to kill him. Do I make myself clear?"

"Crystal. But if you have the shot, take it. Don't let this fangy fuck get away because you're sweet on me." I flash him a smile.

"Don't you worry. Cause when things go bump in the night…"

"We bump back."

"Hoo-Ah." It sounds more like an amen than the army's call back.

# PLANS ARE FOR SUCKERS

Three days is an eternity when you're waiting.

This Rowena woman terrifies me. The first night we spent together, I cracked a joke about runes and tattoos.

This caused her to launch into a lecture about how yanks are the devil and take nothing seriously. She lit up like the Rockefeller Christmas tree and blew me across the room with a rune no larger than my palm.

After that, I stuffed the jokes and buckled down. In the end, I came to appreciate that Rowena Harper is a stern but brilliant teacher.

"Yer human brain cannot understand the complexities of offensive runes yet. We're gonna stick to the stuff yer capable of. This rune is to keep yer mind sharp. Vampires ken how to muddle your thoughts and make ya believe its yer idea."

Her Irish brogue keeps the smile plastered on my face,

even if she's insulting me. It's like listening to the Lucky Charms leprechaun.

"This one, here, it brings the blessin' o' Paul. Givin' ya the strength to persevere."

I nod and trace them with my fingers, going slow at first. Rune magic is all about details. One slight blip and your rune sends a person flying when they should have been encased in a protective shield. My journal is full of the runes we have access to in the archives. These runes are more intricate, commanding more focus to create, and provide far more power than I've ever used before. I'm drained after practicing them for a few hours.

Rowena doesn't explain how she can do them effortlessly, but my guess is she's a Half Divine. Half Divines are descendants of divine beings. Traditionally speaking, it's the Christian Pantheon, but the others could manifest. Cardinal Renford, the current leader of the Iscariot, isn't beyond using whatever holy means he can lay his hands on.

I told Jack I wasn't afraid because that's what he needed to hear. The truth is I'm terrified. That man already carries the weight of the world on his shoulders. I'm not about to contribute to it by pointing out all the flaws in our plan, talking about what happens if it goes wrong, or even that I'm afraid to be put out there alone. This operation is dangerous and terrible. Trevor says he can take the shot, but I'm still worried. If he's even one second too late, then our entire plan goes up in smoke.

I stare in the mirror and barely recognize the woman staring back. I had hoped this dress was for our victory celebration when we caught this vampire.

If you could call this a dress.

I'm a highly trained, decorated soldier who can kill

people with my bare hands. Yet, here I am, in two scraps of clothing that Forever 21 calls a dress. My hot mess of curly hair is pinned into a mohawk, pooling down my back like tendrils of fire. After a quick lip pop, my gloss is perfect. With a sigh, I remind myself this was my idea, so I can't be too put out.

The idea is to behave like an American girl in Venice: party too hard and wander off alone. It's stupid and reckless. Jack was right; I'm trying to prove myself to the guys. Maybe I'm trying too hard. If it weren't for the long hours with Rowena placing protection runes in every viable location of my person, I would not be doing this.

My heels tick on the old stone floor as I head to the war table. My mother comes to mind. Her quiet strength, even when she was dying carries me forward. She had been the glue of our family and passed the torch onto me. Jack, Trevor, and Buck are my family now, and I refuse to let them down because I'm getting cold feet. I fold the envelope in half in my hand. I still haven't decided who to give my just-in-case letter to. The hardest part of being a part of a top-secret special-ops team is not being able to write home about what is going on in my life. The contrast between the men in their tactical gear and this scrap of fabric I'm wearing makes me feel naked.

Buck whistles low and stares at me with narrowed, hungry eyes the entire time I walk down the stairs.

Trevor and Jack exchange money and grin.

"Hot damn, Murphy. You look pretty enough to give candy to," Jack drawls.

Trevor pats his hand rapidly against his chest.

"Yeah. Yeah. Laugh it up. Where's my ride?" My cheeks flush from the compliments, and the bile in my stomach settles down. Covering up fear with brash bravado is this team's go-to coping mechanism. Doc Ford would have a field day with today's plan.

"Waiting outside. Holy rollers already took off to get in position. Your driver will drop you off at the party, and then it's all you. Stick to the plan. Don't deviate. If it gets too hot, abort. We all go home." Jack barks in commander mode.

"Hoo-Ah," we call back.

When Jack and Trevor head to the truck, I catch Buck's arm. "Hey, big fella. Do me a favor?"

He pauses as I catch his arm.

His strength lends me courage and I give him a smile.

"Anything. So long as you let me see you in that dress stateside." His soft green eyes trail down my body and he wriggles his brows at me.

"Cute," I snort. "I'm being serious. Look. In case tonight goes..." I hold the folded letter out to him. "It's for my old man."

Buck's body stiffens and his playful smile fades into a stern grimace as he takes the letter. "You ain't dyin' tonight, Tabitha. If I have to blow up all of fucking Rome, you are not dying tonight." He pulls me into a hug and kisses my forehead.

My heart races and I smile, relishing in his tender gesture. For a massive brute of a man, he knows how to make a girl feel cherished.

We are breaking the rules. Fraternization is frowned upon in the squads because emotional attachments become liabilities in the field. That hasn't stopped us from pretending to just be buddies while fucking like bunnies. So I linger in his gentle embrace enjoying the brief reprieve it brings. Before I let him go, I inhale sharply to get one last scent of Buck to keep with me for the evening..

He catches up with the rest of Shadow Squad, leaving me alone in the foyer to wonder what I have gotten myself into.

My gaze focuses on the crucifix tacked above the door with a motto in Latin. The words bring me comfort, and I cross myself before following the team.

Only a small car with a driver waits for me. On the ride to the piazza, I stare out the window, taking in the ancient sights of this beautiful city of Rome..

"Are you meeting someone tonight?" the driver asks. His Italian accent is so thick that it takes me a moment to recognize he's speaking English.

"No. I'm on an adventure! Just graduated and came to Europe to celebrate!"

"Someone as beautiful as you should never be alone." His gaze shifts from the road to the rearview mirror as he takes in an eyeful. "I hope you enjoy the festivities tonight." He pulls into the drop-off location.

After handing him far too much money, I bounce out of his cab like I can't wait any longer to get to the fun.

The piazza twinkles under the strands of lights strewn across in a hap-hazard pattern. Glow stick jewelry halos figures in the crowd to make them look like neon angels as the young and beautiful pulse to the music. Amongst the angels are demons swathed in black clothes, holding trays full of pill cocktails and booze. Strobe lights flicker above the crowd giving an eerie stutter effect on the otherwise fluid movements of the ravers.

Someone gives me a cold glass filled with liquid as a hand on the small of my back guides me into the masses. I go with it. I have no intention of drinking whatever I'm holding, but I bring it to my lips and look like I am. As the music grows louder and faster, I bump and grind with the crowd, allowing it to slosh out of the cup.

Minutes tick by, and my skin crawls with the nagging sensation of being watched. I push my way through the sea of bodies. Sweaty and breathless, I finally emerge from the masses to see the make-shift bar.

I giggle as Buck jokes in my earpiece about how unfair it is he has to watch from the shadows. Jack scolds him for complaining. I haven't seen a single Iscariot yet, but the crowd is heavy, and they'll be blending in. The nagging feeling of being watched makes me shudder. Even though I know my boys are watching me and will do everything to keep me safe, the hairs on the back of my neck stand on end.

After getting another drink, I fall back into the crowd. My body stiffens when the rune on my hand begins to glow, confirming the nagging sensation that I'm in danger.. Even if it isn't the vampire we're after, something has tried to get me to comply with its wishes.

Leaving the crowd, I head in the designated direction. With every nerve in my body on edge, I decide I need a little liquid courage and take a sip of my drink.. The runes running up my arms flare to life and then flit away like ashes. Any normal person would panic and attempt to flee. My heart beats faster, and I continue forcing myself to walk forward, hoping to draw whatever is pursuing me from the shadows.

"Oh, you precious girl. Did you really think those would work against me?" His voice is rich and purring, like a tiger creeping out of the tall grass. He isn't chuckling, but there's amusement in his voice.

The runes on my chest burn to life, revealing they're providing me what little protection they can offer.

Resisting the urge to stop moving, I swallow hard and fish out the only weapon I have, a small silver stake. If I can pierce the vampire's skin with it, we can track the beast.

The runes on my chest flit away in ashes as I shift to face the monster following me. Averting my eyes from his face, I look at his chest as he comes close enough to slide an arm around my waist.

He doesn't look like a monster. The business suit he's wearing gives him the appearance of a typical white-collar worker..

Runes flare to life left and right. As my defenses fall away. my will's succumbing to the sweet song in my ears.

Obey. Comply. Submit.

"Murphy!" Jack roars, but it's muffled and distant like a dream.

"Fuck. Take the Goddamn shot!" Buck's voice follows.

"Where the fuck are they?"

The vampire smiles at me and it seems odd his chest is warm and enticing. The desire to submit to him grows ever stronger.

"I promise, my little firecracker, you will enjoy this. Be a good girl, and I'll give you what you deserve."

The last rune lights up on my forehead.

I tilt my head and press against him. My body responds to him as though I were holding onto Buck. My heart races. My skin flushes with anticipation. My muscles tighten from fear. I'm helpless to resist now and can only hope Trevor takes the shot.

The vampire's lips kiss against my neck, and I fade into bliss, pure bliss.

I moan. My hand wavers as he sucks against my neck, and my body trembles against him as the best fucking orgasm I have ever had courses through me. My eyes close.

I'm too close to stake him in the chest with how he cradles me to him. I do, however, manage to jab the stake into his side.

The rune on my forehead burns as it disintegrates, leaving me completely defenseless.

When he growls in pain, the bliss I felt seconds ago turns to agony.

I scream in pain.

Our bodies suddenly jerk and I register that it must be Trevor's round that hit the vampire.

I can't catch my breath. Large, hot tears roll down my cheeks.

The vampire pulls back from my neck and snarls at me, his lips stained with my blood. He doesn't let go of me, and I'm too exhausted to fight.

"Go! Go! Go! Where the fuck are they?" Jack shouts. "No! Buck, you'll kill her. Fuck! Buck!"

Wherever the vampire takes it, it's too dark for me to see. White pain racks my body and paralyzes any movement from me. His murderous gaze tells me he has no intention of leaving me here, as he had with his previous victims.

He rips the round from his neck. The UV and silver nitrate concoction spread through his veins like black ink. He jerks me closer and sinks his teeth into me again.

It's pure torture this time. Every fear I have ever had conjures itself at once. Every doubt. Every insecurity. If it brought me any kind of suffering, it's now happening tenfold. My skin burns like it's being ripped from the muscle. I can't breathe or move. I sob, begging for him to make it stop. The agony reduces me from a highly trained soldier to a blubbering young woman.

The movies don't tell you about the dark side of vampire kisses. In addition to insane ecstasy, they can also bring excruciating pain. Vampire venom will manifest your deepest, darkest fears in your mind until you are nothing but a dried husk of insanity.

I cling to my tormentor as my head swims. I have lost too much blood. My heart thunders in my chest as it struggles to pump the blood that isn't coming.

The alcove lights up with a booming bang.

I scream, too terrified for rational thoughts. My body crumples to the ground as it's suddenly released. The last thing I see before I succumb to unconsciousness is a black cloud of bats fleeing like the wind.

## STAY WITH ME

"Medic!" Jack shouts as the team rushes into the building. "We need a medic!"

Cardinal Renford descends the steps. His eyes narrow in disapproval at the four-man team causing a ruckus inside one of the Vatican's sacred spaces. In a blink of an eye, he assesses the situation. With a motion of his hand, his men spring into action. Buck refuses to let go of me, and they're forced to guide him to the treatment room.

My eyes flutter open and all I see is the blurry outline of Buck.

"I got you, baby girl. You're safe." His deep voice whispers to me from far away.

I close my eyes again. He could have been the vampire standing before and I would not have the strength to react. My whole body is heavy and racked by phantom pain.

"Put her there, strap her down." The Iscariot medic

barks at Buck.

Buck obeys. The cold, hard surface feels like stone against my skin and makes me shiver. I barely register the apology he murmurs as he binds my wrists and ankles. A strap tightens   across my chest and I groan.

"Was she bitten more than once?"

"Don't know. Don't think so. We shot the fuck when he bit her."

The Iscariot forces something hard into my mouth and ties it in place. Another medic comes in with bags of blood on one tray and bags of holy saline on the other.

"What's all that for?" Buck growls at the two men.

"We have to burn the poison out of her system. With how much blood she's lost, the process will kill her. Our only chance is to give her both at the same time. Even so, she'll be lucky to survive the night."

"No!" Buck roars. "She can't die! I promised her. I'll fucking gut you if she doesn't make it."

Before he can get around the table to the medic, Trevor grabs him, holding him back. "Calm down, Buck. Ain't gonna do anyone any good if you kill the guys helping her."

Buck continues to struggle. He pushes against Trevor, still trying to get to the Iscariot.

Trevor keeps Buck under control until an Iscariot jabs a tranquilizer into Buck's neck.

He growls in pain, and then subdues, swaying in front of Trevor. Someone produces a chair. He sits roughly, trying to fight the sedative.

"Just relax, man. We got her. Ain't nobody gonna kill our girl." Trevor says to convince Buck as much as himself.

Monitors beep to life as the medics attach electrodes to my body. My heart struggles to keep up with the lack of blood flow, and my heart rate monitor is barely making a sound.

Two medics move around me turning my arm and injecting IV ports. They give me blood first, in a desperate attempt to get my heart rate to a safe level.

Someone turns my head abruptly, while pushing my hair out of the way. The holes from where I was bitten are open and draining. The monster didn't even bother to close the wounds. "We need saliva," the medic calls to the room.

Trevor sticks with Buck, watching the scene unfold.

A young boy races from the room, returning seconds later with a small vial.

The Iscariot pops it open and generously dabs it over the open wounds.

For his efforts, the Iscariot is rewarded with my shrieks of pain. My eyes fly open from the    adrenaline shock, but I still don't understand what is happening. The agony is too great and overwhelms my senses. The only thing going through my mind is I need it to stop as    I struggle like a worm on a hook against the restraints.

The monitor next to me blares an alarm to match the erratic pace of my now-racing heart. The painful burning in my neck radiates through the rest of my body. My pupils are dilated and I can't see anything. All I feel is terror.

"Fuck! You're hurting her." Buck's voice shifts between roaring in rage at the Iscariots and soothing to me. "Tabby, baby, calm down. We got you. You're safe. Come on, baby. Fix her already!"

"Sit down." Trevor shoves Buck. "They can't help her if you go berserk on them. She's screaming. Means she's breathing. She's a tough little bird. Trust her man." He glances back to watch the medics work while keeping a hand on Buck.

The commotion spurs me to struggle more, but my efforts are feeble. Black spots dance in my eyes as darkness threatens to settle in once more.

"Tabitha, I need you to calm down." A stern but soothing voice cuts through the fog of terror. His Italian accent rolls as he speaks, calming me down. "We are replacing the blood you lost. A vampire bit you. If you keep resisting us, you will die. Tell me you understand."

"Under...Stood." I stutter out as I try to force myself to ignore the pain still terrorizing my body.

"You are still under the kiss's influence. Breathe. This is going to hurt."

The room continues to darken. The voices around me are fading.

Why are the lights off?

Oh, God. I've turned. They're trying to stop the process. They're going to murder me.

"Saline's good. Line's open." The same voice penetrates the fog again.

This new pain is far worse than anything the vampire could have forced on me. It's fire searing through my veins. White hot, burning pain seeps from the port and rages like rapids up through my arm. My struggles start anew as more restraints are added.

"Stop. Stop. Please. Oh, God. I don't want to die. Please," I beg. Every new drop of saline in my system is a fiery new path of pain I follow.

"Tabby," Buck calls to me.

"Buck, help me," I croak, unable to see him in the darkness. Hearing his voice makes me want to unleash the beast of a man on every person in here. "Please. Make 'em stop. Please."

"Get him out of here," the stern voice commands.

"Fuck if I'm leaving. What are you fucks doing to her?" Buck snarls like a rabid beast.

"Blessed saline. It burns the kiss out of her system and stops the addiction." The lead medic doesn't take his eyes from monitoring the process.

Buck and Trevor stop struggling against each other and both men stare in silence. The holy saline had not been done outside of the Iscariot. The horror stories of what happens to a person when they undergo the treatment are enough to make both men stare in fear.

"Fuck," Trevor breathes.

"How long?" Buck's voice cracks.

"Seventy-two hours. Maybe more. She's lost a lot of blood. If she makes it through the night, I'll reassess in the morning."

"If?" Buck narrows his eyes. "You had better fucking make sure she makes it through the night."

"Easy, Buck. He's doing the best he can."

"No. Those fucks weren't there to stop him from biting her. They don't get a fucking pass now. Where the fuck were you?"

Trevor squares up against Buck and pushes him out the door before he loses all sense of control. "Not the right people to be pissed at. Let's find Jack and rip that dickhead Cardinal a new asshole."

Buck's soft green eyes burn with rage as his jaw twitches, his nostrils flare, and his chest heaves from the efforts to not turn into the Incredible Hulk and smash every person in this room, Trevor included.

Trevor trying to reason with him is like trying to move a mountain with his bare hands. It's taking all his strength to keep the threatening locomotive of Buck from jumping right off the tracks into murder town.

Tabitha's tormented shrieking is only muffled by the door shut behind the two men. "No. I'm not leaving her side."

"You ain't fucking right, man. You can't stay in there if you're going to kill them for doing their job. Get your shit together! Those men in there are all you got to keep her alive."

Buck's fists clench and unclench. His weight shifts from one foot to the other. He doesn't even care about his self-inflicted wound from trying to save Tabitha. Several beats pass in silence before he grumbles like a scolded child. "I won't kill 'em."

Trevor sighs and shakes his head. "Get your wrist fixed. Calm the fuck down. Our girl's gonna be alright." He hesitates, then turns to find Jack and Cardinal Renford. His search is short-lived. He hears Jack's voice echoing down the hallway as he tears into Renford.

"Where the fuck were your men? We had a fucking plan. If your men had been in place, we wouldn't be in this situation!"

"Language, Mr. Talbett, you are in the house of God. My men were exactly where I told them to be. I knew you gung-ho Americans would try to enact this reckless plan and make a mess of things. So I put my men where they would be most valuable, hunting down the monster at his lair." Cardinal Renford's northern English accent cracks like a whip. Disdain for his American counterparts drips like venom from a snake's fang.

"If it weren't for her, you wouldn't even fucking know where his lair is, you God damn prick! You dangled her out as bait, fully willing to let him fucking murder her to get what you wanted."

"You will not use the Lord's name in vain!" Renford bellows. "I did what was necessary to complete God's mission of eradicating the world of these monsters. One foot soldier in the crusade is an acceptable loss. Her sacrifice will not be forgotten. Now, I have work to do." He waves a delicate bony hand to dismiss the crude soldier before him.

The pistol sheathed on Trevor's thigh sings to him as his hand rests over the holster. He could kill the man with a single shot. This holy roller was anything but holy. After hearing he deliberately left Murphy high and dry, Trevor wants to kill him just to prove that no one does that to his team. When he hears    the telltale slap of skin hitting skin followed by a grunt, Trevor rushes    forward, giving away that he was listening.

Jack stands over the Cardinal with clenched fists, and the Cardinal holding a hand to his eye.

"You had better fucking hope she lives. Or so help me, Cardinal, a black eye will be what you beg for by the time I get done with you." Jack spits on the man and storms out of the office.

# I WANT TO ROCK

Night Ranger Base: Undisclosed Location

I sit at the big oddly shaped table with my guys, two stuffed-shirt doctors, and General Armstrong. Rather than a uniform, I'm in a slashed pair of jeans, and one of Buck's old sweatshirts. My hair is swept up in an unkempt ponytail, and I haven't touched my make-up bag since Italy. I glance at my watch for the millionth time today to remind me what day it is.

Two weeks have passed since the Iscariot let me out of their hell-hole sanctuary. I have not been cleared for duty. None of us are in uniform, other than Armstrong. The guys have been enjoying the down time as I work to get my shit together..

This meeting is an after-action report. They're worried about my sudden onset of night terrors, and Doc Ford is chomping at the bit to document my progress after the holy water treatment.

My biggest fear today is that this meeting is to retire me from service. If that happens, I'll have no choice but to suffer my father's disappointment. He couldn't believe I made it into Ranger training. He was even in more disbelief when I told him I made it. Night Ranger clearance is beyond most Generals' purview, and it kills me that if they kick me out, he'll only know I failed.

"It would seem you succeeded in not only locating the vampire and his nest, but also in enraging the good Cardinal. I believe his words are, and I quote," General Armstrong chortles as he pulls up a hand-written letter. "Your renegade degenerates made a mess of my city. Causing such a commotion that even the Vatican took notice. Between whoring and cursing, your squad's Neanderthal leader accosted me." The rich, grandfatherly voice sputters in mock indignation.

Keeping our composure at the angry words of Cardinal Renford is more an impossible task than bringing a vampire back to life. Jack is the least successful as he makes snorting noises.

Armstrong sets the letter down and turns his steely gaze on us. Having a grandfather stricter than the Ten Commandments allowed me not to wilt under his gaze.

General Armstrong has wavy silver hair that never gets out of place, pale blue eyes that pierce right into your soul, and enough wrinkles to rival Gandalf the Grey. Even though he's been our fearless leader for as long as anyone can remember, he still gives me the heebie-jeebies. Right now his frowning gaze is leveled at me.

It doesn't matter how much training I have had. His piercing gaze makes the holy saline adventure feel like a vacation. "Sir, it was my—." I start to take the blame.

"It was all me, Sir."

I whip my head around to stare at Jack as he cuts me off.

"We had a solid, albeit risky, plan, and I made the call. My team executed to perfection. I accept full responsibility for the shit show."

"It was me, Sir. I made the call saying I could take the shot."

"I threw the UV grenade, causing the alley to light up pre-maturely."

The room has erupted into chaos as all three of them talk at once, throwing their hats in as the guilty party for why this mission went sideways.

Guilt gnaws at me. It was my plan that I forced down their throats.

Jack winks at me before turning back to Armstrong.

Armstrong stairs at us for what feels like an eternity as he silently measures the four off us. His expression is etched in a scowl before a devilish grin appears on his face. "I believe Cardinal Renford is perhaps retaliating to your response to his lack of support he agreed to when we sent you to Italy. After reading your reports, the Iscariot were nowhere to be found when the monster attacked, and Cardinal Renford believes losing a non-Iscariot asset was acceptable in catching the beast."

"I'm truly sorry for what happened to you, Tabitha," his tone shifts to that of a doting grandfather, even if he stares at me with the General's stoic gaze. "Your swift actions allowed the Iscariot to track the beast to his nest. They destroyed not only him, but four other vampires he had sired as well."

I exhale and nod respectfully.

"Now, to the matter of your next mission." He closes one file and opens a new, much thicker one. "Doctor Ford, have you assessed Lieutenant Murphy's progress?"

The mousy woman with glasses too big for her nose and the straightest hair I have ever seen, clears her throat and sits up straighter. "I have. We exposed her to subject mv-438024. The holy water treatment was successful in eliminating any traces of addiction to the kiss."

"Good. Good. So that—."

"However," she cuts Armstrong off. "We noted the subject was immediately drawn to Lieutenant Murphy when presented with six other viable options as well."

"Wait. You're tellin' me those fanged fucks are going to target Murphy now?" Buck roars to life next to me as he slams his hands on the table and pushes himself to his full height. His voice booming off the walls.

Doctor Ford clears her throat and looks nervously from one face to the next.

I'm intrigued. I don't remember being exposed to a vampire in the last two weeks.

"And you are sure this was not due to her being a woman?" General Armstrong asks the doctor.

"Yes, Sir. All patients were women."

It's suddenly too hot. I can't breathe. My ears ring like Buck just threw a grenade. Every voice in the room has turned into a Peanuts adult. It only took two seconds to take me from rockstar soldier to two-bit lab rat.

Jack and Trevor hold onto Buck for dear life to keep him from pulling the good doctor over the table. All three of my guys shouts and chest-puff as this meeting has gone completely off the rails.

I'm paralyzed. The boiling rage burns me from inside out only to be quenched by the tidal wave of fear. My eyes settle on General Armstrong.

His piercing gaze stares right into the depths of my soul,

judging me. He does nothing but stare at me, creating an infuriatingly calm eye of the Shadow Squad hurricane around us.

Doctor Ford cowers in her chair as she pushes away from the table. Her body poised to flee for the door, should Buck get free of Jack & Trevor. The other doctor furiously takes notes.

All the while General Armstrong and I remain locked in our staring contest.

I don't like it. He knows something about me I don't, and instead of putting us all at ease, he lets us bark like hyenas shredding a helpless zebra.

"Enough!" he finally bellows. His voice reverberates off the room like the voice of God coming down from on high.

My guys fall silent and I hold my breath, expecting all of us to be reprimanded.

"Sit," he orders. "We need to assess how compromised your teammate is before sending you on the next mission. That is, unless you would like another support specialist, Major Talbett?"

"No Sir," Jack answers without hesitation.

"Good. As the doctor was attempting to explain, Lieutenant Murphy offers a unique advantage. While she cannot be lured in by the addiction of the vampire's kiss, the creatures will be drawn to her, allowing your team to be in control of the situation."

My life is going to suck from here on out.

When I joined the military, I was planning on one tour and being done so I could go to college and not disappoint my old man. Then Armstrong walked through our front door.

To those without clearance, my uniform says I'm an Army Ranger. Everyone questions everything about me as there are no women in the Rangers.

To those with clearance, the special patches designating my rank would tell them exactly who I am and what I stand for.

Armstrong senses my hesitancy. "Of course, that is only if you believe you are still Night Ranger material, Lieutenant Murphy."

I'm not ready. Nowhere near ready. Every time I close my eyes I'm in that dark alcove in Italy, feeling my body being ripped to shreds, crushed, and set on fire all at once. Shadows shifting make me afraid that vampire somehow survived and is stalking me. My body breaks into a sweat and my hand trembles. I rub my palms on my jeans, hoping no one sees my fear..

Jack looks at me with a grim yet neutral expression.

Trevor looks at me like I'm a victim.

Buck looks hopeful. It will just kill him if we don't get back to work.

The pressure to be strong here is monumental.

Even though it's 2003, women in the military are kind of like pariahs. The Night Rangers is an exception to the norm and women have been a part of the organization from the start. General Sherman, during the Civil War actively sought women as they're more in tune with magic. General Armstrong has not deviated in his recruitment.

Failure isn't an option for me now. "I'm ready to rock, Sir." I flash a grin and put all my normal brass behind it. Sure, I'm a scrambled eggs on the inside, but duty calls.

The collective exhale makes me feel better until I realize I'll have to tell the guys the truth at some point.

"With that settled, your next mission is in New York City." General Armstrong briefs us on the details and scope of our mission.

I furrow my brow. New York City is Patrick Howell's territory. He's the current vampire representative of The Accord.

When General Sherman made his great push to the Atlantic ocean during the Civil War, he was not just fighting the rebels, he vanquished the demons they summoned to win the war. When he won the battle, he formed a peace accord with Mehzebeen, the vampire who helped him, and Jedediah Belmont. They pulled in the werewolves, and the Alpha of the Appalachian pack signed it as well.

This Accord is the peace treaty between the United States and the underworld that has held since Sherman's march to the sea. Savannah is the haven designated to underworld creatures, protected by Mehzebeen, and there are sovereign rights they hold there. However, all members of the Accord are afforded those rights. So long as peace is kept, and humans are not in danger.

Patrick Howell didn't join the Accord until the late 1920s when he murdered the existing clan leader. Lucien Deveroux came in the 1960s but has been in Louisiana since it was sold to the United States. Unless something has happened in the past two weeks, as far as I know Patrick Howell has not violated the accord.

I shift in my seat, uneasy with violating the treaty without a good reason. General Armstrong has no intention of notifying Howell of our presence. Howell's a lawyer, and his ingénue, Sabine, is a viper. She has earned her title, The Blue Dragon.

With a quick look at Jack, he's ticking through the same thought process. His jaw twitches, and his hands are clasped in front of him as he listens.

The Night Rangers already dance a fine line, conducting missions on U.S. soil, and not notifying the leader of a city of our presence violates the Accord outright.

"You will ship out in three days. Until then, you are granted leave." Armstrong closes the file and dismisses us.

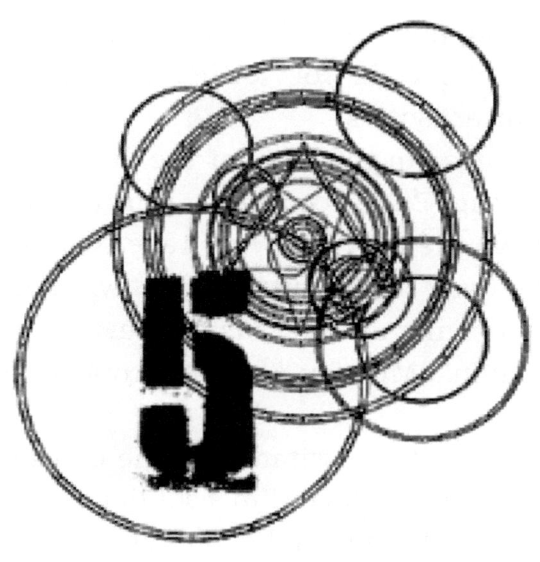

# HEADS, SOUTH CAROLINA

Leave means one thing: Savannah.

Being an elite hunter leaves lots of places less than safe for our kind. Vegas is completely off limits with the state of the vampire politics in the desert. West of the Mississippi and the underworld is the wild west. It's survival of the strongest and money talks. Show your ranger badge in Sin City, and you're likely to become a snacky treat for some whale of a vampire. California is barely better, with the chi-sucking vampires.

Savannah is the Underworld Mecca. Vampires, werewolves, and everything else not human knows that Savannah is relatively safe.

Why Savannah? It has something to do with General Sherman and Mehzebeen, and all the mumbo jumbo of The Accord. That, and Jack's from Savannah. He keeps singing this song about a strip joint with the prettiest girls he has ever laid eyes on, and the old man who owns it is good to his guests. That's code for letting patrons partake in extracurricular activities.

We load our gear in the back of the Suburban Jack and Trevor are taking. Buck accordions into the driver's seat of the Blazer we are in. We always take two vehicles, just in case. Either way, we're hitting up Savannah for a day or two before driving up the coast to New York City.

"How you doin', Murphy?" Buck's tone is gentle and quiet.

I know I shouldn't be irritated by the concern, but I'm sensitive about being babied. I'm a soldier and they should treat me as such. There have been a lot of soft voices and soothing words. Hell, even Trevor has been walking on eggshells around me. If I had a dick, they'd be giving me shit for screaming like a bitch, and we would be clinking beer bottles in triumph.

"Peachy keen, stud." My eyes narrow in warning.

"You were screamin' in your sleep again, Tabitha. You haven't eaten a full meal since you've been back, and the slightest shadow makes you jumpier than a long-tailed cat in a room full of rocking chairs. You ain't gotta be a tough soldier for me."

"I'm fine, Buck." I sulk. "I don't want to talk about it. I just want to have a good time in Savannah. Let's drink ourselves stupid and find a nice hotel room to ruin. Then we can get back to work like it never fucking happened, 'kay?"

"Ah, well, I'm heading up to Charleston to see my folks. Thought maybe..." He hesitates and rubs his hand along the back of his neck, turning an endearing shade of red.

"Do you think that's wise, considering we're not supposed to be fucking?"

"I don't fuckin' care. I want you to meet my folks. If that gets us in trouble, it gets us in trouble. After Italy, I'm not lettin' no dumb fuckin' rules stop what we got."

His confession catches me off guard, but   I don't dare mock it. I have been using Buck as a crutch since we stepped off the plane from Italy. Sleeping in his room, wearing his clothes, and sticking to him like glue whenever we venture out.

He's right. I'm not okay.

As much as I'm looking forward to drinking myself stupid, partaking in the ecstasy Jack always gets his hands on, and thoroughly enjoying a lap dance, the idea of hiding on a farm with Buck for two days sounds like a dream come true.

I smile and lean over the console to kiss his cheek. "Alright, stud, you got yourself a date. Let's go meet mom and pop."

Buck lights up like the Rockefeller Center at Christmas and does a little boogie dance. It's the most adorable thing I have ever seen. His smile fades as he corrects me. "Well, stepmom and pop, and now that you're in, we gotta pick up a carton of Newports."

Buck changes from insane demolitions expert that was blushing a few seconds ago, to an anxious young man about to bring a girl home to his family.

We follow Jack and Trevor to the Denny's in Savannah that Jack likes to haunt. Our meal is thankfully brief and the two of them give us shit about seeing Buck's parents. But I see their grins. Neither of them gives a shit about our relationship so long as it doesn't interfere with work. Our "secret" is safe with them.

For the two hours up to Charleston, we hold hands and rock out to the radio.. At a truck stop just outside of

Charleston, we stop for the Newports.

With all seriousness, Buck hands the cigarettes to me and says, "That is your bribe into Carla's heart. 'Cause if she don't like you, daddy won't like you. Then it's gonna be a real shitty leave."

"How bad could it be?" I shrug, taking the Newports.

"Damn it, Murphy! What the hell? Why did you go and jinx us? You damn well know that shit's real!"

I laugh then. Long and hard. His concern is adorable.. "C'mon, stud. It'll be fine. I got your six. If shit goes sideways, we'll just head back to Savannah, and you can watch me get a lap dance." I trail my fingers along his knee and give him a coy smile.

A shit-eating grin appears on his face. "Nah, baby girl. I got a hell of a closer place for you to get your freak on. Ain't no reason to waste all that gas."

I giggle as we start the final leg to his parents' place. The sun is setting as we pull into the driveway. I'm surprised I haven't crushed the Newports with how tight I hold them. While I have been all smiles and cool rider about this, I'm as scared as I was in Italy when I thought I was a goner. What if they don't like me? What does that mean for Buck and me?

Three giant German Shepherds greet us, howling and barking. The noise makes my ears ring and my pulse quickens. I struggle to keep my composure and not shrink into the seat. My heart thunders in my chest like Scottish war drums.

Buck parks the Blazer and hops out without any fear. "Go on, shut it, you howlin' mutts!" He  laughs as all three dogpile him, forcing him to the ground to shower him with affection. "Get off me. You know I don't like bein' licked. Damn dogs."

"Well, that's news to me," I tease as I slip out of the blazer. Any signs of how I truly feel are well-buried under the smirk plastered on my face.

Buck blushes as red as a cherry and coughs as he gets to his feet. "That's different."

"Uh-huh," I smirk.

Movement behind him catches my attention. My instincts kick in, and I launch the nearest weapon I have at the approaching figure.

"Ow! Shit. Is that a carton of Newports?" a young man's voice calls out. "What the hell, Buck?"

"It's your own damn fault for sneakin'. Now get them damn Newports out of the mud 'fore Carla sees."

The kid, who looks no older than fifteen, rips the carton out of the mud and hastily wipes them off on his clothing to make them pristine again. Buck snatches the cigarettes and hands them back to me.

"Hot damn, she's gorgeous," he says as he stares at me, mesmerized.

"Trust me, kid. That's one philly you ain't ever gonna tame."

"I wouldn't mind dyin' tryin'."

I laugh and offer my free hand. "Hi. I'm Murphy. Sorry for trying to kill you with Newports."

"S'all right. You can hit me with anything you like, Miss Murphy." His sweet Southern drawl is light, matching his boyish grin.

"Still not gettin' that ride, buddy."

"Shut the fuck up, Chester. I'm tryin' to flirt."

"Who in the hell taught you how to flirt? Your left hand?"

The younger version of Buck shrinks in embarrassment for a split second, then he puffs right up like his big brother and gives me a wink. This is going to be great.

"Yeah. I got a sweet trick, you wanna see it."

"No," Buck says.

"Yes," I say at the same time.

"What the fuck is all that noise out there? Thought I told you to pen those mutts, Daniel. Do I need to call animal control and have 'em put down?" A woman's voice cuts across our merriment.

The mirth disappears from Buck and Daniel as their shoulders tense.

"Sorry, Carla. We have guests. I'll get them penned up right away, ma'am." Daniel hurries off, whistling for his dogs.

Shifting my gaze from the scurrying Daniel to the terrifying shrill voice, I'm greeted with a woman who looks to be in her sixties. She has mousy, dyed blond hair that obviously came from a box. Her leathered skin hangs on her with the weight of time. Not to mention the cloud of smoke that hovers around her.

I step forward past the now paralyzed Buck and offer the carton.

"And who the fuck are you, sugar tits?" Her hand on her hip, standing at the top of the stairs like she's the Queen of England.

"I'm the green fuckin' fairy who brought you a carton of Newports. But if you want to keep bein' a cunt, I can just toss 'em in the mud." Confidently, I hold out the carton, daring her to start something. No one makes my Buck unhappy.

"Carla, this is my girl, Murphy." Our banter finally cures Buck of his paralysis and he comes up alongside me.

"What kind of a fucked-up name is that? Whatever, dinner's on the fuckin' table. Get your asses in here." She growls as she snatches the carton.

I cut Buck a look to see if he's okay.

"Well, that could have gone worse." He holds the door open for me, and I follow the nasty haze inside.

The inside of the house is worn down, and stained a dull yellow color, exactly what you would expect from a chain smoker. Everything reeks of her cigarettes.

The stench doesn't get any better when we step into the dining room. Another young man sits at the table, his hands folded together and his eyes focused on the empty spot across from him. A big burly son-of-a-bitch puffs on what I guess are Marlboro Reds. My guess is confirmed when Buck stealthily pops out a carton of Marlboro Reds and hands them secretly to his father.

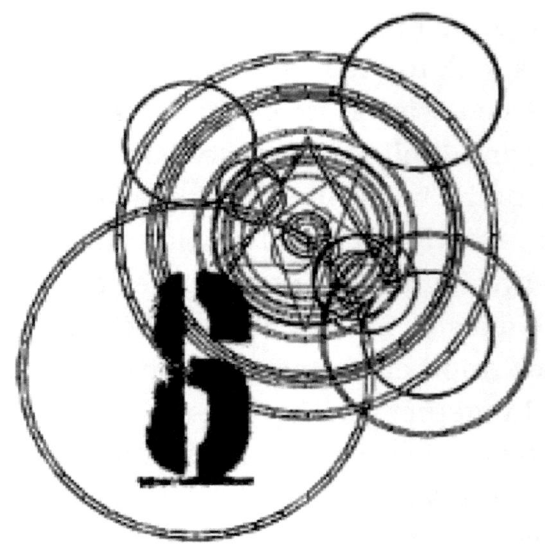

# TAILS, NEW YORK CITY

"Don't just fucking sit there. Get another Goddamn chair for princess over there." She whacks the boy sitting as silent as a mouse at the table about the head.

That silent mouse morphs into a lion before my eyes. "You want a fucking chair so bad, you fucking get it, cunt. Don't fucking touch me, Carla."

"Nate, do what your mother says," says the big, burly man.

I look at Buck again, like he has lost his mind if he thought this was going to be pleasant on any level.

"I got it," Buck says, a surprised look on his face.

I've already concluded that the abusive shit from Carla is the norm in this house.

We all sit down to eat what they call meatloaf and mashed potatoes. Between how greasy the meatloaf is, everything tasting like ash, and the potato flakes being dryer than sandpaper, I lose my appetite. I pray to God Buck wants to get a hotel room for the night.

All the talk at dinner is between Buck and his old man. The rest of us are a mix of silently listening, choking down the food, and staring daggers at each other. His beaming smile and boisterous tone give away how proud he is of his son. Who wouldn't be? Buck's top notch.

The infamous Nate smirks at me across the table. I raise a brow when he finally catches my attention, and he winks at me with a nod.

*Jesus these kids need to get laid.*

I shake my head and snort in laughter, which is a mistake.

"What the fuck do you find so funny?" Carla's voice cracks across the table.

Again, all the mirth and normalcy of the meal evaporates in a cloud of smoke. I look around the table briefly to gander the temperature of the room before I level my gaze on Carla. "Nothing, ma'am. Just enjoying dinner." Not wanting to make waves for Buck, I decide to put on soldier polite mode.

"You know what she found so damn funny, *Carla*?" Nate's voice snaps like a whip. "She's thinkin' about how much better my dick's gonna be than Chester's tonight."

I choke, not expecting that in the least. The sip of water I barely had in my mouth ends up all over my napkin as I sputter and Buck thumps my back. But now I really like Nate.

Buck, who has been timid since we got here, rises out of his seat like a fucking missile to launch, facing Nate. "You want to run that by me again, boy?"

"You heard me, you crazy fuck. She's gonna ride my dick until the sun comes up."

I palm my face. This isn't going to end well. "Don't do it, Buck," I mutter. "He's just a kid."

There's no reasoning with Buck when you fuck with his shit. None, whatsoever. He was already moving when I spoke. His chair scrapes along the worn wood and clanks as it hits the ground. He storms around the table, takes Nate by the scruff of his neck, and drags his ass outside. Daniel hops out of his seat like a kid heading to Disney. The screen door slams behind the three boys.

Buck's old man, Carla, and I are left at the table. I'm not getting in the middle of a fist fight with Buck. He can handle himself. What gets me going is how smug Carla looks. She did that on purpose.

The burly man speaks up without pausing in shoveling his ashy potatoes into his face, "You should probably go and keep your boy from killin' his brother."

"Buck! Don't kill him!" I shout out the door before I whirl on Carla. It's time for someone to unseat the queen. Quick as lightning, I'm out of my chair and have Carla by the ear, dragging her to the door.

She lets out a screech as I throw her into the mud. The chair behind me scrapes across the floor. A door bangs open. Buck's father is going for a gun.

"That'll be the last mistake you ever make, Sir. I suggest you sit your ass down and finish your dinner, while I teach your cunt a lesson on manners."

He doesn't stop. As he loads the shotgun, he says, "You touched my wife. You are no longer welcome on my property."

"Your wife abuses your sons, and you let her, you piece of shit. You want me to teach you a lesson, too? 'Cause that gun ain't gonna do shit to me. Do you really want to find out who's gonna win this? Or do you wanna enjoy an evening with your son before we ship out again?"

The three boys come running from somewhere near the barn, beers in hand.

"Oh damn," Nate says. "She's got balls."

"I'm in love." Daniel thumps his chest.

"What the fuck, Pop?" Buck growls.

"She laid a hand on your mother. I won't have nobody disrespectin' my family like that. 'Specially some two-bit, city-slickin' whore."

I wish he hadn't said that. It breaks my heart that Buck is put into this situation because I couldn't hold my temper. I'm convinced that tonight will be the only night I might have become Mrs. Buck after this. I'm not going to put a wedge between him and his family.

Buck surprises me by swallowing his anger. His fists open and close for several breaths before he says, "Tabitha, it's time for us to go."

"Oh, hell no!" I growl at him. "You're not going to take that shit anyone, much less your fucking father, who values that cunt over his own flesh and blood. She treats you all like shit, and he lets her." I whirl on his father and stalk forward. "She's not their mother, asshole! What kind of man does that? I'll fucking show you city-slicker, asshole. I have put better men than you in the ground. I hope you fucking choke on your cigarettes." Buck has lifted me off my feet and I spit on the ground in his direction as Buck carries me out.

From down the steps, I continue to shriek at her over his shoulder. "And you! You fucking cunt! If you so much as look at those boys wrong, I'll know! I'll come back here and fucking rip your eyes out. You hear me!"

Buck shoves me into the passenger side of the Blazer.

"I'm definitely in love," Daniel says.

"Ditto," Nate echoes.

Buck throws himself into the driver's seat and slams the door.

The tension in the air is thicker than the cigarette smoke of his family home. Guilt fills me as he says nothing while driving away.

Five minutes later, he jerks the car to the side of the road and kills the engine.

I bite my lip, keenly aware we're in the middle of woods, on a two-lane road where no one will find the body. While I'm sure I could hold my own in a fight with Buck, if he gets any good hits in where I can't run, I'm boned. "Hey, stud..."

"I just wanted it to be perfect," he growls. "Just once in my fucking life, I wanted that dumb fucking cunt to shut her fucking mouth for two seconds and let me enjoy something."

I hold my breath, having expected his anger to be directed at me, and not solely toward his stepmother.

He glances sideways at me. "You couldn't just leave well enough alone and come out to the barn to drink with the rest of us, could you?"

"How was I supposed to know that's what you were doing? It's not like you gave me a bat-signal or anything." I pout at him and cross my arms in a huff. "Fuck, Buck. I was sitting there panicked you were murdering your brother!"

"I thought you would've come runnin' after me."

"Almost did, but that cunt, with her smug ass look when she thought you were hurting Nate. No. Nuh-uh. Not going to fly with this bat girl."

Buck gives me a once-over, his boyish smile forming. "You're so damn hot all worked up like that. Come 'ere.

Give me some sugar."

I'm in his lap before he finishes speaking. The Blazer rocks dangerously as we tear at each other's clothing in the confines of the driver seat. My ass hits the horn twice before Buck gets wise and tilts the seat all the way back. Finally free of my jeans and panties, I lift just long enough for him to shove his boxers and jeans down. I line up, grab his dick, and thrust down hard, like it's the last thing I'll ever do.

Our romp in the Blazer is dirty and quick. I don't care that we reek of cigarette smoke and cheap beer. Not any worse than if we spent the evening in a run-down bar. I bounce on him vigorously, and his hands death-grip my hips as if he thinks I would try to escape.

"Fuck, I love you," Buck moans. He jerks my hips down as he thrusts up. His face scrunches into the most adorable orgasm face ever.

It's the first time he has used the "L" word.

I don't say it back, but it doesn't matter. He's lost in the endorphin high of such an intense orgasm.

I lean down and kiss him gently before I get as comfortable as possible on top of him.

This just got a lot more awkward.

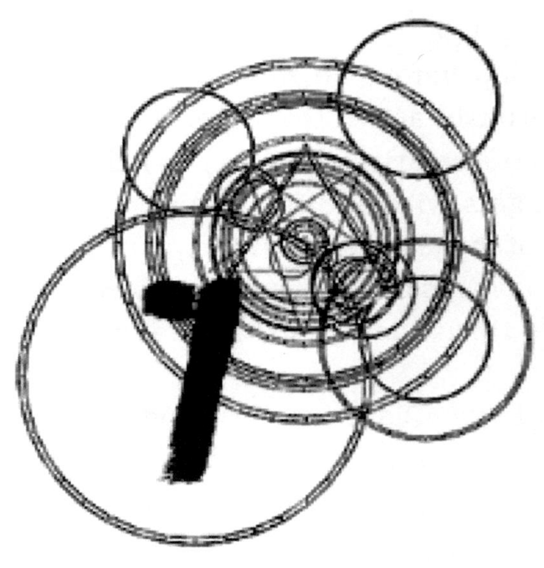

## YOU GOT SERVED

After our escapades, Buck and I hit the road. We rolled through Norfolk to talk to a few of Buck's buddies and take in the sights. I could tell his parents are still bugging him, but I'm not sure how to approach it.

On a whim, we find a carnival with expensive games and cheap toys. The hours and money we waste leaves us both in stitches and carrying arm loads of useless stuffed animals. It becomes a competition to see who can make a kid's night as we hand off our prizes.

I do keep one prize, a small keyring. It's a silver dollar sized circle filled with glitter and confetti in liquid making it look like a lava lamp. It's enough to remind me of the day.

We check into a swank hotel, and Buck orders us room service while I take a shower. The water is hot, and I take my time, letting the high-powered jets punish away the tension between my shoulder blades.

He said he loved me.

Yeah, sure, it was in the throes of passion. Still. He said it.

I should transfer to a different team, put our relationship on record, and then we can do whatever we want. The likelihood of seeing Buck more than in passing drops to almost never and would he still feel the same?. I don't think I could hack it on another team. Italy rattled my cage hard.

When I come out of the shower, the room service cart is waiting with covered dishes.

Buck kisses my cheek before ducking into the bathroom. "I'll be quick."

"You better. Or I'm starting without you." I lie.

Ten minutes later, he stalks out with a towel around his waist and we devour the steaks he ordered.

Finally, we get into bed. For the first time in a long time, I'm not sneaking in to snuggle him on a bunk too small for just him. I fall asleep curled against his chest, listening to the steady beat of his heart.

******

The next day we cover the last six hours of driving, by boondoggling, as he calls it. I'm shaking my head as we pull into our rendezvous point in Atlantic City, a strip joint. We laugh hard that all the places Jack chooses are strip joints. "He must have a stripper in every port."

Sure enough, Trevor and Jack have beat us here. When we walk into said strip joint they're at a booth. Between the narrow-eyed look, twitching jaws, and jabbing fingers pointing at each other, the conversation is heated. When

Trevor spots me, the conversation abruptly ends. We slide into the booth, and a topless waitress brings us menus.

"Bud," Buck orders.

"Coke and water," I say.

Jack stares at me, while I smile from ear to ear at his choice of places.

"You got something on your mind, Murphy?" Jack asks.

"No, Sir. Just admiring the view while we wait."

"Uh-huh," he says. "Enjoy Charleston?"

I give Buck a cursory glance before I answer. "Not as much as I did Norfolk."

Buck laughs and coughs, his cheeks darken with his blush.

Trevor gives Jack a stern look and then shakes his head.

"We didn't fuck in Norfolk, Trevor." I roll my eyes. "We went to a carnival."

"Girly girl, I know damn well you fucked him somewhere between Charleston and here. Damn fool hasn't stopped smiling since you walked in. You two need to knock that shit off right now." He glares at Buck and jabbing his finger at him angrily. "I'll fuckin' shoot you myself, you pull that shit you did in Italy, Buck."

Confused, I furrow my brow and look at Buck. I thought we'd told each other everything about Italy. "Buck?" My voice trembles, despite my best effort to look casual.

"This ain't the place to talk about it." Buck cuts Trevor a dirty look and won't meet my gaze.

"Hey, Candyman, I see you brought friends tonight." The server shuts off any further discussion while she stands next to Jack.

His ears turn pink when she calls him Candyman. Trevor, Buck, and I exchange a glance before bursting into laughter. The tension of Buck's secret is lost while we tease our fearless leader.

"Jesus, Jack. How many strip joints are you known in?" Trevor asks.

"Yeah, Candyman. Looks like you got your own little side gig going. She know about Miss Fontaine?" Buck teases.

"Awe, sugar. I ain't into Candyman like that." The server cheek pinches Jack. "He's just so damn cute and has the best candy. He's a favorite with all the girls."

I groan. "I bet he is. Hey Candyman, what's good here?"

"The rib-eye, mashed potatoes, and green beans." Jack rattles it off like he has ordered it a hundred times.

"Sounds good, I'm in," I say, sliding the menu to the edge of the table.

Buck and Trevor nod to order the same thing.

She struts away, causing her tits to impersonate a bouncy castle.

Jack looks over his shoulder and then beyond Buck and me to see if anyone is close enough to hear us. I draw the rune on the table with water. Now, anyone trying to eavesdrop would hear us talking about tennis, the US Open specifically. I don't know why I picked tennis, but that's today's cover.

"Somethin' is happening to the lycan population in Manhattan." Jack's voice still drops low to keep prying ears out of our business.

"You know they hate being called lycans, right?" I chime in, like a paranormal hunter Hermione Granger. Jack's about as impressed as Ron Weasley was when she called him out on his levitation charm.

When the food comes, we all agree Jack's right about the steaks. This meal's one of the best I have ever had.

Jack's popularity with the strippers doesn't end for as

long as we sit there. They all call him Candyman and whine when he tells them he's out of candy.

Throughout dinner, Trevor keeps giving Buck the dirtiest looks. I pretend to not notice. Something went down between the two of them while I was out of it.

Buck eats slowly and steadily. It's an obvious sign he doesn't want to talk about whatever has him on Trevor's shit list.

When he pops the last bit of steak into his mouth, he chews and avoids making eye contact with me. I drum my fingers on the table, giving a side look to Trevor and Jack who also avoid eye contact.

Buck swallows.

"Spill it, or the romp in Charleston was the last time." I bark like a drill Sergeant.

Jack and Trevor snicker, while Buck's ears turn pink.

"Fine." He grumbles as he wipes his mouth and sighs. "I lost my cool in Italy. All I saw was that fanged fuck sucking you dry, and you dropping to the ground like you were dead. The grenade didn't even phase you." His voice is hollow. "I didn't care if that fanged fuck was still around. I broke protocol and charged in. Those holy rollers were supposed to be there, to protect you. You looked so frail, frightened, and I just couldn't take it." He clenches his jaw.

My heart breaks for the big lug. "What did you do, Buck?" I ask gently. Whatever it was, it crossed a line and Trevor's hot to trot about it.

"I cut myself to give you blood." He stares at the empty plate, chewing against his lower lip.

This is serious. As serious as he saying he loves me.

While he obviously failed in his insane plan, it throws a whole new complication to us having any kind of relationship. I look at Jack and Trevor.

Jack stares down at his beer bottle, fastidiously playing with the label.

Trevor's face has '*I told you so*' written all over it.

I punch Trevor hard and square in the jaw. "You dumb fuck. Why did you let him get anywhere near me? You know how he feels!"

"Ow, shit, Murphy! What was I supposed to do? I was on a fucking rooftop more than fifty yards away. He's the shit-bag that broke protocol." Trevor whines as he rubs where I hit him.

The inside of my mouth hurts from biting against it to keep from losing my cool. My face scrunches into a scowl. "You couldn't just leave well enough alone asshole."

"No. He couldn't," Buck's voice cuts over my angry bark. "He shouldn't leave it alone. I fucking lost my mind in Italy and will lose it again if something happens to you."

Jack sighs. "Well, no shit, Sherlock. Look. You two have been fuck buddies since training. I don't really give a shit. Good for you. Italy was a shit show, and you died, Murphy. Your heart stopped at least twice. They wanted to stake your ass to the ground. Thank fuck you hadn't drunk any blood."

Jack's perfect poster-boy face draws into a grimace. "Which you almost gave her, you dumb shit. Listen. I get your balls to the wall bullshit has gotten you as far as it has, but we're better than this. I'm not fucking covering for you two anymore. So fuck, don't fuck, get married, but if you compromise another fucking mission, you are both out."

"Yes, Sir," Buck and I respond like scolded children.

We tip the lovely server, and I wipe the rune so some other unsuspecting patron doesn't get stuck talking about tennis.

The ride across the bay is quiet. Buck won't even give me a side glance. He fidgets and inhales as if he's about to say something, then stops, and starts the whole ritual over again. It's better to leave well enough alone for the night, so I let him flop about like a fish out of water and stay quiet.

Our motel is a far cry from the swank place Buck and I stayed in Norfolk. Jack heads in and gets the adjoining rooms. We could all fit in one room, but then we would be clustered together. At least in two rooms, we have a chance to duke it out.

Buck and Jack head into one room while Trevor and I go to the other.

I keep the poker face on, trying not to be angry with Trevor, or Jack., "What the fuck?" comes through the door. Trevor and I draw pistols, and I jerk open the between door on our side to let him kick in their side. We tear into the room ready to shoot first and pray later when I see Jack and Buck staring at a young girl.

Her sleek dark hair is pulled into a high ponytail with fringe bangs holding a sharper edge than my boot knife. Ethereal blue eyes stare at the four of us, all with weapons drawn, and she giggles.

She Goddamn giggles.

She's not afraid of us, but she sure as shit isn't any older than fifteen or sixteen. When she stands, I catch a glimpse of blue on her chest. She holds up one hand and in the other is a manila envelope.

"You have been served. Don't shoot the messenger." She chortles again and crinkles her pert nose. "Mr. Howell expects you in his office at 8 sharp tomorrow. Should you perform any hunting duties in the confines of his territory, we will see this as a violation of the Accord and will detain you accordingly. Good night!" She flounces by Jack with too much confidence for someone her age.

None of us move a muscle as we watch her leave the room.

When Trevor starts to pursue, I throw my hand up to stop him. "Let her go. She's the Blue Dragon. You do anything to her and we'll have Patrick Howell to deal with. Maybe even Mehzebeen."

"I can take two fanged fucks, Murphy."

"She's right, Trevor. Stand down." Jack holsters his pistol and locks the door.

Jack frown as he picks up the envelope to read the contents. With a sigh, he hands it off to the rest of us. Four cease and desist letters addressed to us individually, invoking the legal red tape we now must navigate to complete our mission.

I knew not telling Howell first was a bad idea.

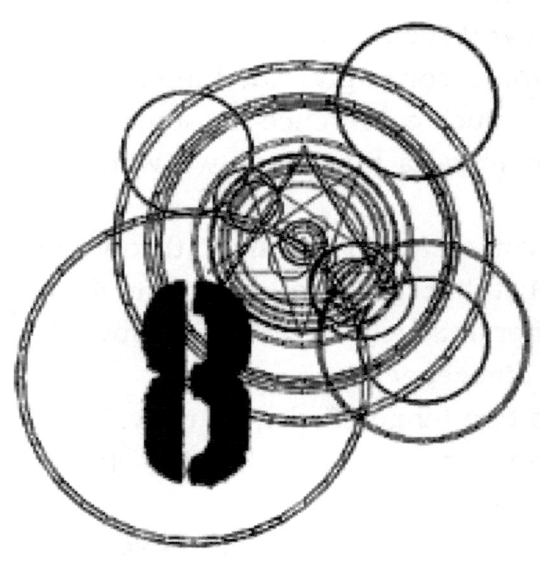

## ANYTHING YOU CAN DO

I used to joke that sleep is for the weak. I used to joke about a lot of things. Italy sucked all the humor out of my sense and left me with this dark, foreboding itch between my shoulder blades. Let's not forget the amount of phantom pain I feel when I close my eyes.

Sure, the holy rollers made it so I don't feel like stripping naked and offering myself to the vampires like a weirdo sushi bar but their torture treatment did nothing for the horrors that vampire filled my head with.

I wonder why he didn't turn me. I keep replaying the night over in my mind. He wanted something, and it wasn't me as a vampire. The look in his eyes when he leaned in to bite me. The way he burned through my runes like they were nothing. All of it makes no sense.

Unable to sleep, I spend the night listening to Trevor wheeze. The high-pitched noise makes me laugh. For such a disgruntled prick of a man, he sounds delicate and small in his sleep. I know better than to mess with him. He keeps his pistol in hand under his pillow. Not the safest of methods, but effective. The man has never misfired it.

I try meditating. Sitting on my bed with my feet touching and my legs butterflying out, I rest my hands on my knees. With slow breaths, I churn in and out all the thoughts in my head. My body starts to relax. Sleep starts to take hold when the sweet moan of Buck saying he loves me filters through my mind.

"Fuck," I mutter and fling myself back on the bed to stare at the ceiling.

Why did he have to ruin a good thing? Sure, I love the big lug. He's perfect soldier boy material for my pop to get a hard-on for, but love compromises the whole team. Love is commitment. Love is marriage and babies, and no more career for me.

I thump my hand against my forehead hoping to find a way to fix this love problem. Sure, I could sleep with Jack, or Trevor, but that will just make even more of a mess. Buck is a jealous beast. I have seen him in action, and while they're brothers-in-arms, there's no sharing of what Buck thinks is his. I should just tell him straight that we can't be in love. If he can't handle that, then I'm putting in for a new team.

At some point, I close my eyes with all the terrible possibilities of dealing with Buck's feelings dancing like sugar plum fairies in my head. Then someone nudges my side.

"Fuck off," I grumble without opening my eyes.

"Rise and shine, Sleeping Beauty. It's seven." Jack says.

"You damn well know they meant eight at night, asshole. Why are you bothering me?"

"You damn well know if we aren't there in forty-five minutes, they'll throw a fit and we'll have an issue with the Tribunal. Now, on your feet, soldier."

I hate when he's right.

My boots are still on, and they thud against the floor when I swing my feet over the side of the bed. I'm the last one up. They let me sleep as late as they could. Damn it, I hate it when they baby me.

We gather our things and head into Manhattan.

The building is massive and shiny, just like every other structure in downtown. There are fifty different kinds of offices. The directory is as tall as Buck when we trudge through the revolving door. It takes a hot minute to get through security with our weapons, but the assistant for Howell, Brigham, and Young finally persuades the portly guard to let us through. We are ushered into the plush office and confined to a conference room with a restroom attached. They don't want us to leave this dedicated space for any reason.

Then we wait.

We wait for twelve full hours before Patrick Howell, his ingénue, and two other well-dressed vampires enter the conference room.

During the half day of idle time, we have made ourselves at home. Buck and I raided the office supplies drawer, and the team has turned the entire conference table into a war zone. Each of us have our Post-it notes castles, paper-clip soldiers, and pen cannons. I sulk at not getting to launch my triangle football assault.

Jack sleeps on the other side of the table. His boots are propped in the chair next to him and he has tilted back as far as the chair will let him.

Trevor hates being confined like this. He mutters as he

ticks all the reasons why on his fingers, burning a hole in the floor as he paces.

"I trust we have not kept you waiting."

At the sound of Howell's Irish brogue, Jack wakes and sits up.

"No, Sir, not at all," he offers a smile and a hand to shake. He doesn't look Patrick Howell in the eyes. He likes not being mind-fucked by vampires.

Buck leans back in his seat and crosses his arms.

Trevor joins us at the table.

I sit up straight in my seat, ignoring the battle scene of wasted office products.

"Why, pray tell, are you soldiers in my city without notifying me?"

Jack shrugs, "It doesn't concern vampires. You didn't need to know."

I raise a brow. Jack has never been so cavalier, and his disrespect to Howell puts us all in danger.

Patrick Howell may look like a twenty-four-year-old red-haired Irish kid, but he's old and powerful. From what the files say about him, I would never want to cross him.

My gaze shifts from him to Sabine Howell, the bratty teenager that served us papers last night. Her response is all over her face and it takes all my control to not laugh. Her pouty face and crossed arms with her cocked hip give away her being offended and fully expects Daddy Howell to do something about it.

Now that I see the two of them together, I'm curious as to why he keeps a human as a daughter. She obviously has not been bitten. Her eyes are sharp and bright instead of glassed over, and she's not trying to mount any of the vampires in the room. So, how does a vampire like Howell convince someone he's a good father figure?

Then I notice the other vampires. None of the normal reactions to being bitten happen. I don't feel drawn to them. The only reason they draw my attention at all is how much they ogle me.

They stare at me like I'm covered in whipped cream and cherries. The lust in their eyes makes me squirm. Each one rolls their head as if to shake the trance the sight of me causes, but it does not ebb. They continue staring at me.

I ease my hand down to my side. My pistol won't stop them, but the silver in the bullets would slow them down.

Howell slaps his hand on the table, and all of us jump. "If you cannot control yourselves, leave the room." He scolds the two vampires with him.

"You cannot order me out, Howell. I'm a named partner."

"As am I."

Those two suits must be Brigham and Young.

"I can and will. She sings because of Sorbolo. I will not tell you again." Howell stares them down until they submit before shifting to us. "As I was saying, all issues in this territory are my issues. I represent the entire underworld in the Northeast at the Tribunal."

His gaze settles on me with eyes greener than the Emerald Isle.

I can't look away, no matter how unsettling him staring at me is.

"I have arranged for a townhouse for you to operate from and provided the information we have obtained about the drug and how it affects the wolves."

"Wolves are affected by something?" I pipe up. "Isn't their metabolism too high?"

"Yes, Lieutenant Murphy. That is normally the case. However, the Alpha of New York has gone missing, along with her sister, and they were investigating this matter. I suggest you start at The Pit. Now, if you will excuse us, we have business to tend to." Patrick Howell stands, followed by those who entered with him.

The entourage leaves first. As Howell nears my chair, he leans into my personal bubble.

"I would not presume to hurt such a lovely creature as you, Lieutenant Murphy. But there's something about you that calls to my kind. I suggest you be careful around vampires."

I nod.

Jack steps in, offering his hand to Howell again, forcing him out of my space. "We got it from here, thanks. Keep your *kind* out of our hair while we're investigating, and everyone's a winner."

Jack and Howell posture, gripping each other's hand tight enough to whiten both their knuckles. The moment is gone as fast as it came, and we are left alone in the conference room. Thankfully, Howell decided to leave Jack's hand intact.

None of us say a word until we are outside.

"What the fuck was that?" Buck growls.

"Let it go, Buck," Jack warns.

"No. They looked like they were going to fucking eat her right there on the table."

"Big man, let it go. Nothing happened," Trevor chimes in.

"That's an order," Jack snaps.

I say nothing as we pile into our vehicles to head to the location Howell gave us. Something deep down inside me wants them to bite me again. I'm not about to tell the guys that. They'll send my ass packing back to the Iscariot for more holy water.

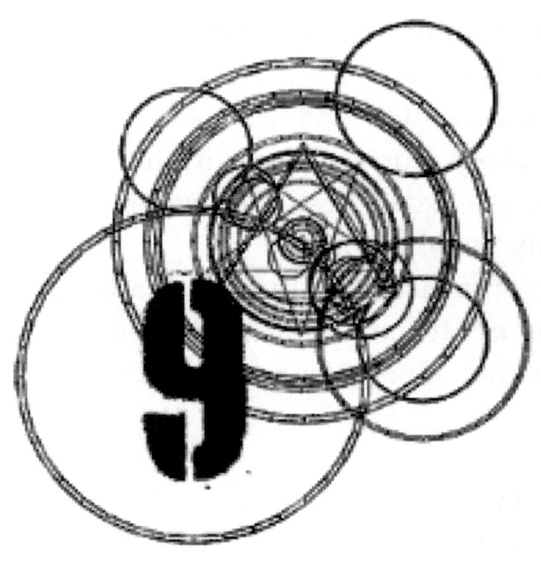

## WE CAN DO BETTER

The Pit is everything I expected it to be. Dirty, dark, and illegal, even for the underworld's messed up law system. The former Alpha's wife haunted the club when she was a kid. She disappeared about ten years ago, and no one knows anything. The loss broke the Alpha. He went mad and absconded with his eldest daughter. Rumor has it they're in Canada, but no one cares enough to track him down.

The Alpha's son also vanished after a trip to Russia, leaving the Malone twins, Dallas and Diane, in charge. I'm not entirely sure what they are, but they aren't just wolves.

Dallas is the official Alpha, but if you aren't smart enough to tell them apart, Diane may be the one you're dealing with. When Howell said the Alpha is missing, it makes me wonder if the daughter is carrying the sins of the mother.

The freight elevator rattles and clanks as I'm lost in the history of a place I have only ever seen on paper. When we read the bottom, Jack snaps his fingers in front of my face, alerting me to the fact I haven't been paying attention. "Murphy," Jack growls. "You good?"

"Peachy keen, boss." I flash him a smile.

"She ain't heard shit you said, Jack. Why ask her a dumb question like that?" Trevor retorts. "Don't start shit. Keep your eyes open. Keep your earpiece on."

"Got it." I reach up and adjust the small earpiece before tucking my hair back in place.

The scents in the Pit overwhelm me. It's mix of booze, cigarettes, cigars, and animal. Werewolves, while looking like humans, give off a scent. To the untrained nose the scent is just musky and nature filled. The longer you are around it, the more distinct it gets, and it stinks. Sure, they look sexy as hell in human form, and practice good hygiene, but this place isn't about being 'good.' These monsters work out all the aggression here that they can't release anywhere else. Before us is a sea of sweaty bodies and lycan-forms.

Trevor perks right up, seeing the fighting ring, a smile dances across his lips and he rolls his shoulders like he's getting ready to be Rocky Balboa.

"Don't even think it." Jack flashes him a grin.

"No hunters allowed," a surly-looking man in a wife-beater and jeans barks at us.

I step forward before the testosterone fest escalates without us even getting into the club. "Then it's a good thing, I'm not a hunter, champ."

The bouncer looks me over and licks his lips. If I were a weaker being I might feel like the rabbit spotted by the wolf.

"Sweet Cheeks, I don't care if you say you're the Queen of England. You stink of hunter. But I'll tell you what," he leans in close, invading my space and inhales deeply. "You pay the entrance fee and last more than a round, and I'll let you and your lap dogs in for the night."

"Deal."

"Absolutely not," Jack, Buck, and Trevor say in unison. All three puff up and step forward, Jack curls his fingers around my forearm to prevent me from dancing on through the entrance.

The bouncer cuts a look to the guy sitting in a booth too small for him with a clear window for protection and flashes him a grin. Whatever conversation they have is via mind link and it can't be good.

"Murphy, you are not stepping in that ring." Jack commands.

"You want in, or not?"

I don't take my eyes off the bouncer. His toothy smile tells me he thinks I won't last a single round.

Silence lingers while Jack mulls it over. None of us are happy about the situation, but we need to find a way inside. Jack is the one who said not to cause trouble.

"Two rounds, that's it." I confirm.

"Buy-in's five thousand. Cash only." The man behind the window smirks and holds out his hand.

The four of us pat down and pool in the cash, only coming up with fifteen hundred. I pout and  face the bouncer, hoping my charm wins us a smaller entry fee.

"Tell you what, Sweet Cheeks, I got you." The surly guy nods to the man behind the window.

"She ain't gonna fuck you after," he laughs at the bouncer.

"We'll see about that. Once she gets this, these boys ain't gonna do shit for her." He squares his shoulders, pimping his physique for us.

"Name's Murphy. What's the rules?"

"Ain't no rules, Murphy. Fight lasts until one of you gets thrown out. Or knocked out."

"Perfect!" I chirp and press by the bouncer who stops the boys. Commotion behind me causes me to turn and see the boys heatedly arguing with the werewolf. He doesn't budge, and they're forced to remain in the tiny entrance.

The further into The Pit I walk, the more varied the creatures are. In addition to werewolves, there are were-cats and a few Fae. The magic teems and a nagging feeling in the pit of my stomach grows.

I avoid the bar and make my way to the ring. The evening is too young for the festivities to have started, which gives me a few moments to survey the club. Taking a slow three-sixty turn, I eye the canopy from which the entire kingdom can be surveyed. No one is up there at the moment. As I ogle the empty catwalks, a dashing beast saddles up next to me, surprising me.

"What's a divine creature like yourself doing here?" His purr sends tingles down my spine.

"Getting ready to raise some hell."

"Ah, you're a fighter?"

"Something like that." I'm eyeballing the canopy still, trying to figure out if there's another way out from up there, and ignoring him.

"Awe, what's the matter, Angel? Just bein' friendly."

I stop my inspection of the catwalk and turn my full attention to the beast next to me "Listen, *babe.* There's nothin' here but trouble for you. If we're not fightin' in the ring, I don't give a fuck what you have to offer. I'm not interested."

When he gives a low growl, I have to restrain myself from giggling and agitating him further.

As he walks away, I admire his ass. He's handsome enough, but I know better. A human in this place is a rarity, and often a snack.

I don't have to wait long before a skittering rat of a man squirrels his way into the corded off ring to gain everyone's attention. "Settle down! Settle down! We have a rare treat tonight." His tongue darts out and licks his lips as his glossy eyes meet mine.

I try to look unphased, but the onlookers don't need a spotlight to know I'm human. A flutter of doubt tickles my stomach, and I roll my shoulders to shake it off.

"First, Gunthar returns!"

The room erupts into roars. Fists pound on tables, and feet stomp on concrete. A man the size of a small house steps up into the ring and his smile is from ear to ear as he eats up the praise.

"Second! We haven't had a human in the ring since Maggie! Let me introduce you to Murphy!" The room stills for two uneasy seconds before erupting in a cacophony of whistles, clicks, and kissing noises.

I saunter toward the ring and purposely wiggle my ass as I bend the ropes to climb in. The cat calls and cheers ratchet up. Looking at Gunther, that bouncer meant for me to get hurt when he made the deal. I'm at least half this guy's size.

"Alright, you mongrels!" the announcer hollers over the raucous crowd. "Settle down! The rules are simple. First one knocked out. Or thrown out. All methods allowed!"

As he scrambles from the ring, I quickly trace a shield rune over my chest.

Gunthar is pacing in his corner, a small frown gracing his chiseled jaw. The shifty glances to me, then to the rat that escaped the ring give away he's irritated by this pairing.

"Don't worry, big fella. I'll be gentle." I wink at him.

He laughs heartily, tears coming to his eyes.

Just because he looks like a big wolf doesn't mean he's any good at fighting. I roll my shoulders again and teeter on the balls of my feet, waiting for the bell to ring.

As soon as it chimes, I see my mistake.

Gunther's massive human form turns not into a wolf but into a were-bear. My situation wouldn't be so bad if he turned into a lumbering large Kodiak. Much to my dismay, a were-bear is pretty much man-shaped with bear features. His legs grow to the size of tree trunks, giving way to a chestnut brown fur torso, arms swollen and ripped, along with a snout and large fanged teeth, stunning and terrifying all at once.

If I let him connect a hit, I'll be dead.

A buzz fills my ears and drowns out the room until the only sounds I hear are the two of us shuffling about the ring. As he moves, I scan over him for any sign of a weakness, hoping he has a limp, can't lift his arm, or a blind spot. The closer he gets the worse I feel about my odds. So, I decide to fight dirty.

In his bear form, his waist is nearly at my eye level. If I'm going down, at least I go down swinging. Leaping forward, I throw my shoulder down like I'm going to collide with a football dummy. His massive paw swings for my head, and I drop to my knee to watch it go over me. Then I come up like Ryu in Street Fighter, my fist connects with his balls.

He roars and staggers back. One hand holds his jewels

while the other swipes wildly at me as I dance away.

I get cocky and dart in to follow up with a left hook.

His open paw smacks my face. I hit the concrete with a loud thump and slide a good ten feet.

The buzzing gets louder.

The shield rune is now ashes.

From somewhere in the crowd, one of the guys calls my name and commands me to get up. I roll away from the voice and the crowd to see Gunthar stand and start limping toward me.

## SIZE MATTERS NOT

I push to my feet and the buzzing in my ear grows louder. My survival instincts say I should be running right now, circling around him until I find a good vantage point to leap on and ride him to the mat. That makes the most sense with our size comparison and well, me not being a were-fucking-bear.

As he turns and lunges faster at me in our whirling dervish of death dance, I assess him and make the calculated assessment to fight, not flee. I push off my foot, and with a one-two-leap step I'm in the air.

Gunther freezes, his mouth open and his paws in the air, his eyes blown wide with surprise at the tiny human daring to leap at him. He widens his stance, like a batter ready to send the ball to the fences.

Time slows as a malicious glee at this madness of me versus a were-bear fills me. This new sensation gives me an unhinged need to be unpredictable and dangerous. I have always been a risk taker, but never at this level.

Power wells in me like God Himself has kissed me. I rear back my fist as I descend upon the waiting Gunthar. My fist connects with his jaw as his paws grapple my waist to throw me. He groans and staggers before he hits the ground, his lights going out.

I manage to snag the top rope of the "ring" and hold on as if my life depends on it. I imagine I look like a damn frog on a lily-pad being bounced around as the ropes are not used to the strain I put them under. When I finally let go, I fall back into the ring.

Strangely, the power still courses through my veins. My heart pounds in my chest like the strength of ten men bursting to get out.

Silence fills the warehouse basement.

I scramble to my feet and back up until the ropes won't let me go any further, keeping my eye on the hulking mass that is Gunther. The rat-faced announcer squirrels his way to the were-bear, now in human form, and checks for a pulse.

"Murph-Murphy wins!" His voice breaks mid shout.

The club roars to life in a mix of excitement, joy, anger, and fear. Not only did a human take down a were-bear with her bare fist, but there are three more humans waiting in the wings. The entire atmosphere is ill-at-ease with this revelation.

Hunters are a joke to the underworld creatures. We have no powers, no back-up, and often our gadgets prove less than useful if we get caught in a creature's abilities. Finding my guys still near the entrance, I raise my fist in response to their cheering. My stomach is in knots, and the buzzing in my ears has subsided. Whatever power I felt has left a nauseating sensation in its wake. I'm not sure I'll make it through round two.

Someone thrusts a large bottle into my hand. I pop the lid off and run a rune around the lip. The rune slithers and dances into the bottle, lighting it up blue, revealing the contents to be pure, uncontaminated water.. So I pop the lid back on and drink like water is scarce.

The Pit staff struggle for a good ten minutes to remove Gunthar. While I'm grateful he's not dead, I now have a pissed off were-bear on my list of pissed off creatures. When they finally roll him out of the ring,, the next fighter gracefully dances in.

"Now, my friends," the rat-faced MC chitters. "Let's see how our fiery human fares against her next predator." He shifts his beady eyes from me to the new combatant.

I follow his gaze and take a slow breath. This tall drink of water is tan, with a long black mohawk braided down his back. Tattoos and scars cover most of his bare chest.. His eyes flicker between a Caribbean blue and stardust gold. Muscles ripple and move with him like this man is not only in command of himself but demands the attention. Every step he takes demands attention.

"You gonna eye-fuck me the whole time, Miss Murphy?" His voice is thick and rumbles like a well-tuned Harley. He could read me the phone book.

"Only if you plan to get naked and fight without shifting." I smirk. I doubt he won't shift.

"Deal." The man unfastens his belt, unbuttons his jeans, and lets them drop to the floor, leaving him naked.

*Fuck, he's hot.*

*When* the bell rings, I'm distracted as hell by the naked

man who closes the distance between us faster than a thought. His fist pounds into my gut, and I double over. I manage to turn my body so his knee connects with the side of my face and not my nose.

I drop to the ground with a grunt.

His foot swings back around. When it gets close, I latch on, using his leg for leverage to sweep around. I'm oddly satisfied with his cry of surprise as he hits the ground.

We both roll away before the other can take another shot.

He's on his feet first, but I'm quick to follow. We race forward to collide again. This time, I monkey up his front to latch my legs around his waist and turbo-punch his pretty face.

He throws hard, rib-cracking jabs from both sides while writhing in my grasp to wriggle free. When my legs won't release, he falls to the ground and squishes me between him and concrete.

"If you wanted me on top, you just had to say please," he growls.

I'm more turned on than when partaking in Candyman's good stuff.

I roll us so I'm on top. "You're a cute pup, but I like my men seasoned." I cheek pat him as I try to spring to my feet.

His hand closes around my throat. He throws me down like a rag doll, squeezing lightly as he leans his weight on me.

The well of power from before returns, that burning hot desire to bring God's wrath upon this beast. Both our eyes widen in surprise.

"What the fuck are you?" He snarls as he rips his hand back like I burned him.

"I'm a mother fuckin' Night Ranger, that's what." I swing up with a left hook that sends him sprawling.

All around the ring is a sea of strange faces, salivating at the idea a human can give them a run for their money. I'm alone, unable to hear or see my guys anymore.

I roll to get up when he jerks my foot from under me and pulls me across the ring. This asshole intends to toss me out of the ring, but I won't have it.

I turn back to him and bend to grab his arm, but it's too late. My move gives him the momentum needed to fling me. I sprawl my fingers out to grab the ropes but miss and crash into a table, shattering it under me.

The roar in my ears makes me believe I cracked my skull on one of the concrete pillars, but no blood or pain comes from where I touch my head. By the time I sit up, the boys surround me.

"Jesus Christ, Murphy. What the hell was that?" Jack asks as he squats in front of me.

"A fight?" I offer a weak smile, and the other two snicker at my sass. We're in enemy territory. It does none of us good to show any kind of real emotions.

"Aw, Jack. She's alright. She's still being a wise ass." Trevor helps me up and dusts me off.

"Hot damn, Murphy! That was some serious power. How did you clean that bear's clock?" Buck's voice is both husky with lust and awestruck like a kid meeting Batman.

"Yeah, Murphy. How did you manage to knock out a full-grown were-bear?" Jack's arms cross; his expression is all business.

I open my mouth to lie about it being runes and a few new tricks learned from Rowena in Italy when the cat who hit on me earlier interrupts us.

"Big man wants to talk with you. Especially you, Red.

Not sure what you're on, but no one knocks out Gunthar like that."

None of like the sound of that. We were supposed to lay low and see what we could find. When I look at the guys, they're all arms crossed and dirty looks. Except Buck, who can't seem to wipe that shit-eating grin off his face.

Jack nods at the interloper.

The walk up the stairs to the catwalks is accompanied by a mix of jeers and curiosity.

"So much for keeping a low profile," Trevor mutters.

"Leave her alone. She got us in the door." Buck defends me.

"At what cost?" Jack grumbles.

Anger wells from the same place the power came from, and I bite the inside of my mouth hard to not pop off at Jack.

We step into the office. Sitting at the desk is one of our top ten wanted werewolves, Maxim Trent.

"Well shit, now it's a party," Trevor's snarky voice filles the room as the office door closes behind us.

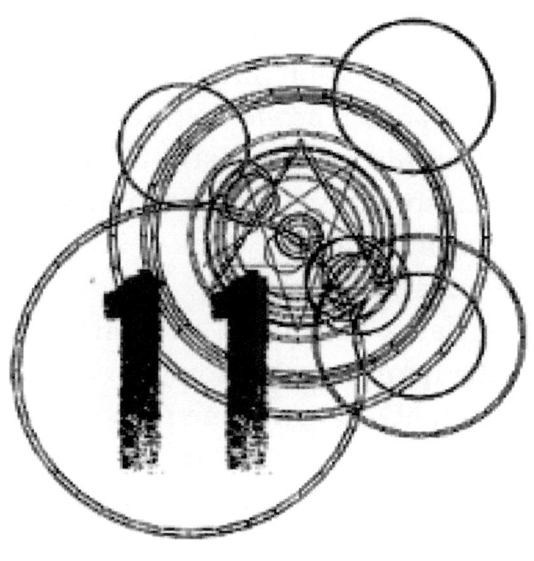

# 11

## IT'S GOOD TO BE ALPHA

Maxim sits smugly in the leather chair behind the oversized desk. Though he's a beast of a man, he must be compensating for something the way he peacocks around here. His dark hair and eyes remind me of Eastern Europe.

His elder brother, Constantine, is one of the most feared Alphas in the States. Being from a breed of wolves that finds humans far inferior, he keeps his pack in the wilds of New England.

Maxim, however, has a chip on his shoulder the size of the moon, and decided if he couldn't run a pack on his own, he would poison them all.

We first learned about Maxim's machinations when he introduced heroin laced with silver to the scene. Normally, The Night Rangers wouldn't give two shits about werewolves poisoning themselves. Then humans got their hands on the supernatural drug and started turning up dead. No one profits when the mainstream United States' government investigates. We fight to protect the truth as much as we do humanity.

With eyes full of mischief, I'm still itching for a fight. I hope Maxim does something asinine, and we get to wipe the floor with his smug face. My lack of self-control is why I'm not the team leader.

Jack, ever cool as a cucumber, motions with his hand open, palm to the floor, to calm down. "What the fuck are you doing here, Trent? Give me one reason to not just end your sorry ass and move on with my night."

Buck grunts in laughter and eases closer to me, making me roll my eyes. I don't need him to shield me. Okay, so I'm still on edge, and to be fair, Buck smells like whiskey and gun powder. I bite my lip to keep from leaning in and giving him a little clue as to what we would be doing if we were alone.

Trevor snorts and wedges between the two of us, giving Buck the stink eye and motioning him across the room. As Buck backs away, Trevor's gaze turns to me. "I don't know what the fuck is going on with you, Murphy, but you're creeping me the fuck out. Knock it off."

Oblivious of my supposed sin, I hold up my hands and shrug my shoulders in innocence.

Jack clears his throat to refocus us and crosses his arms, waiting for Maxim's answer.

"I could ask you the same thing, Hunter. Unlike you, I belong here. What the fuck are *you* doing here?"

Maxim's New England accent amuses and turns me on at the same time. *What is wrong with me?*

"This is Howell's territory, and Malone's. Last time I checked, your name ain't either." Jack retorts.

Maxim's smile turns wolfish giving me a knot in my gut "That fanged ginger fuck doesn't run shit. This is *my* territory and I'm telling you, you're not welcome. I'll give you until dawn to get the fuck out of my city before I put a bounty on all your heads."

"Awe, buddy. We aren't here to fight you." I chime in as if I'm talking to a toddler. "We're just looking for Malone. If she says you're Alpha and we'll be on our way. No one reported the change in power, and you know how the high muckity mucks are." I jerk my thumb towards Jack.

Maxim huffs out of his nose, laughs, and licks his lips as he looks me over. "Murphy, right?"

I nod.

"I'll show you how that transfer of power went." His tone is laced with lust as he licks his lips again, taking me in. "Ditch the boy scouts, and you can stay."

Normally, the sexy talk doesn't get me going with creeps like Maxim Trent. Tonight, though, I'm considering his offer.

*What the fuck is wrong with me?*

Jack shifts his weight to put him in Trent's line of vision between us. "Enough of this bullshit. Where's Malone?"

Buck, I notice, has closed in on Maxim. His face is red with rage and the way his muscles twitch in movement suggests he's about to pound Maxim into a pancake.

Trevor teeters back and forth, rolling his head like a boxer waiting for the bell. He'll definitely jump into a fight Buck starts.

When I shake my head no, I'm looking at Buck. Attacking someone who claims to be Alpha is unwise when we're under geared.

"Malone could be anywhere, Hunter. The pack is fortunate I was here to step into the vacuum she and her sister left."

"Hrmph. So you really aren't the Alpha. Good to know. We're done here." Jack turns on heel and stalks to the door.

Buck, Trevor, and I pause, like we're playing Red Light Green light, but quickly fall in like dutiful soldiers. When we hear a snarl behind us, Buck turns without hesitating and throws his hunting knife.

The hilt vibrates as it sticks out of Maxim's shoulder, pinning him to the leather chair. Steam rises from his body as the silver blade burns his skin. The knife won't hold him for long.

"God damn it, Buck," Jack snarls. "Move!"

At his command, we rush to descend the stairs and gather our things. Buck definitely threw down the gauntlet, and Jack's clenched jaw, along with the vein bulging at his neck says he's pissed.

Trevor laughs and shakes his head.

I pause, glancing back to see if Maxim is pursuing and relieved when I don't see or hear him.

"Hey, Red," the burly bouncer growls in my ear. "He tell you where Malone is?"

My brows shoot up in surprise. "No. Sadly. It was all dick swinging and chest thumping. But tell you what, champ, you let me know if you see anything weird, and I'll let you know what we find about your Alpha." I snatch the bookie's pen and write my cell number on his hand with a little heart.

"What was that about?" Jack demands when I catch up to the boys.

"Nothing." I smile and shrug. "Just wanted to know where his Alpha was."

Jack rolls his eyes, and Buck is frowns.

"I gave him my number in case he hears something."

Once outside, we huddle up to decide our next move. We have two choices. First,, we pretend to track untagged werewolves in a city teeming with equal numbers of people and underworld creatures. Second, we go back to Howell, Brigham, and Young and recruit their tracking services. The idea of dealing with the bratty vampire ward makes me roll my eyes; but again, I'm not in charge.

"Looks like we're going to need a lawyer." Jack chuckles at his own joke.

The three of us groan at his dad joke..

An hour later, the four of us once again sit in the conference room, waiting.

Before long, the pint-sized terror struts in. "What do you guys want?" She pops her bubble gum.

"We're here to talk to your boss." Jack is all business, no Southern charm tonight.

"I don't have a boss." Sabine narrows her eyes.

"Fine, then we need to talk to the big man upstairs, or whatever you call him."

"Uh. You talking to God isn't my problem. That's a *you* thing. Now, if you are done wasting my time, I have things to do." She flips her hair over her shoulder and looks at him defiantly.

"Yah, and one of those things, Princess, is to tell Howell we're here to see him." Jack glares at the girl.

The interchange is hilarious to Buck, Trevor, and me. This little menace definitely is used to getting her way. Howell must spoil her rotten.

We wait quietly while our fearless leader and the Blue Dragon face off. She may be a teenager, and a pain in our asses, but she could get us all in a metric shit-ton of trouble. I learned long ago that even teenagers could really fuck up my day when dealing with the underworld.

"Fine," scoffing in true teenager fashion. "But he'll be pissed." She storms off, leaving us alone in the conference room.

"She likes you." I elbow-jab Jack in the ribs.

"I like her," Trevor thumps his hand against his chest over his heart, causing all of us to stare at him.

"She needs a damn whoopin'," Buck motions like he's slapping someone's ass.

"That's not any of our business, so long as she tells the old man we're here to see him. Now," he swivels back to me with narrowed eyes. "Murphy, what in all that is good and holy happened back there?"

I groan, though I knew this was coming. Jack misses nothing; however, I have no idea what happened. That inconclusive answer probably won't fly with him.

"I did what I had to do," I grouse and shrug.

"You damn well know that's not what I'm talkin' about." He crosses his arms and hits me with that steely gaze that makes me feel like I'm sixteen again and just got caught smoking a joint by my father.

The room goes silent. The tension is wound so tight my muscles ache from being clenched too tight.

Buck and Trevor stopped joking to listen.

With a frown, I submit and look away first. "I don't know what happened. One minute I'm getting my ass handed to me. The next I felt like I could bench press all of Manhattan." I look up to meet Jack's stern face. I gave him an honest answer and there are tears welling.

Doubt consumes me. What if he doesn't believe me? Would he kick me off the squad? Could it all have been just adrenaline and nerves? I've heard of humans committing feats of strength when pushed too far. All of us have been in this business long enough to know there are some things that can't be explained.

"Okay then." Jack nods and turns to take a seat, leaving me feeling cold from the lack of comfort.

## PAGING DOCTOR FEEL GOOD

December 2004

The life of a Night Ranger isn't glorious. In fact, we spend most of our time sneaking around and infiltrating. However, with Maxim Trent making us persona non grata with the werewolves, we were forced to use the vampires.

That doesn't mean we left town with our proverbial tails tucked between our legs. We aren't that kind of hunter group. We bide our time in the townhouse, planning and mapping out the territories claimed with the vacuum of Dallas Malone's disappearance. My gut tells me she's still in the city and Maxim Trent knows exactly where.

I staked out The Pit, marking comings and goings for months.

Buck took the docks. He came home smelling like the sea and raw fish. The putrid smell has turned me off of sushi forever.

Trevor stuck to the unions. Fun fact, most of the labor unions are organized by the underworld. The creatures are better able to integrate with society using them as a front.

Jack, being the Candyman, took the roll as party boy. He's a man who knows how to get what he wants when he wants it when it comes to drugs. How that man networks so well and doesn't scream government spook is beyond me. But he comes back to our townhouse with more 'candy' than any dealer I have ever seen.

Even with all our efforts, we keep coming up empty-handed. The scouts from the vampires always lose Trent in the big, bad city. With every new report of failure from them, Trevor insists they're lying.

Things between Buck and I have cooled since coming to New York. I wouldn't say our feelings stopped. But I haven't been laid since that damn night in South Carolina, and it's make me antsy.

Tonight, we get our first big lead in a while. A couple of she-wolves vanished from a night club on our list. Two missing wolves wouldn't be suspicious, except that the security feeds were wiped at the time of they disappeared.

In the spirit of blending in, I go all out for tonight and wear a little blue number that shimmers. After slipping into matching stilettos, I tuck my weapons into places only Buck ever sees.

The fellas cleaned up nice each in their own unique suits. Buck wears a sleek black jacket with a black dress shirt. Jack dons a steel gray ensemble with a light blue dress shirt. Trevor went full on rock god in a deep dark red suit with no dress shirt underneath, leaving his tattoos and muscles on full display.

We each take a moment to inspect the others, and I'm all smiles as Buck can't take his eyes off me. If we weren't working tonight, I would give him his Christmas present early.

"Alright, listen up. No earpieces tonight. I'll see if I can get my hands on product. Trevor and Buck, you're on the lookout for anyone slipping things into drinks. And Murphy." Jack gives me a once over. "You do what you do best. See if you can find us a party."

I'm amused as I step up to Jack. My fingers trace over his forehead lightly, making the rune glow to life. Next, I draw one over his chest and then the inside of his thigh. He stands still, his eyes forward, but I still notice the boyish smile on his face. I repeat the process for Trevor and Buck.

"What about you?" Buck's amused look turns into creases of concern as he looks down at me.

"Already put mine on, Stud. Don't worry. I won't be swept away by anyone but you." I pat his cheek roughly, and the other men cough to cover their laughter.

We have no trouble getting into the club, thanks to Jack slipping the door guy more money than was necessary.

The place is hopping. Music thumps as lights flicker to the beat. Sweaty bodies glisten and shine in the vibrant lights. Scents of booze and sex linger in the air. This club is a place for the young and beautiful to forget about their woes.

We part ways and head for our preselected locations. Any person who dares to enter our townhouse while we aren't there would find all sorts of building plans, maps, and scouted locations marked. An outsider would think we were planning a heist.

I feel Buck watching me from the bar. His eyes

practically burn holes into anyone who dares to dance with me. I smirk and throw my hands in the air like I don't have a care in the world. The plan is to look for that party boy, the one who will take it just a step too far in wanting to show a girl a good time. I'm not afraid. All the runes I wear tonight will keep anyone from getting too far into my bubble. I don't want a repeat of Italy.

"Well, aren't you a pretty little bit of stardust," a deep, rumbling voice purrs in my ear as strong hands rest on my hips to pull me into his movements.

I laugh and dance with him. No sense in being rude. When I look over my shoulder, he's easy on the eyes, with a scar. His eyes are a piercing blue, and his five o'clock shadow only adds to his handsome visage. He's too old for the normal crowd, and he screams naughty from a mile away. But nothing sends up red flags as we dance.

After several songs, I'm sweaty and hot. I find myself clinging to the burly stranger like all I can think about is ripping his clothes off here on the dance floor. The music picks up pace and the entire crowd grinds in time.

One of the runes flares to life and fizzles out, alerting me to something being done to my person.

"I'm gonna get us some drinks. Don't go anywhere," I giggle at my sexy dance partner before slipping into the crowd.

The music is too loud, as my heart races. Something isn't right.

I quickly recall every detail of the man I was dancing with. Those smoldering eyes, the scar, his suit. I glance over my shoulder as I make my way to the bar for another look and he isn't hard to find. He's easily a foot taller than most of the women around him.

This is different than what happened in the ring. In the

ring, it was pure power and a desire to punish. Here, I'm struggling to catch my breath, and my heart beats hard enough I could be having a heart attack. Then I level out, and my heart slows. The aching need to ride Buck like a pogo stick fills me.

As I approach Buck, I realize I'm compromised. The imprint of my dance partner is on my mind. Even if I don't remember, the vampires can pull it from me. My body isn't showing any signs of distress. I press into Buck and nuzzle his chest.

"Take me home," I mewl and kiss his neck.

His pulse quickens with my touch, and his dick hardens against me.

"Murphy?" Buck peers down at me.

"Take me home and fuck me." I pull him into a forceful kiss and grind against him.

"Yes, ma'am." He wraps an arm around me and walks me to the door, pausing long enough to tell Trevor we're leaving.

The cab ride back to the townhouse is cramped, as I try to climb into Buck's lap. Finally, he pulls me into his lap, grabs my wrists, and holds them behind my back as he stares at me, awestruck. I whine and grind against him, feeling his desire threatening to destroy his pants.

"Fuck, Murphy," he gasps.

In my frenzy, I barely notice as he pays the cabby and carries me into the townhouse. Buck backs me to the bed in my room, peeling me out of my dress as we walk. He tosses me on the bed and pauses to unfasten his belt before he follows me and presses a knee between my legs, parting them as he crawls up my body. Wet and wanton for him, I open like a book. I squeak in surprise when Buck whips his belt around and ties my hands to the headboard.

"Buck?" I mewl and tug against the restraint. A mix of irritation and excitement fills me, and I whine again.

He kisses my stomach before pushing back and binding my ankles with the sheets. When he steps away, I'm furious with lust.

"What the fuck? I need you, Stud."

"Jesus, Murphy. I want nothing more than to fuck you until you see stars. But you ain't right. You just be a good girl until Jack gets here."

I writhe and squirm, panting in my need for him to fuck me. "Buck, please, I want you to fuck me so hard."

Next thing I know, Trevor is standing next to Buck. I shift in the restraints offering my body to him without any inhibitions.

"Trevor, please. Buck won't give me what I need." I moan against my arm.

Trevor says nothing, crossing his arms, his eyes glued on me.

Buck snorts.

Our fearless leader enters the room. I don't register the icy blue latex gloves, even though I see them. I only register he has a needle in hand.

"We going to have ourselves a good time, Candyman?" I purr at him arching my back to offer myself up like a buffet.

"Sure, honey. Just lie still, so it only pinches a little."

I comply because I need Jack to touch me. He always brings the good stuff. When my buzz doesn't get any better, I furrow my brow in confusion.

"Good girl," Jack patronizes me as he pats my arm. Turning on heel, he walks to Trevor. "Take this to the vamps and have them analyze it. I have a feeling we're onto something."

## IT'S ALL ABOUT BLOOD

Jack sits at his desk, flicking through his email. Murphy weighs on his mind. Based on the words coming from her mouth, he'd failed her a second time by letting her go on a mission before she was ready..

He takes a sip of coffee before setting the mug back on the pretentious coaster to preserve the too-expensive desk.. The bitter, hot liquid is soothing.

The hour is too early for the rest of the team to be awake, and he takes a few minutes to enjoy the peace and quiet. His phone vibrates, and he flips it open to see a Savannah number.

"Well, Miss Fontaine, what do we have here?" When he opens the attachment, he spits out his coffee. On the screen is an eyeful of Evie Fontaine's assets. With a smirk, he closes his phone and cleans up the mess he made with his coffee.

That stripper tugs on his heartstrings, but he's working. The last thing he needs is to get her hopes up. He's a Night Ranger, and going up against monsters is a losing prospect. What kind of man makes a widow of such a pretty girl?

A light knock at the front door pulls Jack from his morose thoughts. With a pistol in hand, he makes his way to the door. A quick glance out the window reveals Howell's courier.. He opens the door and watches the kid fish around in his messenger bag.

"Mr. Howell says you were right. Also said he gave you a present." The young man hands him an envelope and waits expectantly.

Jack looks up from the envelope and raises a brow. "You need something else, Jerome?"

"C'mon, man. I rode halfway across town to deliver that. Seemed kind of important. Least you could do is give me a fiver."

Jack reaches into his pocket, fishes out a ten, and hands it to the kid, thinking Jerome has to be an oblivious human based on how he talks. If he knew he ran around town for vampires, he would probably do something stupid, like try to become one.

After closing the door, Jack heads back to his office and sits down to read the results. Damn, vampires work fast. He wishes the military worked with any sense of urgency. He would bring up the subject to Armstrong when this mission is complete. Setting the coffee mug on the coast, he fishes out the lab results.

Subject: Female
Age: Unknown
Pregnant: Negative

Subject Species: Demi-Human*
Foreign Substances: DNA traces of vampiric origin
Source of Substance: Unknown
Genetic Ancestry of Source: Middle European
Age of Source: 200-300 human years
*potential specimen contamination


Jack stares at the piece of paper as though it bit him. "There's a lot to unpack in this," he says to the empty room. How would the vampires know where that blood came from?

He shifts to his laptop and pulls up Murphy's last medical file to examine the blood work clearing her for duty. The notes clearly label her species as human with an affinity for the arcane. Humans inherently can use magic. Some are born with too much access to it and end up being hunted down by the likes of The Night Rangers. Others have to work at it. But Demi-Human means that she's part human, and part not human.

Jack has to believe the specimen was contaminated. The drug in Murphy's system somehow messed with the species results. Jack starts to pull up the paperwork to requisition her entire family history but stops. If he sends this request, command will pull Murphy from the mission, assuming she's a vampire. Jack knows what happens to those that are turned.

"Fuck!" He slams his fist on the desk. He damn well knows she's not a vampire.

For the last year, he has seen her out and about during the day. The only way she's a vampire is if she was turned last night.

Suddenly worried, he grabs his flask and trots upstairs. Without knocking, he enters the room.

Buck is passed out in the chair next to the bed. Murphy is still naked and tied to the headboard. Someone had enough decency to pull a sheet over her.

"Sir?" Buck blinks the sleep from his eyes and sits up.

"Just seeing how Sleeping Beauty is doing?"

"I gave her one of the pills Doc gave her to help her sleep. She hasn't moved since."

Jack is relieved to see the sun's rays playing over her fair skin as it slowly rises. He steps forward and dabs a bit of holy water from a flask on her forehead.

Buck's eyes widen as he realizes what Jack is testing for and frowns. "Fuck, you think they turned her?"

Jack watches the water dribble down her forehead. "I don't know what to think, Buck. Blood work came up with some weird results. Just wanted to make sure our girl was alright."

Buck nods and stretches. "I'll keep an eye on her. Trevor's been working on the footage."

With a curt nod, Jack turns and heads to Trevor's room. "Find anything good?"

"I sure the fuck, did," Trevor grins.

"Our girl got him to look right at the camera." He pulls up saved points of the feed.

The two men watch as Murphy and the party boy dance like there's no tomorrow.

"See, right there." Trevor points. "He pets along her skin."

"That doesn't mean shit. They're just dancing, Trevor."

"Yeah. Well, look at this. Murphy goes from moving to the beat, to moving with the man. Her entire body language changes. Then she goes straight to Buck. But that's not the best part." Trevor leans back and spins around in his chair, a smug look on his face. "That club is in on it. You should have seen the look on that fuck's face when I showed up and demanded the footage."

"Okay. Still doesn't show him slipping her anything. For all we know, she didn't get drugged on that dance floor."

"Some days you fuckin' kill me Jack" He rubs his hand over his face. "Fine. Look at this." He pulls up another section of the video feed. "When Murphy disappears, you would think he would look for her, right?"

"Yeah."

"He doesn't. He dances with a couple of other girls and then–." he motions like Vanna to the screen.

On the screen, the guy from the club is dancing like everyone else. Then his fingertips brush along another girl's arm. Just like Murphy, the woman's entire posture morphs, and she dances in sync with him. They watch in fascination as he pulls her in and guides her off the dance floor, out of view of the cameras.

"Rewind it back to when he touches her and zoom in," Jack commands. "Slow it to half speed."

Sure enough, upon closer inspection they see him make a motion, like he's retrieving something from his pocket before touching his fingers against her skin, leaving a tiny film behind. Trevor hits the space bar to pause the image on screen.

"It's a fucking contact drug." Jack's voice is low and full of menace. If he could get his hands on that asshole, no one would find the body.

"Yeah. I sent the guy's mug to the Vamps. They said it might take a few days to figure out who he is. I told 'em we needed it yesterday."

"Good work, man."

"How's our girl?"

"She's still sleeping. Buck hasn't left her side."

"Yeah. What are we going to do about that?"

"I don't know yet." Jack sighs and rubs the back of his neck in frustration. "I like Murphy, and we all work well together. They've been behaving since we called them on their shit last year."

"That ain't gonna last, and you know it. You want my opinion?" Trevor leans forward and rests his elbows on his knees.

Jack knows he'll regret hearing what Trevor has to say but they're like a family. Trevor and Buck are his brothers, and Murphy's their weird, smoking hot kid sister. Reluctantly, he nods.

"Find Buck another girl. What about that stripper with the super perky tits in Savannah?" His hands make a subtle motion of squeezing said tits.

"You think he could be swayed? Something tells me they're way beyond just fucking. He took her to fucking Charleston. To his old man's place. You don't take the stripper bouncing on your lap home to meet mom and dad." Jack smacks the back of Trevor's head. "And that stripper in Savannah is off limits."

Trevor snickers and shrugs. "Then kick her off the squad. Send her to go work with the asshats in Vegas."

"What do you have against Murphy?" Jack presses his lips together in a grimace.

"Not a damn thing, man." Trevor holds up his hands in surrender. "She's hot as hell. I'd tap that in a heartbeat. If she's in Vegas, they can fuck all they want. Get married, make fat little fuckers, and all that shit. Her old man'll love Buck. And shit, they might actually live happily ever after. But if she's stayin' they're not fuckin'." He shakes his head. "It scrambles his brain and makes him do stupid shit."

"I never took you for such a romantic."

Trevor winks and crosses his feet on the desk.

With a heaviness in his chest, Jack heads back down to his office. At least Murphy's risk got them a solid lead.

Sliding into his chair, he examines the lab results again. While he wants to believe it's just contamination in the blood, he cannot get the image of Murphy fighting at The Pit out of his head. For now, she's a benefit to the mission, but he'll need to keep a close eye on her.

# THE WITCHING HOUR

Five Days Later 3 AM

It's called the witching hour. Some believe at 3:33 AM the bridge between Heaven and Hell opens and all manner of holy and unholy roam free.

Religion is one of those funny things that has been twisted and turned over numerous times until you cannot recognize what it was at its origin. Sure, truth exists in a good deal of it. A man named Jesus rose from the dead. Angels and demons, all who believe in the Father, abound. These beings don't call him God. They call him Father.

Full-blooded angels died off millennia ago, or so the Night Rangers thought. There's a rumor that Gabriel is alive and kicking somewhere in Australia. Last thing I want is to come face to face with an Angel. They aren't these pretty boys with wings, or whatever hell else Hollywood paints them to be. Angels are terrifying to look upon. Human brains can't comprehend them, and those who encounter the true visage of a divine being go mad.

The witching hour has me on edge tonight. Since that night in the club, visions have plagued me. These can't be dreams. They're too vivid and real. Something is trying to connect with me, and I'll be damned if part of me isn't curious.

I wanted to start this raid at two, but our party boy was still in his apartment when we arrived. So now we are in a holding pattern until he steps out. The little girl he brought home is handcuffed to the bed, unconscious. Just like me, she threw herself at him, wanting nothing more than sex. Only, she kept asking him to bite her.

Party boy happily fucked her into oblivion, but he refused to bite her. He shifted while fucking, confirming he's a wolf. A wolf's bite turns you into one of them. He wants the girl for something else, so he left her on the bed. Now we are waiting to verify that he leaves the building.

"We're a go," Trevor confirms in my earpiece.

As Jack and I exit the security room, I glance at my watch. I circle my finger in the air and show him five. We don't talk to make it harder to identify our gender.

With the tactical gear, I look just like the guys. My unruly hair is braided and cleverly hidden under a cap. We all wear full coverage masks. Night vision glasses complete the ensemble.

The two of us move like Peter Pan's shadow through the hall until we come to the door. If all goes well, we'll be in and out in five minutes with no one the wiser. Jack picks the lock, and we slip into the dark apartment.

Inside is a sparsely furnished studio. Opposite the door

sits a king-size bed with the sleeping girl. The kitchenette is gutted aside from the sink and some cabinets.

We split up and move silently to install the cameras and mics. We stop at the bed, looking the girl over without touching her. She's out cold but breathing steadily. Though I know Jack is torn, our mission isn't about rescuing anyone. He's got that boy-scout complex I lack.

With a light shake of my head, I remind him that it's not the mission objective. Saving her might compromise the greater good. Jack knows this, so I'm thankful when he gives me a curt nod of acknowledgement.

I step into the tiny bathroom and carefully place a mic. When the door to the apartment opens, I freeze.

"Fucking blood suckers," Party boy snarls from the other room.

This apartment's too small for Jack to hide out there. Even with the anti-scent gear, any werewolf worth his salt will detect him.

Thankfully, I have a bit of shelter and can get the jump on him if needed. I'm more worried Buck and Trevor didn't alert us. They're supposed to be on lookout. I pull the silver hunting knife from my boot and slowly move to get the lay of the land.

From my vantage point, I see Jack pressed against the wall. The wolf freezes in the middle of the room, sniffing lightly. His low growl tells me Jack is about to have a shitty night when the wolf turns and looks at the bathroom instead.

I narrow my eyes. Not daring to move, I hope to get lucky, and he'll think he's paranoid.

When he stalks toward me, I inhale slowly through an adrenalin rush of anticipation. This pup is about to learn you don't fuck with Night Rangers. My lip ticks up in a smug smile, though he can't see it. Unable to run or hide, I stalk forward, my knife shifting around in hand to an offensive position.

Jack takes the advantage of our element surprise to leap on him from behind, plunging his knife in rapid succession to multiple locations. Nothing lethal, but it's sure as shit going to hurt. Jack's knives are silver laced with Wolfsbane.

Without hesitation, I leap into the fray. Party boy doesn't go down easily. In a tangle of limbs and knives, the two of us wrestle him to the ground. He's oddly quiet and doesn't call for help. I find his quietness strange, but crazier shit than this happens during the witching hour.

He shifts, throwing us both off him. In his wolf form, he can pump silver and Wolfsbane out of his system faster.

Fuck, the situation got harder.

Jack and I circle the lycan. At over seven feet tall, he looks like a giant cramped in a doll-sized apartment.

We stay in a flanking position. If he chooses to strike one, the other will attack.

The lycan's head swivels to the girl in the bed. When he takes a step forward, I hop up to stand over her protectively. Jack swings around behind him.

"Listen, doggo. You can save yourself a world of hurt if you point us to Dallas Malone, and where you got the shit you dosed me with."

With no Trevor or Buck in my ear, and Jack forced to keep himself opposite me, I gamble this guy isn't really the aggressive type.. He strikes me as a lady's man more than a fighter. His job is to lure the girls in. If I had to put money on it, he's not more than twenty-four and has no clue what the drug actually does. Maxim's too smart to spill his secrets to a guy like this.

Party Boy snarls and swipes at my mid-section.

The strange surge of power rushes through me again, threatening to rip my skin apart.

Rather than dancing away from him, I leap into his arms. This confuses the hell out of him and makes Jack curse. My legs lock around his waist, and I throw an uppercut that causes his jaw to clack shut. My chest heaving from the surge, I ride the furry train all the way to the ground where he lands with a thud.

His eyes roll to the back of his head and his tongue lolls to the side as I stare down at him. Slowly, his body shifts back into human form.

As I get to my feet, Jack stands next to me.

"Bind him before he wakes," he barks at me. The way it sounds like he grits his teeth as he issues commands alerts me to how pissed off he is. Jack is the level-headed one. When he loses his cool, heaven help us. "Trevor, Buck, report. Right fucking now."

When we don't hear a response, my gut feels like it's holding a rock. I roll party boy over and zip tie his ankles and wrists. The restraints won't hold for long but hopefully long enough. I hogtie him and leave him face down on the tiled floor.

His phone buzzes in his shredded pants pocket.

Jack retrieves the phone and tosses it to me. "Looks like it's for you."

With a raised a brow, I flip it open and read the message on screen.

*Answer the phone, Red.*

When it buzzes a second time, I answer. "You've reached the party line."

"What the fuck are you still doing in my city, Miss Murphy?" Maxim Trent barks on the other end.

The fact he knows I'm here tells me the apartment is under surveillance.

"I just couldn't miss Bye, Bye Birdie! And then there's the statue, and that one pointy building. Not to mention all the places I can get coach purses on the cheap!" I try not to laugh at him roaring into the phone. "Besides, champ, you're not the boss of me."

When I turn, Jack, Trevor, and Buck are talking quickly. Jack went from stiff and rigid to his normal relaxed stance. I assume the other two had good reason for going radio silent.

Jack motions for me to wrap it up.

I purposely giggle at Maxim, who's still ranting. "Okay. Great! Been fun, see ya around, champ." I press end and toss the phone at Party boy, who's still out cold.

"Did you have to antagonize him that much?"

"I don't know what you're talking about," I strut toward the guys "What are we going to do about her?" I motion to the unconscious girl on the bed.

"Unfortunately, she's not the priority. We'll alert the authorities when we're through."

"Uh, Jack, if you haven't noticed this place is compromised. We're not getting any further intel from here."

"Well, lucky for you, Trevor and Buck found the grand goose to cook."

I wonder what Southern people mean by their weird phrases, but I speak Jack. This means they've located Maxim. He's the only goose we care about right now.

"Great. What's the plan?"

Buck steps in and grins, "Ready for round two?"

"Buck, I'm not fucking you in this werewolf's apartment." I waggle my finger at him.

All three men erupt in laughter.

"We're stormin' the castle, sweet cheeks," Trevor cuts in. "Unless you think you can't handle it, princess."

"I love storming the castle. Try to keep up short stack." I jab back at Trevor.

"Alright, button it up. We need Maxim alive." Jack cuts in.

His words act like a switch.. All joking stops. We check ourselves, and the four of us peel out of the apartment. Split two and two, we make our way up the stairs. Taking the elevators when storming the castle is out of the question. Jack refers to them as murder boxes.

After only a few minutes, we reach the penthouse on the top floor of the building. I'm mildly disappointed at the lack of resistance we met getting here. Maxim is arrogant and probably thought we would never find this place. Or he thought the pudgy guy with a rent-a-cop suit was enough protection.

After a brief huddle outside the penthouse, we each give the go ahead signal and take positions safely away from where Buck plants the explosives.

Seconds later, the door explodes inward with a loud bang. Trevor tosses in two smoke bombs laced with silver and Wolfsbane. These wolves don't know what's about to hit them.

## STORMING THE CASTLE

Buck goes first, followed by Trevor. I'm next. Jack brings up the rear. We move in time with each other, keeping our backs to the center, pistols drawn. My gaze flits over the chaos, searching for threats.

Buck and Trevor step over two men thrashing on the ground. Just moments ago, they had been wolves. The silver and Wolfsbane laced smoke bombs forced them back to human form as it burns through their blood and lungs. They won't die, but boy will they regret messing with us.

I palm another grenade as we clear the antechamber to the penthouse. I launch it into the center of the sunken living area and the dense smoke billows up as massive beasts of flesh, fur, and claws barrel out of the side rooms.

Our sidearms snap into action, lighting the wolves up

with silvered rounds. We fall back, luring them into the dense smoke, and the fools follow like mindless brutes. They snarl and snap at us before collapsing, gasping, and grunting on the floor. Their fur recedes revealing tanned skin. We push past them, and Jack signals us to break into two squads.

Buck and Trevor head to the left. Jack takes my six as I lead us toward the closed door at the end of the hall on the right. Our backs snap to the wall on either side of the door as Jack pulls another smoke bomb. I gently try the knob, and find it unlocked. With a nod, I crack the door; and Jack whips the grenade into the room. I pull it closed and hold the door shut.

Silvery smoke billows out from under the door, like wispy fingers trying to grab our ankles. At Jack's nod, I pull into the cover position. He kicks open the door to breach the room and force back anyone who dared to get too close.

Through our night vision goggle, the room is pale greens and reds as we sweep it. We are in a bedroom with an attached bathroom. Two human shapes lie still on the bed. We ignore them as we push to clear the bathroom.

Jack is instantly jumped as he clears the threshold, knocking the gun from his hand. As Jack stumbles away from the mountain of beast flesh, I snap fire one round to draw the animal's snarling muzzle toward me.

This beast is one of the largest wolves I have ever seen. His roar echoes in the small space as he leaps at me, ignoring the silver-laced smoke filling the room.

Any normal person would be pissing their pants. I unload my pistol, flinging it when it's empty to draw my hunting knife. We are trained to not react, or to feel. The mix of torture and technique has left any Night Ranger hunting machines. That, and werewolves are only scary because of their size. I've seen Fae the size of my pinky more terrifying than the beast snarling at me.

Claws slash at my midsection, tearing into the heavy vest and gear, knocking the air out of my lungs. My back wrenches with the sudden change in direction.

I stumble to the side, closer to the danger zone of this monster than I would like. The proximity allows me to drive the blade into his arm, ripping deep into the beast's flesh. I thrust my shoulder into his damaged forearm to keep his claws from ripping my back open.

My breath comes quick and the power wells in my core. I want to rip off my helmet to gasp for air but know better than to expose my face and neck. His massive arms squeeze around me, threatening to bear, or wolf-hug, me to death. I grit my teeth, kicking and struggling to get free.

Thankfully, the beast forgot about my backup. Jack leaps on the beast's back, his arm snaking around the thick neck. Again and again, the tactical blade flashes into the upper chest of the beast.

He bucks up and roars, but Jack locks his legs around the werewolf's waist, his blade digging ever deeper into the creature's chest.

Finally, the beast stumbles to a knee, and his human flesh reveals Maxim as the smoke begins to clear.

Jack rides him to the ground.

Maxim coughs, struggling to handle the poisonous gas. "You're going to kill them," he gasps, motioning to the bed.

I wait for Jack to confirm he has Maxim under control before I lean down and retrieve my pistol. Then I edge to the bed and check the two people there. They appear to be identical female twins and are unconscious. Both twitch from the poisonous smoke. Upon further inspection, I guess we have found the missing Malone twins. Great, one mystery solved.

"Alpha Malone located. Maxim subdued. How are you boys doing out there?"

Gunfire and grunts sound from the other room. I wait patiently for a response. In the meantime, I begin attending to the closest Malone sister. She's foaming at the mouth and her pale pallor suggests an overdose.

From my utility belt, I pull out a lock pick kit.. In ten seconds, I've popped the lock on the collar about her neck. In case they're faking, I plant my knee in her chest while I retrieve the NARCAN. Jabbing it in, I administer a full dose.

The antagonist does the trick, and the woman gasps awake. She struggles and swats at me, which I deflect easily. She's not at full strength. Her body flickers from shades of full human to partial wolf, as she tries to shift, while she screams in pain.

"Take it easy. You're safe. Just breathe." I lean my weight on her enough to restrain her, but not to crush her.

This girl is messed up. When she curls and mewls, trembling, I ease up and move to the other side of the bed.

Jack keeps Maxim on his knees, facing the bed via gunpoint. I mostly ignore them while keeping Maxim in sight. From his size, I know he has Alpha blood, even if he's not an Alpha. His eyes follow me from woman to woman, and his brow is creased as he slowly heals.

From the way the second woman is breathing and how the tendons in her neck stand out, she's playing opossum.

"If you attack me, I will put you down."

As soon as I pick the lock on her collar, she leaps at Maxim, snarling. Since she's smaller than me, I get an arm around her waist and easily throw her back on the bed. She snarls between a wolf, then a cat, and back to human. From how her pupils are dilated, she's high as a kite , which is the only reason I can hold her down.

With how rapidly she's healing, I guess that she is the Alpha.

"Calm the fuck down, Alpha Malone. I'm Lieutenant Murphy. We were sent to locate you; don't make me hurt you."

Maxim growls and struggles against Jack. With a quick turn of my head, the way he stares at the two women, ignoring Jack and me, tells me he at least cares for them on some fucked up level.

"Start talking, Trent, or l fill them both with Silver."

The threat enrages Alpha Malone, and she swipes at me. My gear is pretty well shredded from Trent, so I grunt in pain as she gets her licks in. After a hot minute, I get Alpha Malone pinned on the bed, facing her sister. The sister trembles and remains silent with a thousand-yard stare on her face.

"Last chance, Trent. Hope you made your peace with these women." I bring my pistol to Alpha Malone's temple, knowing full well it's empty. I gamble he doesn't know that, and has more concern for their life than saving his own skin.

"Fuck! Okay!" He whines. "What do you want to know?"

Jack steps forward, blocking Maxim's view of the three of us. "Who gave you the drugs?"

A growl is his only answer.

"How about you, Alpha Malone?" I ask the woman beneath me. "You care to share where the drugs are coming from? Or are you fine dying for your fuck buddy?"

"He's not my fuck buddy. He's a dead fuck when I get

up." Alpha Malone hisses at me.

"Well, you can shred him to pieces once we get what we want from him." Jack offers.

"Some Southern prick in a red jacket." Alpha Malone snarls and struggles against me.

When I notice she's gaining some of her strength, back, I lean my full weight against her.

"You had better be certain, Alpha Malone. Are we talking some asshole in a red blazer? Or do you mean one of Deveroux's goons?"

"Shut up, Dallas," Maxim whines with a slight tremble to his voice.

"Fuck you, Maxim. I'm not going down because you got a hard on for drug dealing. I'm the Alpha here, and you will tell them what they need to know."

I have never seen the Alpha command in effect. Thanks to the Accord, the Alpha of the Appalachian pack educated us on how it works, and I'm thankful it doesn't affect people not related to the pack. As her tone changes, Maxim, despite all his bravado, buckles under her demands.

*If she is this strong, how did she get into this predicament?*

I keep my weight and most of my attention on Alpha Malone while I risk checking out the other Malone girl. She's not responding like Alpha. Her wounds aren't healing, and she hasn't moved a muscle from where she crumpled. Her eyes stare blankly ahead. The only sign she is still alive is the faint rise and fall of her chest. Taking advantage of my distraction, Alpha Malone bucks me off and scrambles to her sister.

Jack keeps his hold on Maxim. I back away from the women on the bed and move to the other side of the would-be Alpha. We watch the tiny Alpha pull her sister into her arms.

"If I see you in New York again Maxim, mate bond or not, I'll kill you. Now all of you get the fuck out of here."

Jack and I hoist the naked Maxim off the floor and he sags in defeat. Between his injuries and the silver lined zip ties, he comes along quietly. Based on our research, we know mates are bonded on a level humans can't comprehend. To be rejected by his mate has to be a huge blow.

As we pass through the main living space of the penthouse, I let Buck take over for me and follow behind with Trevor.

We load Maxim into the truck, throw a bag over his head, and drive around for the next hour before hauling him back to the townhouse. I snag a pair of Buck's gym shorts and help the man into them. Trevor gets him a bottle of water.

We don't remove the zip ties, knowing he could be playing dejected puppy to win us over before shredding us to pieces. The five of us cram into Jack's office. Maxim sits in a folding chair, while the four of us stand around him, still in gear.

"Now, we don't give a shit about your lover's quarrel. You give us the info we want, we'll cut you loose." Jack shrugs as he crosses his arms.

## PINCH THE TAIL

February 2005 - Malone Mansion

If we thought Maxim Trent was a large werewolf, his brother, Alpha Constantine, now Beta of the Appalachian Pack, is easily a hundred pounds larger.

The werewolves had their first change of power in their hierarchy back in November. While there are countless packs with alphas, anyone who lives east of the Mississippi river rolls up to the Appalachian Pack, now run by Susie Coeh. Each Alpha runs their own pack, but they defer to the laws set forth by Susie and the Appalachian Pack.

Between Howell still punishing the Night Rangers for encroaching on his territory, and Maxim having wreaked havoc amongst the werewolves, we were asked to stay and assist Alpha Malone.

When Constantine shows up at Alpha Malone's home and causes quite the stir. All four of us are forced to dogpile Alpha Malone just to get her off of him.

Ol' Constantine was not giving it his all and could easily wipe the pavement with the pygmy alpha. The pain in his eyes and prominent frown on his face as she attacks him makes me want to ask what the story is. He doesn't even swat her away, letting her get her licks in. Having to restrain an angry Alpha without putting her down, forces me to get my gossip later.

Jack finally subdues her with a tranquilizer dart. In response Constantine picks Jack up and throws him into a wall. he massive beta tenderly scoops up Dallas Malone and carries her inside.

After making sure Jack is alive and that his gear protected him, we follow. Diane's reaction to seeing Constantine is vastly different. She eagerly teeters and waits patiently for him to lay down Dallas before she leaps into his arms, which he reciprocates with a tight hug.

"I'm so sorry, baby girl." He nuzzles her.

For the first time since she came out of the hospital, Diane is showing emotion. From what Alpha Malone told us, she lost her wolf.

I'm not exactly sure what that means, but it doesn't sound pleasant. I always thought wolf and man were the same. Which would make Diane Malone a zombie. On the sly, Trevor confirmed she isn't, in fact, a zombie. Jack had a bad mission straight out of training that makes him shoot first and ask questions later when it comes to Zombies. Had he gotten any kind of notion of her being a zombie, she would be dead.

Just when we think everything is going to settle down,

Constantine stalks from the main room, slamming the door open. The bang is followed by growling, whining, and the sounds of something heavy being dragged across the floor.

Everyone draws a weapon.

Diane whimpers in fear, as Constantine shakes a ragged-looking Maxim by the scruff of his neck.

"Wake her up," Constantine demands.

"Your funeral." Buck waves the smelling salts under her nose.

Dallas comes up swinging and stops dead when she sees Maxim kneeling on the floor, held in place by Constantine. I have to give it to Alpha Malone. I thought she would go full lycan on us. Instead, a dark auburn colored tabby cat leaps through the air with claws out.

Constantine, like a fucking Jedi, catches her by the scruff of her neck and holds her at arm's length.

The four of us stand there in awestruck silence, watching this unfold.

Constantine pulls her in close, letting her bite, hiss, and latch on to his arm. The man leans his face down into the maelstrom of teeth and claws to gently head butt her. The gesture is followed by a plaintiff mewl from the cat.

"I know. I'm angry too, but Alpha Susie sent me to settle this matter. So you're going to change back, listen to what he has to say, then what I have to say. When I leave here, this feud is over. That understood, Alpha?"

She transforms without leaving his arms into a naked, petite, woman curled against him. "Fine."

The four of us are still standing between Diane and Maxim, weapons drawn, unsure of how to proceed. This is pack business and we should not be here.

Constantine ignores us as he shakes his brother without

setting Alpha Malone down. "Apologize," he barks at Maxim.

"Sorry," Maxim mutters.

Constantine shakes him hard enough bones crack, and Maxim winces.

"I'm sorry I tied you up and forced you to take those drugs."

"And fucking pimped out my sister," Dallas growls.

"You did what?" Constantine's hand clamps down harder on Maxim's scruff causing the smaller wolf to whine. "You told me it was just drugs and sex with you. I'll fucking kill you myself." He's crushing Maxim's neck.

My eyes shift to Dallas. She trembles with a grimace on her face, as if she's feeling the pain herself, but keeping a brave face.

Behind us, Diane whimpers.

All of us look at the meek Malone.

Tears stream down her face as she speaks. "You can't. He's her mate." She points to Dallas.

Constantine pauses in his death grip to look down at Dallas.

She snorts and shrugs. "So what? I don't want him here."

Constantine sighs. "We both know that killing him hurts you."

"It's worth the pain," she shouts at Maxim.

"You are a fucking idiot." Constantine growls as he throws his brother to the ground. He then gently sets down Dallas. "As much as I understand your fury, you are not strong enough to withstand the mate bond breaking. Whatever he gave you has weakened you."

"I fucking know that! He fucking killed her wolf!"

"I didn't do that. The fucking hunters did." Maxim

protests.

When Constantine kicks Maxim in the ribs, I wince.

"No. Every other wolf exposed to their poison clouds survived with minimal damage. Maybe if you hadn't caused her to overdose, her wolf would have been strong enough to survive. You're not only a murderer, but guilty of mate abuse. I came here to get Dallas to make peace with you to give you our fucking pack. Now, I can't even do that, as you will have to answer to Alpha Susie for your crimes."

Fascinated by all the nuances of werewolf politics, I wish I had popcorn.

"Does he really have to go before Alpha Susie? She'll kill him." Dallas grumbles.

Constantine's head whips around so he can stare at her fully. Two seconds ago she wanted him to kill Maxim.

"There's only one way to stop it. You claim him for your pack, and he becomes your responsibility."

"Well shit, this is better than a tele-novella," Trevor pipes in.

Constantine's growl rattles in my chest. The fury and power radiating off him smothers the room and any jovial jabs we might have are silenced.

Buck elbows Trevor. "Not now, man. I think he could eat us."

Jack barks, "Shut it."

Constantine stands to his full height and crosses his arms, waiting for Dallas to decide.

Dallas and Diane go still, their eyes glassing over, to have a conversation only they're privy to.

Boy, to be a fly on the wall of their minds.

Still naked, Dallas stalks toward Maxim. Her jaw twitches and her eyes are razor thin as she stares down at him. Her hands on her hips makes her look like a kitten trying to be menacing and I have to bight the inside of my mouth to keep from laughing aloud.

"Dallas, baby, please." Maxim yelps as Dallas sinks her teeth into his shoulder.

Maxim's pupils dilate. He yowls in pain, before relaxing against her.

Constantine grunts in disapproval but accepts her choice.

I look at Jack with furrowed brows. Our intel doesn't talk about any kind of claiming ritual. A werewolf's bite turns their victim into one of them. What the fuck does this do?

Dallas motions, and two strapping guards appear from nowhere to drag a subdued Maxim away.

"Put him in my room," she commands.

Dallas crosses her arms and turns to Constantine. "What the fuck do you mean I'm too weak? I am Alpha here."

I bite my lip to not laugh again at the juxtaposition of pygmy Alpha versus mountain Beta.

Jack nudges me hard.

"Exactly what I said. That Kiss shit gets past your metabolism and corrupts your healing abilities. It's poisoning your wolf. Which is why I'm here to see them." He motions to the four of us.

"What the fuck can a bunch of humans do for us? You hate humans."

"These humans have a way to flush the vampire taint from their own." Constantine focuses his piercing gaze on Jack. "Which is why I allowed you to stay. So I'm asking if we can try your miracle cure to help restore our pack members who have fallen prey to this drug. They're suffering, and it would be in the best interest of the Accord if we can help everyone."

The Iscariot need to approve a request like this, and the likelihood of them relinquishing their secret for werewolves is slim to none. Jack nods, ever the confident leader, "I'll make some calls and see what we can do. No promises."

Three Days Later - Malone Mansion

We stand in a massive master suite, geared up and weapons hot, next to a Catholic priest. A native New Yorker, Father Michaels is a grizzled, battle-worn Iscariot exorcist.

"I have no way of knowing what will happen to your beasts, Beta. This is a first for the Iscariot. We have only performed this on humans tainted by a vampire."

Constantine's clipped tone cuts across the room, "Listen, Father. I just need you to hook up the drip."

"Okay. If it's working, you will know immediately." With that, he tightens the restraints on the twins and nods to his assistant.

They inject the IVs. As soon as the liquid passes under their skin, both girls scream as if they're being flayed alive. Dark blue streaks dance under their skin as their blood boils from the holy water.

I flinch and shift, recalling my three days of hell. With a lump in my throat, I observe Constantine, worried he may attack the priests. The wolfman is an unreadable stone-cold statue as he stalks out of the room.

When he returns, he's dragging Maxim with him. "Watch them. See what you did to your mate. Your fucking mate, Maxim. Look at her!" He screams at Maxim with rage while shaking him like a rag doll.

# SUCK THE HEAD

March 2005 - On The Road

Until we are satisfied that Alpha Malone and her sister survive, we cannot leave New York. As thanks, Dallas makes Maxim give us every detail he could think of about the Red Jacket and the operations related to his drug ring.

Buck has been acting strange since Christmas. The way he avoids me stings, and I couldn't figure it out until I followed him during our down time.

Then there she stood, perky and sweet, waiting for him. Her flouncy blond hair curled to perfection. She giggled at all his jokes. She hung on every word. He ate her up like candy with smothering kisses and pulling her under his arm. He took her to Coney Island. They went to the movies. He won her stupid carnie prizes. With how easy and familiar they are together, I realize this has been going on for some time. When he greeted her parents with warm hand claps and slaps on the back, like he's part of the family, I walked away.

Seeing him with someone else stings. As if in response to my heavy emotions, the steady thrum of power roars inside me. I hate every damn second of knowing what I know now.

*Why can't that be me? Am I only good for fucking? Am I not pretty enough?*

Jealousy shifts to anger, and I need to burn this energy off without hurting the team.

*I can do this. We knew it had to end.* I lie to myself.

So I put on the brave face and throw myself into studying the rune magic Rowena sent with me. I complete all my reports; I hang with the guys. Because, in the end, I choose my career as a Night Ranger over my relationship with Buck. He did the same, and I can't fault the man for that. I pretend like nothing at all has happened.

When we load up and Buck volunteers to ride with Trevor, it's a nail in the coffin of the relationship. I climb into the passenger seat of Jack's SUV and crack open my laptop, typing up our final report to send to Armstrong. After-action reports are boring, but it takes my mind off the stinging pain of rejection. When I finish, I toss my laptop in the back seat and stare out the window.

"You want to talk about it?" Jack's voice cuts through my morose fog.

"I already told you, Jack. I don't know where the power comes from."

"I wasn't talking about that, Tabitha."

"I'm fine."

"If I have learned one thing about women is that fine

means anything but. Come on, talk to me. Just between you and me."

"Jack, I'm fine. We were just fucking, remember? If we were having a relationship, you would have had to report it. So it's fine. He's allowed to have a girlfriend. Let him take her home to that shit-show he calls a family. I hope little-miss-sunshine has a strong backbone and thick skin. Buck's family will chew her up and spit her out for a snack."

"Right. You keep using that 'fine' word. I don't think it means what you think it does."

Did this asshole really quote The Princess Bride to me?

I snort like a dragon about to singe that fucking smirk off his face. "What do you want me to say, Jack? He told me he loved me. He said he couldn't live without me. He tried to fucking feed me blood to save my life. How am I supposed to feel? Please, tell me, you fucking boy scout. Because right now, I'm obviously not feeling whatever I'm supposed to feel. I just want to fucking do my job and finish the mission, alright? Don't worry about the team. You're my boys. I'll do my fucking job like a God damn rockstar, and my personal life is none of your fucking business anymore."

He gives me a side glance. "Feel better?"

"I'm FINE."

"We definitely need to expand your vocabulary. But I'm happy you at least understand the state Buck left things in. For what it's worth, I don't condone what he did."

"What do you mean what he did?" I turn in my seat to face him, narrowing my eyes. My fists clench with the sudden desire to clean Jack's clock for him.

"Leaving you for a two-bit bimbo."

"You don't know shit about her. She might be smart," I

grumble.

"Doesn't mean she's not a bimbo."

"Jack, it's fine. Really. I'm not the kind of girl you take home to mom. I'm the kind you fuck stupid and walk away before the crazy takes hold. It was my mistake to fool myself into believing otherwise."

"This is where I have to disagree."

I shrug and turn back to look out the window, shutting myself off from him.

"The girls I run with, those are the ones you ride hard and put away wet. You, you're definitely keeping material. He's a damn idiot for throwing you away. He's the one making the mistake, Murphy, not you. If the relationship between the two of you were an issue, I would have put a stop to it before New York."

Great, now I feel like an asshole. Jack always knows what to say. Whether he means it is another question, but I'm too raw to go down that rabbit hole.

"So, on a lighter note," Jack takes the hint and changes the subject. "You manage to figure out anything from that cryptic gobbledy gook you call a training manual? The one you got from the Iscariot?"

I laugh. Rowena would punch him if she heard him call it gobbledy gook. "It's rune magic. And it was gibberish to me until after our night at The Pit."

"Rune magic. Like, that angel shit? And you didn't understand it until that night?" He drums his fingers lightly; a tell-tale sign he's working the puzzle of my knowledge gain out.

"Before then, I had to use a translator Rowena gave me. After that night, the words just started making sense."

He nods and fishes out his cell phone. "We're taking a small detour. See you at the hotel." He hangs up, and we drive for another hour before he turns off the interstate.

Next thing I know, we're in the middle of fucking nowhere Tennessee. He turns onto an overgrown deer trail. We bump our way through the winding road/trail until we come to a gravel driveway with a "Trespassers Beware" sign tacked to a tree. Another five minutes of even worse winding gravel road and we come upon the cutest cabin.

"Stay here. She doesn't like strangers." Jack steps out but stands inside the open driver's side door.

I'm fascinated as Jack removes every single weapon on his person. The process takes more than a minute as he carefully unloads each item onto the driver's seat. Then he stalks up to the door, knocks, and steps back.

It cracks open only enough to let me know there's a person peeking out. They appear to exchange words before the door closes. He walks back to my side of the truck and raps on the window. I roll it down, and he says, "Disarm, and follow me."

Now, I'm curious. Jack goes nowhere unarmed, even when he seeks solace in a stripper. I take a few minutes to strip all the weapons off my person before I ease out of the truck.

As soon as my feet touch the ground, I shiver like someone walked on my grave. My body is immediately on edge, and my hackles are up.

Magic permeates every inch of this place. Old and powerful magic wards this cabin and surrounding grounds. Every inch of my being screams to run back to the truck. Because I trust Jack with my life, I ignore my instincts and follow him.

As we ascend the steps, the door opens. Before us stands a petite woman with wild, gray, curly hair. She's dressed in faded jeans and a flannel shirt. After examining us both with her eyes, she motions us in.

Jack steps across the threshold.

I hesitate because crossing a threshold has consequences. Depending on the being inviting you in, you could lose so much more than your freedom. How is Jack staying so cool about this?

"It's alright, Murphy," Jack gestures for me to follow.

I swallow hard and step across the threshold.

The old woman's eyes crinkle in malicious amusement. Slamming the door shut, she moves by me. "You sure you want to squander your favor on this girl, Mister Talbett? She must be somethin' special to you."

"You could say that." He winks at me.

"Jack, if she owes you a favor, don't waste it on me."

"It's my choice where I spend my favors, Murphy."

The old woman cackles. "Well spoken, Mister Talbett." She claps her hands together. "What is it you wish to know about... Murphy, right?"

"Something like that," I mutter, not wanting to give her my real name. Names have power, even without most people knowing it. Those who follow the 'Old Ways' especially use names to weave their magic into a person. Giving my full name is like signing my life away.

"The favor I ask is I need to know what lies beneath."

"Knowledge is a dangerous thing, Mister Talbett. Are you sure this is what you seek?"

"I am." Jack is careful to not move, or touch anything, staring directly at the old woman.

"Even if the knowledge makes you an enemy?"

"For my third consent, I defer to the lady."

They both turn and look at me, who's staring at Jack open- mouthed.

*How the fuck does he know the old ways? Who the fuck is this woman?*

My head swivels from him to her and back.

Jack has tricked me into the presence of an old one. I know I can refuse and we walk away none-the-wiser, but Jack's trust would be broken.

Jack has not come out and said he doesn't trust me after the night at The Pit, but his actions speak volumes. He short with me, and tense whenever we get around supernaturals. He has barely let me out of sight.

The kid gloves treatment for my well-being has reached a point where I'm snippy with him all the time. I can't blame the guy. The safety of the team comes first. My feelings aren't the priority. I frown and stare at him, trying to gain what he meant by what lies beneath.

*What happens if the old woman is right, and it makes us enemies? What if I'm a monster now?*

I break the staring contest to hide the hurt and isolation caused by Jack's detour. Maybe the rawness of this shit between Buck and me is making me too sensitive. But the idea that Jack could be preparing to abandon me too is more than I want to face in this cabin with a creepy old woman waiting for my answer.

"Fine. Whatever."

The old woman cackles again and disappears into her kitchen. She returns holding a mushroom that sparkles in the sunlight between tongs.

"You want me to eat shrooms?"

"No, you suck the head and leave the tail. It's important to not take the stem with it."

"Or what?"

"Or it gets interesting. Now be a good girl and eat your veggies." She eagerly motions to the sparkling mushroom.

I grumble about mushrooms not being a vegetable but gingerly take the tongs. I give Jack a final look then shrug. "What the hell, down the rabbit hole we go." I suck the mushroom head off the stem.

## ON THE ROAD AGAIN

The shit-kicker music blaring in Jack's SUV makes me blink and groan. Rubbing my eyes, I realize we are on the interstate again. The clock on the dash reads two in the morning.

"Hey, sleeping beauty, got your favorite." He motions to the Lemon Lime Gatorade in the drink holder. "How are you feeling?"

I start to say like shit but pause. The realization dawns on me that I slept for at least six hours uninterrupted. My body is free of any aches or pains. Even the lingering desire to fuck everything in sight from Kiss is gone.

"I feel pretty damn good, truth be told."

"Yeah. Bobbi has some surprisingly good shit. I would strongly recommend not having another one of those for at least a decade."

"Killjoy," I tease.

"No, I'm serious. Catastrophic internal organ failure. It's not something you mess with, Murphy."

"Okay... So, did you learn anything, Major Killjoy?"

He chuckles. "I did. First, I have to tell you something verbatim. Bobbi made me recite it before I left. She said, and I quote, there is some knowledge better learned of your own volition rather than told by another."

"What the fuck does that mean?"

"It means I won't tell you what I learned until you have discovered it yourself. Until then, I'll tell you this much. You keep studying the gobbledy gook the Iscariots gave you and you keep doing what you're doing. I trust you with my life, Murphy. That and every other member of this team, but I'm willing to turn a blind eye if you want to let a mutt take a chomp out of Buck's ass."

"Fuck no. Then he'd be big, stupid, *and* furry."

"Ain't that the truth." A smile forms as he stares out the road.

He holds up his fist and I bump it. As we are bumping fists, we both say, "We bump back," like a toast to our success.

"Now, about your after-action report. Did you finish it?"

"Why do you think I put it in the back seat before you attempted to mansplain the word fine to me?"

Jack chuckles and shrugs. "Want to write mine?"

"Not a chance." I grin. "Unless you plan to bend me over a desk and treat me like a naughty secretary."

Jack sputters and snorts his drink. "As much as we would both enjoy that... No. I'm your superior officer."

"You're definitely Major Killjoy. Guess I'll just have to entertain myself over here." I settle back and let my hand fall on my thigh like I'm about to rub one out in front of him.

"Keep the moans to a minimum. I'd like to make it to the hotel in one piece." But I see him cutting a side look without turning his head.

While I laugh in response, I reminisce that it's good to hear Jack back to how he was before I got bit in Italy. Whatever happened in the creepy woman's cabin put his mind at ease. God, I hope she didn't whammy him.

Meanwhile, at the motel in Knoxville, Buck angrily paces in the room he shares with Trevor.

Trevor lies sprawled on the bed, flipping channels on the television. "I thought these motels had booby channels."

"I know he's fucking her!"

"Yes," he says without stopping his channel surfing, "I'm sure somewhere there's a man, fucking a woman."

Buck thumps the dresser and snarls. "You know who I'm fucking talking about. Why else would they take so damn long to get here?"

"So what if he is? She's fucking hot."

Buck turns to Trevor, the veins on his neck pulsing as he rages. "Don't you fucking touch her." He grits through his teeth.

Trevor calmly sets the remote down and gets off the bed, strolling towards Buck. "And what if I do?"

Buck roars and steps toe to toe with him, even with Buck towering a good head above Trevor. "I'll— "

"You'll what? Run back to that dumb bitch in New York? You're the one that made her a free agent again. I might fuck her in front of you. Hell, she might even like making you watch."

Buck swings and Trevor dodges deftly. The next ten minutes turn into the WWE Motel addition until Trevor gets Buck into a sleep hold. A knock at the door between the rooms causes both men to stop dead.

"We're finally here. Open up," Jack barks.

The two men right themselves, and Trevor answers the door.

Jack eyes them questioningly. "Everything alright in here?"

"Ship shape, Sir," they say in unison.

From behind Jack, I chuckle. We had listened for a few minutes before knocking. The gist of their fight is clear. I can't touch that with a ten-foot pole.

"Good, get some sleep. We ship out at o-five-hundred." Jack turns and starts his bed routine. He pulls out his toiletries bag. Next all the weapons are removed from his person. Boots get unlaced and set neatly at the foot the bed. He works as if he didn't just disrupt a brawl between squad mates.

I'm left staring at Trevor and Buck. The urge to say something is strong, but I resist as I'm still riding the high of the mushrooms.

The next morning, Buck storms into our room, snatches up my bags, and stomps back out.

Jack peeks around the corner, toothbrush still in mouth. He witnesses the little tantrum before retreating to finish brushing his teeth.

"Well, so much for you being a white knight!" I joke as I get up to follow my bags.

The scene outside is right out of a rom-com. Buck snarls at Trevor. "You're in the other truck. Murphy's with me."

"You're an idiot. I'm riding with you." Trevor gives him a smug smile, crossing his arms.

"I swear to God, Trevor. I'll blow your ass to pieces if you get in my truck." Buck jabs his finger in Trevor's face.

"Whoa, fellas. Let's not do any blowing until we've had

coffee." I tease as I hold up my hands.

"Who's blowing what now?" Jack asks as he comes out with his gear.

Trevor pretends to toss a grenade. "Buck! To pieces!"

Buck palms his face. "Just get in the other truck, asshole. Murphy, you're with me."

Thinking this is a terrible idea, I raise both my brows. I look hopefully at Jack to give him a chance to redeem his white knight status.

He just shrugs. "Your call, Murphy."

With a groan, I scrutinize Buck for a moment. "Fine." I yank open the passenger door and hop in, slamming it behind me.

Once we're on the road, I cross my arms and stare out the passenger window, ignoring Buck. Every few hours he tries to start a conversation.

I say nothing the entire way to New Orleans, even when he asks me what I want at the drive thru. He should damn well know what I like.

He's upset and frustrated. Despite being the asshole who broke shit, he wants me to fix it.

The problem with being a soldier is my resolve is ironclad. He made it clear I'm no longer what he's looking for. Falling back into that sweet dream is a mistake. I'll eventually talk to him again, but not today. Today, he gets the "Fine" treatment.

We roll into New Orleans early in the afternoon and arrive at the safe. How The Rangers pulled off acquiring one in this city is beyond human comprehension. We grab our gear and head into the house.

When Jack suddenly stops in the doorway, I run into him. "What the fuck, Jack?" I try to walk around him only to practically be clothes-lined by his arm up and extended, signaling danger.

Straight ahead of our fearless leader is a young girl sitting on the island in the kitchen. Her hair is as black as a starless night. Her figure is petite with pale skin. She can't be more than five feet tall.

My brow furrows. Why is a teenager waiting for us? Then I feel power surge inside me. Whatever is going on with me really doesn't like this girl.

"Deveroux." Jack nods.

I blink in disbelief and then narrow my eyes. This girl is the infamous Louise Deveroux? "What is it with supernatural creatures and young girls? It's creepy."

"Major Talbett." Louise hops off the island, and shadows blossom in front of her to blot out the sunlight we are letting in. Her French accent is thick.

"To what do we owe this pleasure?"

Adrenaline pumps through me. Buck and Trevor twitch and shift their weight.

*How the fuck is Jack always the calm one?*

"Do you think you can enter my city without me knowing? You little hunters think you do not have to follow zhe rules?" She prowls toward us.

"We literally just go here. Lucien is aware of our presence."

The shadows roil and boil around Louise, before engulfing all of us. Any sunlight in the room is shrouded in her shadows. Before me, Jack goes in the air as this young girl lifts him by his throat with her shadows. The damn fool signals us to hold position.

They appear to stare each other down, but I know better. We've been trained to look at the center of their forehead not into their eyes.

"If you object to our presence, it sounds like you need to

have a discussion with Lucien. Not with us."

I count four heartbeats before she sets him down. I have to give her props for not backing down. Lucien Deveroux is the leader of New Orleans. He lets his little protégé run amuck, and she likes to pretend she's the ruler of New Orleans.

She remains right in his bubble. "Why are you in my city, hunters?"

"As we told Lucien, we are looking for a Red Jacket pushing Kiss to werewolves." Jack stands, unmoving, his weapons still drawn. Even if he is in pain, he won't show that weakness in front of an enemy.

"So you come to hunt one of my people?" She rests her hands on her hips.

"Not hunting, information gathering. Your people only move the product. I want the source. Give me the info, and we'll be out of your city."

"Fine. You have my permission to play with my toys. Zhe Red Jackets who deal with zhe drugs work at zhe docks." With that, Louise Deveroux vanishes, leaving nothing but sunlight streaming heavily into the now brightly lit living room and kitchen.

# 19

I HATE GEESE

July 2005 - New Orleans

I don't know which God's Wheaties we pissed in when we came to New Orleans, but I have never been so sick of the color red in my life. Four months of the same old shit. Each sundown, we come to the docks and stalk every fucking Red Jacket that dares to show themselves. Everyone in New Orleans owns one of these fucking fashion nightmares. Louise Deveroux did us no favors in pointing us to the docks.

"Cheer up, Murphy. At least we get fireworks tonight." Buck moves to touch me and pauses when I cut him a dirty look. Buck's still trying to make nice. I'm still not in a forgiving mood.

Trevor laughs every time he fails.

Just when I think we can move forward, that girl calls

or texts him, and my jealous soul flares back to life. Even after four months, I want to scorch the Earth every time I hear that damn ring tone she put on his phone.

"I'll take the south. Don't follow me," I jab my finger in Buck's chest.

He holds his hands up in surrender while wearing a pained look on his face because I still won't give him the time of day. He has no idea how much it hurts to know he wants to make nice with me while also keeping that girl on the hook. Maybe I didn't know Buck at all.

Trevor frowns at me and shakes his head before heading to the east side of the docks.

Buck is left standing alone.

I make my way to my perch.

I feel like a gargoyle, watching over the night shift workers. Thankfully, the docks are large enough we need to spread out. I flick on my earpiece and enjoy the otherwise silence my observation point gives me.

Outside of New Orleans

Jack pulls his truck into the parking lot of the seedy motel where the message said his mission dossier would be waiting. He thought it strange that the paperwork wouldn't be sent to the safe house, but Armstrong has never been predictable, or conventional.

He rubs his hand over his face, half expecting this to be a trap. His team didn't like him coming alone, but Armstrong was insistent. Before he left, he told Trevor where he was going and if he didn't check in by midnight to come looking.

Easing out of his truck, Jack makes his way to number seven. After knocking three times, he waits. Instead of a message courier peeking through the cracked door, it opens wide to reveal Armstrong himself standing in all his military glory. When he steps back to allow Jack to enter, Jack's brows lift to his hairline with surprise. Sitting prim and proper on the edge of a bed is Mehzebeen, the de-facto leader of The Accord.

"Sir. Ma'am." Jack nods as he steps into the room thinking how completely unconventional the whole situation is.

When Mehzebeen offers him hot tea, he politely accepts. He keeps the frown off his face as the commander of the Night Rangers settles into a seat next to the ancient vampire.

"Talbett, we have an eyes-only request that you and yours are perfectly positioned to undertake." Armstrong begins as he fishes a folder from the small attaché on the floor next to his chair. "This request has been made of us by Mehzebeen, and I have deemed this target enough of a threat to allow this request to be executed."

Jack takes the folder from the older man and leans back in his chair. The other two patiently sip their tea while he flips it open. He takes a moment to study the headshot paper clipped to the top of the first page before lifting it to skim the dossier.

The man's name is Jackson Pruitt. He was a member of some biker gang before being turned into a vampire by a Red Jacket. Jack's eyebrows raise when he reaches the part where an Alpha werewolf ripped the vampire to shreds, only to have said vampire re-emerge a few months later.

"Is this accurate?" Jack cannot help himself at how unbelievable this file is.

"It is." Mehzebeen confirms, her voice calm and soft.

"We have decided the time to act is now. Lucien has taken this abomination under his wing, and with the winds behind us, we will have the perfect chance to strike." Armstrong states plainly as he sits like a king on a throne.

"What's the play, Sir?"

"The Tropical Depression forming is going to be... encouraged to grow into a full-blown hurricane. When it makes landfall in New Orleans, your team is to use the harsh winds and lack of population to remove this scourge from the face of this planet."

"Sir? How can you be so sure there will be a hurricane for us?" Jack's eyes flit between the two of them as he ponders his team's ability to complete the high-risk plan presented.

"I will make certain it happens." Mehzebeen's matter-of-fact confession is quiet. She maintains the prim and proper posture from her position at the end of the bed.

"I... see. Ma'am." Jack coughs gently to clear his throat.

Weather manipulation is high-level magic frowned upon in the supernatural world.

"Talbett, this is a priority alpha target. You and your team *will* proceed with this operation. Memorize the file. It will be destroyed after you are finished. Do not involve the werewolves." Armstrong's stern demeanor leaves no room for argument or disobedience. "As well, this operation is off the books. If your team is compromised, we will deny any involvement."

Jack hates black ops. Something always goes wrong when it was so hush-hush that even your bosses want their hands clean. But soldiers follow orders. He spends the next thirty minutes memorizing the file. One small tidbit sticks out. Tucked away in a small footnote is the information that this Pruitt fellow is a drug runner. Or was when he had a pulse.

When Jack stands to leave, Mehzebeen also rises and approaches him. In another life, he might have fallen for her pretty face and exotic charm.

"Ma'am?"

"Should your mission go astray, you will need this. You will know when you need to present it." She hands him a small card with a red rose on the card and in elegant handwriting on the other side, Jackson Pruitt.

Jack leaves the hotel with a gnawing in his gut. Armstrong working hand in hand with Mehzebeen is the first of many issues he has.

Hurricanes are unpredictable, yet they claim to know exactly when this hurricane will happen. They gave him dates and times for the mission to be carried out. Now, he just had to tell the team.

Why are the vampires asking the Night Rangers to remove their trash? How did this blood sucker survive a werewolf shredding him to pieces? Why doesn't Armstrong want the mutts involved?

Once back in the city, he radios his team in so they can discuss the additional mission.

******

It doesn't take us long to get back to the safe house. I'm relieved this dumb goose chase is called for the night.

"Have a seat," Jack commands. "We have a second mission." He's sitting at the dining room table.

We settle in, like points of a compass, and reach for the notepads.

"No. Off the books," Jack informs us. "You got anything

in your bag of tricks, Murphy?"

Buck, Trevor, and I frown at each other and sit up straighter in our seats.

"Sure do, champ." I push up and move from one to the next, carefully marking the rune with my fingernail on each guy's forehead, then using the hall mirror to trace the marking in my forehead.

Once I settle back into my seat, Jack begins relaying the entire contents of the file to us.

"Shit," Buck blows out. "You think he might be our guy? For the other shit?"

Jack shrugs. "He was a drug runner before he was turned. Doesn't seem too far-fetched that he would push underworld drugs as well. Taking after his sire."

"Fuck. Where's that bastard?" Buck pushes up like he's going to go take on said vampire right then.

"*Her* name was Adelaide. She's dead. It was in the file. She violated Mehzebeen's hunting rules in Savannah."

"But this Pruitt asshole was dead too, right?" If vampires can come back from being shredded to pieces, we're doomed. Vampires are no fucking joke. Where werewolves can at least be reasoned with, vampires are pure evil. I don't care how nice they play with humans. They're all monsters in the end.

"That's where we come in. We're the only ones who can take him out permanently."

"What are you thinkin', Jack?" Trevor lightly knocks on the table in thought. "We've been chasing our tails harder than Buck chases Murphy and gotten about as far."

I snort.

Buck punches Trevor in the arm.

Jack shrugs and leans back. "We're looking for Jackson Pruitt, and I have a few last known locations. We'll start there, and who knows, maybe Lady Luck will be on our side. Mission date is August 29th. So we need our ducks in a row by then."

The wide-eyed looks of Buck and Trevor must match mine, looking at Jack. We have never had a hard date to complete a mission. Whatever happened during his little rendezvous has left Jack sitting across from us with an etched scowl on his face.

When Jack dismisses us, we hop up, and head to our rooms.

"Murphy, a moment."

"Sir?" I pause and turn back to face him, leaning in the doorframe.

"I need a full perimeter sweep and every defensive rune on this place reinforced. Think you can handle that?"

"Yes, Sir."

## MISSION HURRICANE

August 28, 2005 - New Orleans

From the time Jack came back until today, we have been all over the Red Jackets. After identifying our target, we focus on his every moment. Watching him work on his bike, polish his bike, and the countless women he gives joy rides to rivals Jack's strippers. I don't think I have ever met a man that loves his bike as much as Jackson Pruitt loves his. We've experienced more than one sleepless night as we stalk him across the city on his precious motorcycle.

Pruitt is sexy as fuck. When he was alive, I bet he smelled of leather and cigarettes. His skin holds the hints of a tan, telling us that he's a newly minted vampire.

Two weeks into our stalking, we are back at the docks where we had wasted time chasing our tails. The target meets with two men, and I snap more photos than the Paparazzi stalking an A-lister.

Jack and Buck intercept the little thing Pruitt met up with after she picked up her package before she can hop on the greyhound, and it's like even the Man upstairs wants us to succeed. She had no idea that we tagged her. When she showed up on Malone's doorstep to deliver to Maxim, we knew we had our guy.

The ship manifests, along with information from our Night Ranger tech rats, gave us a location, Bogota. Once this mission is complete, we are cleared to head to South America.

The dining room table is covered in photos, maps, and blueprints. The four of us stand like points on a compass around it. There's no good way to approach without being seen.

"I don't know, Jack. This feels like a setup." I thump the table lightly. "The road's narrow. Buildings are tall, and this storm's fucking serious."

"I know. It's because we're getting ready to raid a lair. Apparently, this area is our target's stomping ground. We are under direct orders, though. Whatever this Pruitt kid is, we're to take it out."

"I've got clear shots from here and here," Trevor taps the map, "but only if you pull them outside. None of these buildings have windows for me to save your asses through.".

"How long will it take you to rig it to blow, Buck?" Jack asks.

"Two minutes, give or take. Rain's gonna make it difficult, but not impossible."

"Do what you do best, Buck. Tell us when you're rigged, and we'll breach."

"Jack, I got a bad feeling about this." I shake my head, seeing no good way to complete this mission. We go in too soon, they know we're there and pick us off as we go through the door. If we go too late, the hurricane sweeps us away. I can't place it, but there's something gnawing at me, telling me to talk the guys out of this.

Lightning cracks, and the wind howls. It's been raining since the twenty-third, and the city is being evacuated.

"You got all the wards up?"

"Yes, Sir. Doubled them up. Nothing is getting in without a lot of effort."

"Then we got this." Jack tries to reassure me, but he always exudes the confidence of success.

******

August 29, 2005 - New Orleans

Jack has us lined up at the corner of a building near Pruitt's hideout. I'm thankful our gear is blocking most of the rain.

"Everybody in position?" Jack asks over the comms.

"Yeah, if by position you mean having a fucking hurricane shoved up my ass," Buck growls back.

"Awe, we both know how much you like shit up your ass," I chime in.

"We've been over this. The hurricane provides cover to strike and washes away the evidence we were ever here. Quit fuckin' around and get your game face on," Jack barks.

The rain blows sideways as the storm rages into the city. Our intel suggested the vampire's lair was near the water's edge; but by near, they mean fifteen minutes from the ocean.

"Overwatch is green." Trevor finally clears us.

Buck, Jack, and I move with practiced precision. Jack pulls us into position near the door. Water streaks across his visor as he pulls out a UV grenade. He pops the door open, chucks the grenade in, and pulls the door closed to shield us from the light. Standard grenades would make one hell of a bang. Not these. The UV grenade is a staple of their arsenal. It has a UV light core enclosed with spring triggered shield plates. After bursting with a pulse of massive UV light strong enough to give anyone second degree burns if not protected, it slowly burns off with a purple UV glow. The blast is like a lightning flash. When it subsides, we filter in. Bullets whiz in the air. The wind howls more as Katrina descends upon the city. We move without hesitation and fire without remorse.

The four vampires had been sitting around a card table. One was instantly ashed by the grenade. Another springs to action only for Jack to slam a heavy stake into its chest.. Rifle fire rips the third to shreds. The fourth, wearing a red jacket, snarls at Jack but then levels his gaze on me and he smiles like a kid in a candy store. Ever since Italy, Vampires are instantly drawn to me. They call it singing. The notes from Ford confirm that their test subject said it was like a siren song calling them to me.

When his eyes lock with me, I freeze. This isn't a vampire singing kind of thing. It's something much worse. Thanks to those three shitty days of Holy water, I'm not supposed to be attracted to them;, but all I can think about is ripping of my clothes and fucking this smoking hot blood sucker.

Jackson Pruitt has pretty boy eyes with a devil may care smile. The look on his face tells me he doesn't give a shit about hunters, or hurricane. He would bend me over the card table and make me scream his name in a heartbeat.

"Shit. Murphy!" Jack shouts to pull me out of my daze.

Pruitt bolts toward me and forms into mist before our eyes. I stumble back, trying to, but it's everywhere.

Suddenly, my head aches like someone drove a stake into my temple. I let go of my rifle and grab my head, shaking it, and ripping off my helmet. Something is trying to tear through my runes to take control.

I hadn't realized I stumbled to the door until I found myself outside in the pouring rain and in Trevor's sights. I'm not sure what made him decide to shoot at me, but he does.

Trevor fires several UV grenades at the entrance. They flare to life, and the wind twists them into a purple vortex of sunlight in the otherwise black sky.

Jack and Buck barrel through the door to witness the gruesome sight we have seen to date. In the midst of the flashes and swirling purples of the UV light, tiny bubbles of blood explode and spray the entire area in gore.

Just like that, Jackson Pruitt spends his last life in New Orleans.

Jack turns to me with narrow disapproving eyes.

I stand frozen, blinking in confusion, covered in gore bubbles, and half blind from the flashes. I yelp when I feel the prick of a needle. My body grows heavy and numb. I slur my words as I try to speak to tell them something is wrong, and in my head.

The tranquilizer works fast, and my pain subsides. The world tilts and I groan as I see the buildings turn upsides before I lose consciousness.

******

Jack and Buck bolt for the truck. Buck presses the go button and the building implodes behind them, just one more lost to the hurricane.

Trevor packs his gear swiftly and takes his vehicle back to the safe house.

The men unload silently. Jack carries Murphy inside to the safe room and lays her on the cot. Buck and Trevor follow closely with the gear.

Once the door seals, Buck rushes to Murphy's side. "What the fuck happened, Jack? Why did you tranq her?"

"She was compromised. I knocked her out to prevent her from freaking out. Looks like Kiss is still in her system." Jack lies smoothly. He isn't sure if it's what he learned about Tabby, or if it's Kiss. Either way, he isn't willing to kill her or leave her behind.

Jack turns to get a blanket and finds himself held in the air by his throat.

Trevor and Buck leap into action, but are thrown against the far wall, pinned by the shadows billowing from Louise Deveroux.

Her black, soulless eyes pierce Jack's, stopping him from looking away. Fury rolls from the petite creature in relentless waves.

"How did you get in?. You don't have permission to cross the threshold." Jack's voice is raspy and strained.

Louise laughs at the balls on this human. "You are an incompetent fool, Major Talbett. You promised there would be no hunting in my city."

Jack slowly lifts his hand, moving to a small pocket on his vest. "I need to show you something."

Louise tilts her head with amusement at how brave this little soldier is. He doesn't cower in fear or beg to be released. If she were inclined to touch him beyond murdering him, he would make a great Red Jacket. So, she allows him to fish out whatever he believes might save his mortal life.

When he holds up a business card, her eyes narrow at the rose emblem on it shining bright in the fluorescent lights. She hisses and looks at him again. "I didn't issue any such bounty."

"I never said *you* did," Jack rasps again.

In the blink of an eye, Jack sails across the room into Buck and Trevor The card and Louise Deveroux are gone.

"Pack all our gear in one truck," Jack croaks. "We're moving out."

"Tonight? Jack, are you off your fucking rocker? We barely made it back to the safe house and you want us to go back out into the storm?" Trevor snaps.

Jack cuts them a hard look. "That card only bought us the time she takes to find her sire. We need to be outside of the city limits, yesterday. Now move."

# DREAM A LITTLE DREAM

We made it to Houston in no time. Thanks to the hurricane, we have a few days before we can book flights to Bogotá.

When I came to, the three of them were arguing about what to do with me. I listened, pretending to still be out, as Jack defended me with a ferocity I didn't expect. Trevor wants to put a bullet in my brain. Buck cradles me in his lap and threatens to blow Trevor up if he even looks at me wrong. His remark makes me giggle and destroys my ruse.

"You know, you three are terrible for a girl's beauty rest."

Silence fills the cab and I sigh, wriggling out of Buck's lap. Pursing my lips and narrowing my eyes at him, I waggle my finger no at him. He damn well knows better. Turning to face Jack and Trevor, I'm greeted with stern and angry faces. Trevor would have more impact if he didn't have a soul patch.

"What the fuck happened, Murphy?" Trevor jumps in before Jack can smooth is all over.

"I don't know. Some asshole threw two UV grenades at me."

"You were actin' weird," he grumbles in defense, all the wind in his angry sails gone.

"So you thought giving me a mega sunburn would help?"

"Well, if you were turned, you'd die. If you were being attacked, they'd die. If you weren't, we have aloe." He crosses his arms and faces forward, sulking.

We all laugh at that logic. He's not wrong.

"Besides, I was right. There was some kind of weird vampire mist all around you. It blew up like a tsunami of blood."

"That explains this," I grumble as I look down at the dark splatters all over myself.

Jack clears his throat. "Are you alright, Tabitha?"

*Shit.*

He used my real name.

I hate the dead air as I mull over my state of being. I have no idea if I'm alright. Everything feels fine, other than I need a hot shower and some tequila. "I'm good, Jack. Just need a shower."

"Fair enough. What happened back there?"

Our eyes meet in the rearview mirror.

He hasn't told the rest of the team what we learned back at that cabin in Knoxville. Neither of us likes keeping secrets from them, but the lack of details concerning it will only result in a fight. That's the last thing we need right now.

"I wanted to fuck Pruitt like a porn star. Then my head felt like one of you assholes staked me in the temple."

I stop talking as I look at Jack. I had more I wanted to say, but the words would not come to me. About how it felt like someone forcing their way in and then I passed out. But my lips don't move, and my expression is noncommittal in the mirror. While my pulse quickens to terrified rabbit speed, I give no indication at the level of fear welling inside.

Whatever is happening to me doesn't want to talk about it and my body responds with heat. The fire builds in the pit of my stomach and blossoms through my body, as if it's trying to purge whatever is holding me silent.

The control on my mouth relaxes.

"I..." I pause as I mull over the consequences of telling them the truth about what has happened. I need to confirm before I drop that grenade. "I don't know, maybe I looked in his eyes. Maybe I just panicked and froze. This is the first vampire hunt since Italy. It won't happen again."

Jack's face goes completely blank and unreadable, but he only nods, turning his focus back to the road. The other two settle in their seats.

Buck opens his mouth to say something, closes it, opens it again, and he shifts around to face me.

"Don't. You made your choice. I'm good. I hope you find happiness." I cut him off before he starts, and as much as it pains me to say it, I mean every word.

Buck opens his mouth. "Tabby, I was wr—."

"You heard the lady." Jack cuts him off. "I don't want to hear anything else on this matter, is that understood?"

"Yes, Sir," he mutters and frowns.

I slump back into my seat and stare out the window.

We pull into the hotel and we each get our own room. The clerk behind the desk says nothing at our state. They fastidiously avoid looking directly at us as they process our rooms. I'm grateful they don't give us a hard time. The elevator ride to our floor is eerie in its silence.

I rush into my room before any of them can ask any further prying questions. Jack won't let this slide forever. I know I need to come clean with what has happened, but when I start down that line of thought again, my body burns and my jaw clenches, keeping me silent.

As soon as my room door closes, I peel out of my gear, kick the shower on as hot as I can stand it, and I step into the scalding halt water. It's the only time I can let loose and cry. Sure, the guys would be sympathetic, but what kind of soldier would I be if I broke down in front of them? My body shakes from my sobs. I scrub until all the dried blood is off my skin and my fingers are pruned.

When the water finally runs clear I shut off the water, brush my teeth, comb my hair, and hit the bed, barely getting under the covers before I pass out.

The door opens and closes with a click. My eyes fly open and I roll over, ready to dive for my gun when I see Jackson Pruitt standing in the doorway. My throat tightens and I feel like I'm set on fire for a third time this evening. "How the fuck are you here? You're dead!"

"Awe, darlin'. You got it all wrong. Ain't no rain and sunshine gonna kill me. Especially now that I found such a pretty little thing as yourself." His voice is smooth and rumbles, reminding me of a fine-tuned Harley Davidson.

My heart races. I shift to my knees, not wanting to be on my stomach when he moves to attack me. The hot, burning need to feel him inside me flares. All I want is to lay down and welcome him with open arms, and that's a problem I need to rectify pronto.

He prowls toward me, the confident predator.

I clench the sheets and bite my lower lip, trying to hide that I want him. I'm unable to force myself to get any of the stakes in my gear, which ratchets me to eleven.

He stops just a few feet from me, peeling out of his red jacket, followed by his clothes. His skin is smooth and sun kissed. His muscles are ripped. His chest rises and falls like he's breathing. His smoldering gaze never leaves mine.

"Darlin', you're the prettiest firecracker I ever did see. I knew the moment we met we were meant to be together." His southern drawl adds to the sex on a stick that is Jackson Pruitt.

The bed dips with his weight as he eases closer. When his hands rest on my hips, they radiate warmth.

I'm coming undone. The more he touches me, the more I want him to touch me. I'm going to hell; I have to be. I know he's a vampire. Or he was. Right now, he's every bit human. His raging hard on presses against my thigh as he pulls me against him. Our lips collide, and it's like a volcano erupting.

I moan, and any thought of killing him goes out the window. The heat rises. My skin burns everywhere he touches. His devouring kisses leave me drunker than downing a fifth of Jack.

His hands slide down and part my thighs before lifting me up and laying me down. His lips trailing down my neck and torso until he draws a nipple into his mouth.

"Jackson," I moan. My mind is muddled. He's making me feel like I'm the only woman in the world.

When he thrusts into me a moment later, it's divine. I gasp and rock my hips to meet his thrusts.

"That's a good firecracker, take it all," he coos.

We're panting and sweating as we pick up the pace.

Moans shift to screams of pleasure as he gets increasingly deeper inside. He swells and fills me like only Buck can.

Buck. My sweet Buck. How pissed he'll be to discover I fucked someone else, especially a vampire.

"Don't think about him, firecracker. You're all mine. Only I can give you what you need." He bites my shoulder and pumps harder.

I shudder as he brings me to an explosive orgasm.

Propping up on his knees, he grips my hips and bucks into me like there's no tomorrow. This isn't lovemaking, it's fucking. Pure, unadulterated fucking.

I gasp when he flips me over and pulls me up to my hands and knees before thrusting back in. I swear he has gotten bigger as he spreads my thighs and drives me into the pillows.

"Fuck, firecracker, you're so fucking tight." He growls.

My body is slick with sweat, and all I want to do is push back like a bitch in heat.

Then the icy cold of a metal stake burns my hand. The silver metal cylinder with one end crafted down to a fine point manifests out of nowhere. My brow furrows in confusion.

*When did I get a stake?*

In the distance, Buck calls my name, and I stiffen. Was he trying to get in? Jackson rips himself from me, causing me to yelp as he flips me like a pancake.

"I told you not to think about him." His lips part and his fangs elongate. "I'm all the man you need, Tabitha. And we're gonna be together forever." The icy pallor of death replaces the heat from his body. He leans down to sink his fangs in, and my instincts kick in.

I force him over, pinning him under me before stabbing

the stake into his chest with all my might.

My eyes fly open. I jump out of the bed, throwing fists and battling with the sheets entangling me.

Standing at the foot of my bed is Jack, not Jackson, or Buck, holding his gun. Behind him, the door is broken from him kicking it in.

Our eyes meet only for a fleeting second before I frantically search the room visually for the vampire.

"You're safe. It was a dream, Murphy. Just a dream." His strong arms wrap around me, grounding me in what I hope is reality.

## GAME ON

The intimacy of his arms around me causes my cheeks to flush. I shove off him and shoot out of the bed like a rocket. Fury fills my veins and venom spews from my mouth, "Quit fucking treating me like a Goddamn broken doll. I'm a fucking soldier, Jack!"

"Then start fucking acting like it," he calmly replies.

"Maybe if you and Buck weren't so fucking concerned with swooping in and saving the fucking day, I would be able to do just that." My voice rises in pitch and volume. "But no! It's oh poor Murphy's been through so much. Buck's so mean to her. Let's not upset her because she might go off the fucking rails.".

My eyes go as wide as saucers, and my body jerks as I fight to gain control of this person spewing craziness out of my mouth. These aren't the words I want to say to him at all. I was starting to tell him exactly what happened in my dream, and that I'm not okay.

*I need to be off this shit mission right the fuck now.*

Jack stands, narrows his eyes, and crosses his arms. His stare is the cold look of a commander, not a friend. "That so? Well, how's this for you, Lieutenant? Get your shit together, or you're on the next flight back to Doc Ford. I've been beyond fucking patient and tolerant. Breaking all the Goddamn rules for you and Buck. I even gave you a pass because of Italy. But you don't want kindness, soldier? Deal. From here on in, you fuck up, you're out."

I inhale deeply, like a dragon winding up to blow fire and my fists clench. The harder I try to say I'm possessed the more my teeth grind together, keeping me silent. "Yes, Sir," I hiss.

"Now grab your gear and get your ass downstairs. It's time to go." He turns on heel and storms back to his room.

My insubordination has finally pushed him to the limit.

*I don't know what the fuck you are! Get the fuck out of my head!*

*Oh, darlin'. But you've got such a pretty head, and it's awful comfy in here. Don't worry. I ain't gonna hurt you much. I just need a ride until I find somethin' better.*

*Better? Oh, hell no! You're gonna pay for that.*

*Bring it on, baby girl. Ol' Jackson ain't afraid of your little parlor tricks. I'll see ya in yer dreams, sweetheart.* He blows me a kiss.

The hold on my mouth and mind releases. For a moment, I have half a mind to scream for Jack. But, as soon as I open my mouth, Jackson's voice fills my head again.

*Tsk. Tsk. Can't have you goin' and ruinin' all my fun, darlin'. You ain't tellin' nobody shit. Now be a good girl and get your gear. We got a plane to catch.*

I have two choices.

Walk away, just disappear and not compromise the mission further. Jackson Pruitt has possessed me somehow, and I can't even hint to the guys there's a problem. When Jack looked at me, his face told me he believed every word I said. Or I do something drastic to force them to take me back to base. Then Armstrong can deal with this body-snatching fuck. This move would also end my career in the military. I would go home a failure to my father, something I would never recover from.

After packing up my gear, I head downstairs to help load the SUV. I fume the entire ride, sitting with my arms crossed, and perform my best Daffy Duck impersonation while I stare out the window. This prick thinks he gets a free ride, can mind fuck me, and do whatever the hell he wants.

*Alright, you arrogant prick. Game. Fucking. On.*

The only person I'm pissed at for my current situation is myself. I froze in New Orleans, and now I have this damn vampire screwing with my head. Oh, he's gonna pay. It takes all my willpower to not think about the things I'll do to him. I don't want him to even have an inkling that he's in for a world of hurt.

Once we pass through security, I buy the beer while we wait for the flight. The round is a silent apology for the shit we've been through on this mission. The tension between us is pulled tight.. I don't want it to snap.

We drink in silence, none of us wanting to talk about the recent shit. Jack and I look at each other once. I avoid looking at Buck altogether.

Trevor fastidiously plays with the label on his beer bottle.

The announcement calls over the speakers for the first

flight to board. Part of our safety protocols is to take separate planes. Buck and Jack have four hours to kill before they follow. By the time they land in Bogotá, Trevor and I will be settled into the next safe house.

I plop into my seat in the first row of the plane and force myself to relax. After the flight attendant finishes giving instructions for emergencies, I close my eyes.

Before I entered the Night Rangers, if you had told me I could control my dreams, I would have laughed in your face. All this hogwash of focusing your mind and making the dream yield to your whim was for people who believed in psychics and mediums.

Yet here we are.

With the hotel room freshly imprinted in my mind, I conjure it easily. I settle into the plush hotel room with a barely-there robe tied loosely around my waist.

He appears around the corner but isn't hidden thanks to the well-placed mirror.

Jackson Pruitt is a dangerously handsome man. My arousal grows as I gift him one of my award-winning smiles. "Hey, champ."

"Miss me, darlin'?"

"Always," I coo as I lean into his open arms. My fingers trail along his wrists to pull them forward. I have to lean up on my tiptoes to plant a soft kiss on his mouth. A smirk forms on my lips as I click the silver handcuffs in place. He hisses in pain.

"What the fuck?"

The room changes in a hurricane of shadows. The soft whites and hues of warm, rich colors fade into drab grays and harsh green colors washed out by the fluorescent light above. A metal table thuds between us, and his cuffs are now securely woven through the jump ring on the table, forcing him to bend forward.

I step back and lean against the two-way mirror wall to enjoy the shock and fury on Jackson Pruitt's face. "Awe, champ. Did you really think we didn't know how to deal with your vampire Jedi voodoo? Two can play the fantasy game. Sit down and be a good boy. You're going to answer some questions and then get the fuck out of my head."

"Feisty," Jackson purrs like a Harley again, forcing me to concentrate harder to resist the unusual desire to fuck him back into existence. "Just what do you think you can do to me, darlin', iffn I don't comply?"

I push off the wall and flash him a devilish smile, as I reach over to the recently conjured desk lamp and flip it on with the light shining right at his hands.

He yowls in pain and jerks the whole damn table toward him to flee the burning sunshine my lamp produces.

"Now, you fanged fuck, you listen to me. You either answer my questions, or I'm going to enjoy watching you fry in my dreams like a Goddamn marshmallow."

"Marshmallow? Shit darlin'. I got a six-pack, and ain't an ounce o' fluff on this body. What the fuck do you mean marshmallow?"

I pull up a chair and take a seat across from him, easing in close, like I might reward him with affection. "Marshmallow. Burns up fast and melts into a pool of nothing."

"Fuck." Jackson's demeanor morphs from arrogant to afraid. He isn't looking right at me, but around me.

Whatever he sees scares him, so I lean into his fear. "Now, first question. Why the fuck are you in my head?"

"Well, sugar. Seein' as your boy tried to blow me up with that grenade, I needed a ride, and you were the only train in the station."

"Why only me? There were two other men with me."

"Ah, see, now I can't go spillin' all my secrets."

I flick the lamp to put the light on his hand again.

"Ow, som'bitch. Alright! Alright!"

I ease it away.

"They're just humans. Can't hitch a ride in humans."

"We both know that isn't true." I reach for the lamp.

"Fuck. It is! My girl was somethin' special when I hitched a ride with her."

"Your girl?" Confusion washes over me for a fleeting moment before I recollect his ex-girlfriend, Shelley Baxter, from the mission details. "So you can only possess supernaturals?"

"Yeah. Somethin' like that."

"Why can't I tell my commanding officer about you?"

"Cause that fuckin' boy scout would ruin all my fun."

I laugh as he pegs Jack to a T. "How did you learn to do this? I've never heard of a vampire that can body hop like this."

"Well, darlin', let me tell you a little story about a boy, a girl, and a fuckin' werewolf."

# ONCE UPON A TIME IN SAVANNAH

I lean back in the seat and cross my arms, letting him have his story time. His emotions roll through me like a run-away rollercoaster.

"It all started a couple years ago. My girl, Shelley Baxter, is the prettiest thing you ever did see. I had just been made a runner in the Angels of Wrath, and she was comin' of age to become club property. Her no-good father was draggin' his feet 'bout her and her sister joinin' the club's assets. Hell, after the first time he tried to kill me, I asked him for her hand proper. She was gonna be all mine and only mine."

Jackson's devil-may-care smile fades in a sad expression. His entire bad boy demeanor crumbles before me, and for the first time he looks like a kid who got a shit deal and has been left holding the bag. "I just wanted to love that girl. She was all I could think about. I did all the shit I did so I could take over the club and be with her. Picket fence, makin' babies, and shit. She was into it too before I left for some fucked up run to California her daddy cooked up."

I would feel sorry for this guy if he weren't freeloading in my head.

"While I was out runnin', that fuckin' prick, Billy Coeh, did somethin' to her. Between him and her daddy, she hated me when I got back. I became obsessed. Wanted to show her I was the best damn man for her, but the old man sent me on a mission to South America. One he thought I wouldn't come back from."

"I guess he was right, since here you are."

Jackson snorts and shakes his head. "Nope. Not even close. I showed up, and sure, they wanted to kill us all. Shitty at the prices old Silas was settin', so I made a new deal. Told 'em we'd run drugs too, no extra charge and I would be the one they dealt with from now on. That I would take care of the old man for 'em. To guarantee I would make the deal they *put up* my friends." He air quotes the put up part of his little tale.

I motion for him to continue.

"It was all goin' great. I felt smug as fuck as I crossed back into El Paso where I ran into one of those inbred Coeh fuckers with his hands all over Faye Baxter, my girl's older sister. Ain't no way Silas Baxter let his eldest girl run off with one of those Wolf Pack biker boys. I stepped in and started headin' home with her. I was gonna make it big. Her daddy was gonna pay. That Coeh fuck was going to sit there with his dick in his hand. I was gonna be in charge, and my girl was gonna be with me."

"What happened?" I'm interested now. How does an upstart kid like Jackson Pruitt go from low-level gun runner to mutant vampire kingpin in less than two years?

"Jasper Coeh, that's what happened. Turns out, those inbred Coeh fuckers are werewolves. Werewolves! He destroyed my load and proceeded to maul me to death. Let me tell you, ain't nothin' scarier than a massive werewolf shreddin' you to pieces. I ain't too proud to admit I screamed. He left and took Faye Baxter with him. If I find him, I owe him an ass whoopin'."

"That still doesn't tell me how you turned into a mutant vampire."

"Adelaide," he whispers her name like a prayer. "She was a cute little thing. Looked to be about thirteen, or fourteen years old, but she was a wild creature, a couple hundred years old. She was there somehow and turned me. Taught me how to be a vampire. Adored her to pieces once she quit makin' fun of my bike." He shakes his head.

"She helped me get my boys out of South America. She protected me from that cunt, Deveroux, who still blames me for Adelaide's death." He frowns and shifts in his seat. "Suppose she should. It was my fault."

Silence falls between us as he gathers his thoughts. I give him the time he needs. The guy looks defeated and broken across from me. Try as

"We went back to Savannah to claim what's mine. I killed Silas and left his wife waitin' for me to come back and claim her. Chased my girl down in the woods. Everything was perfect. I had her beneath me. Was almost in her mind where I could take away all her fear and get her back to lovin' me."

"You mean, mind fuck her into being your slave."

His eyes narrow and he opens his mouth to say something dumb when I hover my hand over the lamp.

"Whatever," he grumbles. "That Coeh fuck that had been

messin' with her head and turned her against me, comes out of nowhere. If I thought bein' mauled as a human was some shit. Let me tell you, being mauled as a vampire ain't no better. That fucker literally put my head on a tree branch like it was a pike." He laughs.

"Somethin' happened that night. Don't know if it's my Shelley's doin', or that Coeh fuck's, but the next time I had a thought, I was inside my girl's head. It was like bein' in heaven. There wasn't nothin' I couldn't do with my girl."

"Wait. You're telling me Billy Coeh put you in Shelley's head."

"No! I put me in Shelley's head. You know that hoodoo voodoo where I can make you girlies drop your panties with a thought? It's that kind of shit. Only I was on the inside. With no one able to stop me."

I have a sinking feeling about where this is going.

"I made myself at home. Only that damn fuckin' Coeh started catchin' on. I figured, if I could get in her head, I could get in his. I planned it all out. Make him weak and then take him over. I was gonna be the Coeh Shelley threw her hat in with and enjoy makin' that fucker watch as I made pretty little puppies with my girl."

"I see. What went wrong?"

Jackson shrugs. "Don't know. Don't care. Shit went sideways, and he ripped me right out of Shelley. I wasn't stickin' around to find out. She made her bed. Chose to be a dog fucker, so I skedaddled out of there. Ran right into a scary motherfucker called Lucien. He's Deveroux's daddy, or something."

"Sire. Like Adelaide to you." I correct him.

"Yeah. Well. They have the same last name. There's some kind of weird shit between those two." He makes the handcuffs clank and hisses again as they burn his skin when he waves his hand dismissively.

"Alright. I'm guessin' the rest of the story is he taught you to use your new mutant powers ala Professor X, and you decided ridin' in my head was a good idea."

"You bet. Darlin'. You're my ticket out of New Orleans, and after what we did the other night, I'm good to ride until somethin' better comes along."

"What the fuck do you mean by that?"

"I mean. I'm gonna enjoy makin' you scream my name in your sleep."

I'm not sure what happens then. Rage fills me, and I'm screaming at him. My arms come up, and the light in the room grows bright, like the sun is burning down on us. I thrust my hands forward, and Jackson flies back, slamming against the concrete wall.

"No! Don't! I answered your questions! Fuck! Please!" He begs me as if I'm killing him.

I stare at Jackson, and don't feel like myself at all. Filled with fury at him enjoying the idea of mind-raping me. If I have to burn everything to nothing but ash I'm not going to let this fanged fuck abuse me like that. I suck a sharp breath in, and my hands raise again, as if drawing walls out of the ground. This isn't me. This is something else. Is he doing this?

Fear washes over me as I see him disappear into the shadows, leaving me alone in the interrogation room.

"Ma'am! Ma'am!" The flight attendant's voice rings above me, sounding miles away.

With a jerk, I start awake. My hands come up to swat away whoever is touching me until I focus on the flight attendant. I say nothing to her because Trevor stands next to her with a stern look on his face. His brows are drawn together in concern with a hint of annoyance. We're making a scene on an airplane. Trevor likes to blend into the background.

"I'm sorry. I was having a nightmare," I mumble.

The attendant looks relieved. "Sir. Please return to your seat. We are about to land."

"Murphy?" he asks in a low tone.

"I'm fine."

"The fuck you are. Can you keep your shit together long enough to stop scarin' this asshole?" He jerks his head towards the man sitting next to me.

My row-mate stares at me wide-eyed.

My palms are sweaty. My heart races, and while I have slept the entire flight I'm even more drained than when we started. Whatever happened at the end of the dream was not me trying to scare Jackson.

"I'm good, just a bad dream." I mutter at Trevor.

He nods and heads back to his seat.

As I resume looking out the window, one thing is for sure. I need to get as far away from my team as possible.

# THESE BOOTS AIN'T MADE FOR WALKING

Projecting yourself into the mind drains you. Thanks to all the lovely "therapy" sessions I attended with Doctor Ford as part of Night Ranger training, I acquired what I needed from my hitchhiker. The fear that he could catch me unaware at any time and force me to betray the team is enough to make me decide to go AWOL. I'll find that head-shrinker Ford always talks about living in treehouses in South America. They'll push this prick out of my head and then I can report back in.

"Awe, darlin', I ain't that bad. 'Sides. I like what you got goin' on. We ain't goin' nowhere." Jackson's voice is muffled.

The sharp pain in my head tells me he's still in the box the creepy version of me trapped him in. For the time being, I'm still in control.

From my gear, I select the items with trackers and set

them on the dresser. My cell phone, watch, and helmet make a morbid shrine of my life. My body jerks to a stop, turns abruptly, and drops my pack. "What the fuck do you think you're doing?"

"I'm preventin' you from makin' a mistake, darlin'. Listen. You're fun and all, but I'm only here until I find a better ride. I'm not an in-the-box kind o' guy. Besides, I want a body that can ride my bike. You're too damn short. So we're gonna take ourselves a little nap, and when we wake up, you're gonna keep doing your job like you're supposed to. When I find what I'm lookin' for, I'll check out."

I yawn in response. If he were not in my head, I would punch him for this. My little stunt on the plane has sucked just about all of my willpower from me. "Stop it. I'm not tired."

"The fuck you ain't. Look, I don't know what the fuck you did on the plane, but that bitch is scary. I'll be a good boy from here on out. But you gotta quit tryin' to be the big damn hero. You're gonna get us both killed."

With a disapproving grunt, I sit on the bed. He's *making* me lay down. So much for him being locked in a box.

"See, now this ain't so bad."

I look over my shoulder to see him sprawled on the bed. Thankfully, he's still clothed, so I scrunch my face up in concentration. Not being able to outright banish him, I shackle him to the bed. Feeling smug that he won't be able to do any funny business, I lay down and turn my back to him.

"I knew you liked this kinky shit," he chuckles.

Did he just nestle me? The burning energy surges, and I snarl, "Don't touch me."

He bounces away in an instant, "Yes, ma'am."

I'll give him one thing. I definitely did exhaust myself on that flight. Try as I might to stay awake, my eyes are betraying me to sleep.

The next thing I know, the alarm on my watch blares from across the room. I groan and there' s warm body spooned to me with the weight of his arm around me. With a shake of my head, it dissipates.

"Fucker," I grumble and stand up.

He's right about leaving, and I hate it.

As I clasp my watch and inspect myself in the mirror, I can't deny I look like shit. The dark rings under my eyes say that the few hours of sleep I just got isn't enough for doing battle with Jackson Pruitt. Rubbing my hand over my face, I sigh. It's after sundown.

Two thumps pound against the door, meant to wake me if my alarm hadn't. I snatch my toiletry bag and duck into the bathroom across the hall. A hot shower and no interruptions from my hitchhiker leave me feeling a hundred times better.

"Good of you to join us," Jack teases when I walk in the main room.

"Yes, well, I knew you couldn't stand to be without me."

"Hrmph," Jack grunts.

Buck and Trevor snicker at my sass but straighten up as soon as Jack cuts them his "commander" look.

"So what's the plan?" I change the subject.

"First, we're going to enjoy our coffee and eat something. Our liaison is going to be here," he pauses to glance at his watch, "shortly."

In Jack speak, it means they're late. Jack also shows up everywhere fifteen minutes early.

I shrug and head into the kitchen to get some cereal and a cup of coffee.

I eat in silence. The tension between the four of us lingers, and I hate being the cause of it. Guilt weighs heavy in my heart. Several times I open my mouth to speak, only to close it again, knowing anything I want to say would fall flat.

The knock at the door pulls me from my pity party. Jack moves to greet our guests. In walks a man with a James Dean bad boy vibe, followed by his biker mamma. When I say mamma, I mean it literally. She's pregnant. They're followed by three other burly looking pretty boys. I'm definitely not lacking for eye candy tonight.

"You're late," Jack growls.

"You're compromised." Mr. James Dean growls back as he gives Jack a cocky little finger gun.

"We knew we were coming in hot. That's why you're here. Where are my guns?"

The pregnant biker mamma rests a hand on her hip. "Keep your panties on. We've got your toys."

"Good. Let's get this mapped out 'cause we're doing this tonight."

The room explodes into a cacophony of voices. Everyone has an opinion to spew except for me.

My head pounds as I stare at the pregnant woman.

Over the noise, Jackson's loud and clear.

*I'll fucking kill him. Fucking inbred, no good, Goddamn Coeh.*

My body jerks as Jackson surges with ire, wanting to attack the man and woman. I grit my teeth and grip my coffee mug tighter, keeping us in place.

*Calm the fuck down, right the fuck now. You agreed to sit there and look pretty.*

*Yeah. That was before I knew you were workin' with the fuck that killed me.*

I blink in surprise as I recall the tale he spun on the airplane. Assessing the state of the two people in front of me, Jackson deserved what happened to him.

*Don't think about me like that! I didn't deserve to have my throat ripped out by a fucking Coeh, who turned out to be a fucking werewolf! How was I supposed to know they were together?*

*Uh, huh. You don't strike me as the knight in shining armor kind of guy.*

*What? Just because I picture myself in a black duster doesn't mean I'm not a good guy.*

Then, he makes himself appear in said duster, looking like a dark sheriff from some cowboy drama.

*This one.* He points angrily at Mr. James Dean. *This one right here. He's not the good guy, Didn't try to talk. He literally slammed into my truck, knocking it on its side while I was driving down the highway. He hurt my bike!*

*I see. I mean. It couldn't be that you kidnapped his woman, or anything like that, could it? Wolves are territorial about their mates.*

*Well, now I know that! At the time, they weren't mates. They were fuck buddies, and she belonged to the club I was taking her back, simple as that. No kidnapping.*

*Ever think maybe she didn't want to be property?*

*It would have been between her and her fuckhead dad.*

*That you killed.*

*After this prick killed me.*

*So, wouldn't you say you're even?*

*Well, it's not like.. I mean. I didn't kill him!*

I snort at Jackson's childish behavior, forgetting I'm the only person in the room who can see and hear him.

"You find something about this funny, Lieutenant?"

I blink, and Jackson disappears, leaving me to face all

the confused, staring faces around the table. During our little chit-chat, the room calmed down and moved on to planning. I have no clue what they have been talking about.

"No, Sir."

Jack studies me for a hard minute before he continues. *I'm definitely getting a talking-to later.*

He turns back to the maps on the table and gives them a good thump. "We both know this is the more valuable target. My team should take this one, and your crew the other."

Mr. James Dean, or Jasper Coeh as I now know, rolls his eyes. "I'm sure it is. But last I checked you little marines can't go traipsing through the jungle at over a hundred miles an hour. Which means if you want both, in tandem, you need my men taking the far one. You're the asshole that wants to go tonight."

# STILL NOT A DEMOCRACY

"Commander. This is a bad plan," I mouth off once I realize what Jack is proposing. The quick seconds I had to see he plans to storm the compound right at sunrise without perimeter checks, and only a few werewolves for back up is making me sick to my stomach. This must be how he felt in Italy.

"It's the only plan we got."

"No. We wait. Scout like we're trained to and make a better plan, Sir," I growl at him in irritation.

"If we wait, we lose them. They know we're here. Which means *if* we don't strike tonight, they'll be in the wind and we have to start all over again. It's now or never."

"Then we start over again. They can't throw up that kind of operation overnight. We'll be able to follow the trail and catch them. Without putting us at risk. This is suicide, Jack."

"The only reason we got this far is luck. Without Jackson Pruitt, we would have never found this operation. If we send them to ground, they're only going to get smarter. We'll never find them again."

"You can't know that."

"It's one vampire." He shouts at me. "All the toxicology reports point to it being one vampire. You damn well know how good they are at hiding."

"I also damn well know how good we are at hunting them. Jack, we don't have— "

"Lieutenant," he says with a sharp snap to his tone, ending all discussion.

I clench my jaw and look to Buck and Trevor to back me up.

Buck speaks up, "She's right, Sir. It's a shit show." For a massive guy he's trying to make himself as small as possible while going against Jack.

"I'm fully aware it's a shit show. Which is why we are trying our damnedest to do it right. So everybody goes home."

Trevor rubs his jaw, looking over the maps again. "We don't know the terrain."

"That's why we the locals are helping. The Accord has been working with the pack here. That's why we waited for them." He motions to Jasper and company. "They're our eyes and ears. Simple as that."

"And *they're* going to be three hundred miles away, Jack," I counter.

"Not all of them. We'll have pack members too." He leans up and crosses his arms. "This isn't up for debate, Lieutenant. These are your orders."

No one responds.. While we are close, we are his subordinates, and to argue further would be insubordination.

I shake my head and frown. This has to be payback for me ram-rodding my bad plan down his throat in Italy. Jack's not the vindictive sort, but it's like he has tossed all our training out the window for the "golden ticket" of a chance at this vampire.

"The mission is to find the source and destroy it."

"Well, how do you plan to determine who the source is?" Faye finally speaks up. "I mean, do you have a magical vampire DNA device" She makes jazz hands to insinuate a device appearing out of thin air." Or maybe your weirdo girl here can do somethin' to make the vampire light up like a Christmas tree? Or, I know, you just kill everything and hope the one you want is there."

Like table tennis, I snap my gaze from Faye to Jack. His jaw twitches like a bird on a wire with the effort to hold his temper in check. He lets out a heavy sigh. "Best as we can tell, the master of the coven is who we are looking for. If we take him down, we take out the source."

Trevor, Buck, and I ping-pong our looks back to the werewolves and shift to stand next to Jack in silent support of our commander.

"Just how in the fuck do you plan to figure out which one is the master?" Faye retorts.

"I assume that means you have never taken down a coven. The master always tries to protect his domain. Especially when it's the *pitiful little humans* attacking."

"Enough. We're here to help, Faye. You know how momma would be if I didn't do this." Jasper finally decides to interject.

Irrational rage bubbles inside me as I stare at the Alpha.

"You should have threatened to not let her see the kids." Faye sulks.

The tension breaks, and everyone laughs.

This is the worst plan we've put together, but Jack has a point, and he's in charge.

The rest of the meeting goes smoothly as the tactical options are laid out and finalized. Jasper and Faye will lead a group of warriors to hit the location out of our range, taking what is in production out of commission. Our team will hit the primary compound to eliminate the head of the coven. While the wolf intel suggests he'll be at the remote location, our intel advises otherwise.

Once the wolves leave, we strip down so I can place runes on each of us. With my fingernail, I trace them in place. Rowena suggested there might be more power behind contact in runes and I didn't put any credence in that before today. These aren't the Christian runes that Rowena showed me, which scares me. My finger moves of its own accord and with confidence in knowledge I was not aware I possessed until this moment. I hope to God these aren't some satanic vampire control runes that Jackson knows.

*No, darlin'. You're out of my league when it comes to the voodoo hoodoo nonsense. This is all you, that scary version of you from the plane. You got someone else in here I don't know about?*

He projects an image of him looking around with a waiting room behind him. While it makes me chuckle internally, it doesn't improve my mood.

"Gettin' kind of frisky there, aren't ya, Murphy?" Buck squirms under my ministration.

"Stand still," I mutter and continue. These runes are being drawn on instinct and look archaic. They burn bright when complete before seeping into the skin.

Trevor squirms and whines the entire time I work on

him. "Hey now, what the fuck, Murphy? These never hurt before."

"You want it to work, right?"

"Wait! Are you saying the ones you put on before didn't?"

"I'm saying the ones before aren't as powerful. Now quit being such a bitch and let me finish."

The other men chuckle, and Trevor grumbles, but stands at attention to let me finish.

As I place them on Jack, he takes it like a champ, never flinching, or complaining. When our eyes meet, I see trust in his gaze. Whatever he knows about me tells him this is good. So I have to put my faith into his judgment.

We gear up and check everything three times before we meet with our wolf counterparts. Everyone is on high alert as we load into the armored jeeps. Knowing we're compromised makes everyone tense and edgy, unwilling to crack the jokes like normal. When we ditch the vehicles, we split up. It's Jack with Trevor, Buck with me, and the wolves are on perimeter duty.

"Radio check," Jack says into our comm units.

"Overwatch green," Trevor replies.

"Boomtown green," Buck responds.

"Magic show green," I answer.

"Good. Wolves will give three short howls if something is amiss. You hear the howls, you get out. Remember, we're after the master, not the buildings."

"Hoo-Ah," we reply.

With a confirming ready nod, Buck and I reach up and flick on the spectrum goggles. They're designed to show supernatural or paranormal juju signatures and can take a bit of getting used to.. We originally used heat sensors but, the older the vampire, the more like a human they can make themselves appear, and the heat signature doesn't work.

With rifle in hand, I let Buck take point.

We move in perfect silent tandem, using hand signals to communicate. After cutting the perimeter fence, we make a break for the first building. Nothing shows on the sensors. So far, so good.

A glance at my watch tells me we have a few minutes before sunrise. The pinks in the sky cast eerie shadows on the buildings, but we're waiting until the sun fully peeks over the horizon.

Buck stands still as a statue next to me.

My stomach's twisted tighter than a pretzel with worry for my guys.

There's no movement, no chitter chatter. In fact, the only sounds are those of the nearby jungle, natural chirps and rumbles of creatures stirring for the day. These are noises you don't hear when predators like vampires are nearby.

Buck taps my arm twice for go, and we move. Kicking the door open, Buck tosses his first grenade. We count to three for the flash of UV that follows while holding the door closed. Then we come storming in with our weapons up.

Only, there's no one in here. Nothing at all, other than long tables with boxes of baggies on them.

On high alert, we walk through the room, keeping our backs to each other. No one has been here for some time. The place is missing the telltale hints of hurried movement to hide product.

Buck breaks protocol. "Where the fuck is everyone?"

I shrug.

We tread from this building to the next and repeat the

process. Still not a single vampire to be seen.

"Maybe the intel was bad," taking my turn to break protocol.

"Maybe. But the wolves were convinced."

"Or Jack and Trevor hit the jackpot and need our help."

Buck gets on the radio. "Sir. We got nothing here. Place is abandoned."

I swallow hard when there's no reply. The hairs on the back of my neck stand on end and the pretzel twisting goes into overdrive.

"Command. Come in." Buck says with more authority.

Still no answer.

"Overwatch, report." He demands.

## MURPHY'S LAW

Jack knows Murphy is right, and this is a bad plan. He wishes he could have agreed with her and taken it slow. However, from the intel the Amazon Pack provided, this vampire is smart and has moved his operations three times when he even gets a sniff of trouble. None of the locals have been able to pin him down.

Not to mention, a small part of Jack worries the longer this mission takes, the worse Murphy's predicament will be. He knows something's not right with her other than the answers he got from Bobbi. She quit confiding in him and won't look him in the eyes. Even her temper tantrum in Houston was off.

Bobbi warned him Murphy would do things her own way, but that she would never betray him, which is why he doesn't ship her back to base. He knows they would put her with Doc Ford again, and from what he has gathered the first round of "therapy" didn't go well.

Despite all his concerns, speeding up the timeline still feels like the best play they had. At least he thinks that until they kick open the first door to find the building abandoned.

"Shit," he grumbles.

A blur of a man bull-rushes them.

Trevor fires his rifle at the streak and separates from Jack to prevent them from both being hit by one shot.

The next thing Jack knows, Trevor is flying to slam into the concrete wall on the far side of the room. Even with their combat gear, the impact is enough to knock a human out.

"Shit!" Jack shouts. He catches movement on the edge of his peripheral vision as it pivots to come straight for him. He drops his rifle and snags a grenade off his belt with one hand and a silver hunting knife with the other. At the last possible second, he drops and rolls away, leaving the grenade on the floor to go off in his wake.

The blur snarls and leaps back.

Hopping to his feet, Jack's gifted the sight of a small man who about the same size as Murphy with dirty brown hair and pitch-black eyes thanks to the purple light. His ivory cotton suit is stained with blood. Sizzling skin on the being's shoulder heals before Jack's wondering eyes. Taking advantage of the man's slow, stunned movements, Jack assumes the offensive.

He dashes forward, moving his center of mass low to the ground. The silver knife flashes in the eerie off-purple light still emanating from the UV grenade. The vampire's clawed hand crashes against his forearm, deflecting the blade away from the creature's soft core. Jack swings with his off hand to connect with the vampire's jaw. As soon as the gauntleted fist connects, he triggers the UV diodes embedded in the knuckles.

The vampire's laugh mocks Jack until the shotgun blast of UV light burns through his jaw. The vampire hisses and smacks his fist against Jack's helmet, cracking it. "I'm going to enjoy killing you and your friends."

Jack grunts at the heavy impact, stumbling back from the beast. His free hand drops to his belt, and he quickly drops another UV grenade. He waits for the distinctive snap of the springs before reaching up to rip off the useless helmet, letting the blast of UV radiation keep the creature at bay.

A few blinks later, his eyes adjust to the dim light now hued purple from the two grenades. He scans the battlefield, looking for the enemy. In one raised fist, he holds a knife. In the other he grips a smoke-bomb mixed with garlic, silver, and holy water. Even with all his toys, Jack doesn't like his odds.. The vampire heals from the UV blasts like they're nothing.

What is worse is Jack knows this vampire is toying with him. If he wanted Trevor and him dead, they would already be in body bags. Jack spins, keeping his body low, at the whoosh flitting past him, tracking the enemy's movement. He needs sunlight and bad. The door is too far away to make a dash for it. He tightens his grip on the hunting knife and focuses on the circling man's shoulders and hips.

The vampire watches this wily human, impressed by the hunter's skill level. It has been at least a century since a human has entertained him this much. The last time he had this kind of a fight was with those blasted Van Helsings in Europe. He'll keep this one for himself and turn the other as reward for such entertainment. He isn't sure what the man is holding but knowing these hunters it's something that will irritate him. "You hunters are alike. I was minding my own business and here you are attacking me."

"Don't play the victim bullshit with me. You're the one who sent your vampire spit into the wild. I'm just the tax man comin' to collect his due." Jack growls as he circles with the beast.

The vampire laughs. "You sound like you want money. If that's all you desire, you could have just asked."

"The tax is your life, asshole."

"Are you so certain you can collect, little man?" The creature's voice hisses sharply.

"Ain't failed yet, short stack."

Jack realizes he's in trouble. Young vampires usually take the bait when their stature is attacked. This vampire is the worst-case scenario. Not only is he old, but he's also powerful. Jack knows from the toxicology reports this vampire is well over three hundred years old, but he had hoped he was a weaker vampire's chylde. "Shit," Jack mutters.

"What? Giving up already?"

"We never give up."

"Ah, what bravado you have. It's going to be so much fun, stripping it from you layer by layer until you are nothing more than my puppet."

Jack grimaces. "So much for the easy way." If he gives the beast more time, it will only end in his death. He grunts as he pushes off his back foot, leading with the tip of the silvered dagger as he lunges at the vampire.

Meeting him halfway, the vampire manages to grab the dagger before Jack plunges it into his chest.

Jack immediately slams the smoke-bomb in the

vampire's burning face, rewarding jack with a snow-globe shower of silver and garlic mist. To finish out his attack, he brings his knee up to buckle the vampire's core.

The vampire hisses in pain from the smoke bomb and rakes his claws down Jack's neck as he grips hold of the collar protecting him. He snarls as he rips it away from Jack, causing the armor to shatter and leave Jack defenseless.

Jack throws another gauntleted punch to blast him again with UV light in his last desperate attempt to destroy the vampire.

"Too slow," the vampire taunts as he sinks his fangs into Jack's throat.

Searing lava flows through Jack's veins, followed by a crushing mental mountain of emotions. Jack buckles. Every fear, every doubt, every nightmare Jack has ever had comes flooding into his mind all at once. Even the great, stoic, Jack Talbett cannot withstand this level of torture. His screams echo through the abandoned building before he finally passes out.

The vampire lets his hunter trophy slump to the ground. He drained just enough to keep the hunter alive but subdued. His hands flash, stripping the hunter of all his gear, and he's surprised that this very military man isn't wearing dog tags.

"How interesting. I was sure you were military." He leaves the unconscious man on the floor to attend to his first victim who is waking up. The stirring groan of the man means he's easy prey.

Trevor pushes himself to his feet and struggles with removing his helmet to give him a fighting chance to see what is happening. Everything moves in slow motion for him and the helmet protected his head but is too damaged to keep using. As the helmet clangs against the floor, Trevor looks up to see gloating eyes and a sly grin right in his face.

"Awe, fuck," Trevor groans as the vampire captures his eyes and prevents him from looking away. Trevor's body floats downward of its own accord until his collared vest hits the floor.

"Good boy," the vampire coos as he leans in to sink his fangs into Trevor. He doesn't worry about the pain, instead letting the pleasure of his bite seduce the other man. The vampire cradles Trevor, like a lover, as he drains him to unconsciousness.

Again, he finds no dog tags or other military insignia. "This gets more interesting by the minute." The gaping hole from the knife wound finishes sealing, while the silver and garlic rolls off his skin. "I do hope the rest of your friends are this entertaining," he purrs as he moves further into the complex.

## LAST WOMAN STANDING

With no reply from Jack or Trevor, our mission turns into search and rescue as much as search and destroy. I hate being right.

*Don't lie, darlin'. Ain't no woman hate being right.*

*Shut the fuck up.*

*Alright. Alright. No reason to get shitty with me. What do you see in He-Man here, anyway? He's kind of a dick and smells like shit.*

*I don't think you have any room to talk, asshole. He has a pulse...and a big dick. Now quit fucking distracting me.*

*I have a big one too.*

I ignore his sulking comment and focus on keeping Buck safe. Our progress takes longer due to Buck stopping every so often and leaving "gifts".

"I feel like Hansel and Gretal leaving breadcrumbs on the trail."

"Assuming those breadcrumbs are self-destructive incendiary devices...Then sure!" I can hear the smirk over the radio.

"Listen, Murphy. Shit goes sideways, you get somewhere safe and call for backup."

"Fuck you, Buck. I'm not leaving any of you behind. Besides, which one of us took down the were-bear?"

"No one gave me the chance!"

"Uh huh."

"I'm being serious Murphy. You run twice as fast as I do, and I got explosives to at least take some of the fanged fuckers with us. So, I'm making the call. If it goes sideways, you get backup while I hold them off."

"Then it's a good thing, I out-rank you, Sergeant. If shit goes sideways we rip open this building like a can of sardines and find our guys. We don't leave people behind."

"Hoo-Ah," he replies.

I'm thankful he doesn't put up more of a fight.

*You damn well know he's gonna pull some shit to protect your pretty ass.*

*I thought I told you to sit there and look pretty.*

*You can call me pretty all you want. But you can't shut me up.*

I growl out loud and then I do just that. Leaving Jackson in a box again.

"You alright, Murphy?" Buck stops us before we go into the next part of the complex by blocking the path.

"Peachy keen, champ," I lie. The effort to contain Jackson is draining. My mind is foggy as I follow him through the hallway.

We come to an abrupt stop again.

"Hey, LT," Buck signals into the room.

If Buck is using my rank, shit is bad. I peek through the

doorway. All the lights are on in stark contrast to the darkness pervading the other areas we've searched. What draws my focus in are the two naked men unconscious on the tables in the center of the room; posed like dead warriors of old.

"Trap."

"No shit," replies Buck. "What's the plan?"

"You pull the ripcord. I got the guys."

"One trail of breadcrumbs going boom in three... two... one..."

I don't wait for the button push. I take off at a dead run for the two men. As soon as I cross the threshold, the lights die. Thankfully, my tactical helmet keeps my vision steady.

With each footfall, I feel the vibrations of Buck's handy work. Rather than looking back, I focus on Jack and Trevor, murmuring the words for the defensive shield to keep us safe until Buck can get us sunlight.

I come to a skidding halt between the two of them and I let the rifle fall as I finish the ritual to call forth protection. The barrier flares to life and from my vantage point I see Buck charging toward me while chucking grenades over his shoulder without care. Buck knows he can't get in without putting us all in danger as I would have to drop the shield and there would not be enough time to put it back up. He pulls his best Rambo moves and slides over an open table, taking it with him to set up as cover. Seconds later, he's on one knee, his rifle pointed the direction he came from.

"That thing at full power."

"Yeah... Why?"

"Good!" Buck snatches two grenades and tosses them out as he ducks behind his table.

Thousands of tiny silver needles spray into the air in all directions. That crazy son of a bitch is trying to kill us. He damn well knows the barrier can only take so much damage. It holds for now, but we are definitely not alone in here. The howling hiss of whatever is in this room with us leaves me as tense as a long-tailed cat in a room full of rocking chairs.

"God damn it, Buck! We need sunshine, not silver!"

"You just aren't ever happy, are you? Give me a second. I'm about to blow my wad. Then you can bitch at me!"

"Fuck! Do it already!"

Buck's grinning. Fighting bad guys and blowing shit up is his happy place. Only, he's a little too good at the blowing shit up part. He chucks a baseball-sized clump at the ceiling.

My eyes widen as I put two and two together and realize it's C4. My hands fly frantically to reinforce the barrier though it's tapping all my energy to keep it up and keep Jackson locked in his box.

The massive explosion rips the roof right off, raining debris down on us. The barrier I set is the only line of defense keeping the three of us alive. The shimmering blue shield of protection finally fades under the onslaught of debris. Smoke fills the room, and the charred remains of ceiling litter the floor.

Buck comes rolling in with a big grin on his face until he looks at me.

I swoon.

Buck's arm slip around my waist. "Shit, Tabby," his voice fills the radio. "Shit. Shit. No. No. No. Stay with me, baby."

"You're a lucky son of a bitch, Buck," I giggle as sunlight floods the area around us.

He rests his helmeted head against mine. "What now?"

"I need a minute."

"Well, isn't this just adorable. Lovebirds."

Buck chucks three UV grenades at the source of the quip with his free hand.

I lean against him as I reach into my pant pocket and retrieve an adrenalin shot issued to all magic users. I yank the cap off and jam the needle into my inner thigh, plunging the stimulant into my system. My breath hitches. My heart races. Everything is ramped to eleven and I push off Buck. My eyes dart around the room to find our enemy. But every time I get a bead on him, Buck forces him to move.

*How many grenades does He-Man have?*

*Not now!*

*Fuck, your heart is gonna explode. What was that shit?*

*I said, not now!*

Buck makes the worst possible choice for us. "I'll hold 'em off, and you get those two out of here."

"Are you fucking insane? They're dead weight, Buck. How strong do you think I am?" Drawing on magic saps your energy faster than a toddler hyped up on sugar.

"Apparently strong enough to take on a werebear."

"Don't you fucking step out of this sunlight." I stomp my foot at him.

"You damn well know I'm the only one who can hold him off. You're not in fighting shape."

"What the fuck makes you think I'm in carrying shape, then?"

"Fuck. Tabby. I'm not arguing. You get them to safety. All you have to do is drag them to the far hallway. Should be plenty of daylight over there."

"I'm not fucking leaving you!"

"Will one of you decide? Some of us have work to do." The vampire grumbles from the shadows.

Buck, being the fucking idiot he is, pulls his knife. "You got this. I believe in you. See you on the other side." He flashes me one of his cheesy, all-teeth smiles and disappears into the shadows.

"Damn it, Buck!" I shriek.

He leaps into the shadows toward the creature.

Jackson's howling laughter in my head makes it hard to concentrate. I hoist Trevor off the table, as he's the lighter of the two.

*You know, darlin'. This ride has been fun.*

*What the fuck are you on about now?*

*You see. The only way out of here for you is if I hitch a ride with him.*

*Him who?*

Jackson forces me to first drop Trevor to the floor then jerk my head up to stare at the monster draining Buck.

*Don't do this. You're not the monster they made you.*

*Awe, sugar. I am.*

*You fucking prick!*

*I knew you liked my dick.*

I struggle with Jackson as he tries to force me to give up the good fight. The words of Dr. Ford warning me about side effects echo in my ears. My ability to resist the mental intrusions left with the lizard brain of adrenalin. Moving without my permission, my hand comes up and removes my helmet, letting it fall to the floor. Soon after, my vest joins it, leaving me an open target to the vampire.

"Well, well. You, my dear, are quite exquisite. Now, come here." The man covered in blood and tattered cotton suit steps over Buck as he wipes his blood-soaked lips on his sleeve.

My body jerks as I try to resist his mental command.

*Don't fight me. It'll only hurt worse if you do.*

*Fuck you.*

The heavy weight of the vampire's control casts its net over me . My body relaxes as I walk to him.

"Much better. Not like those muscle heads before. I am going to keep you." His fingers trail along my cheek as he gently turns my head.

Fear rushes my person, and rage fills me. Memories flood my mind of Italy, and I tremble in front of him.

"You've been kissed before." The vampire raises a brow in surprise. "And yet you continue to fight that which you sing to. How peculiar. Now, be my good girl and show me your neck. I promise you will enjoy it."

I comply, tilting my head. His lips brush along my neck, and then I feel nothing but pleasure, overwhelming pleasure. All the fear, and rage, subsides. My heart settles into a steady rhythm as he filters out the stimulants, and I cling to the vampire for balance, wanting him to claim me on the spot.

*Don't worry, baby girl. I got you.*

Jackson's voice is distant and fading as he leaves my mind. The last thing I remember is the vampire licking my neck before he staggers back to clutch his head, causing me to crumple to the floor.

"What have you done to me?" He hisses in disbelief.

## THE ALPHA RIDES AGAIN

"I can't fucking believe you went along with this shit plan. You don't owe those soldier fucks shit."

"Faye," Jasper growls in warning. The rest of the wolves in the vehicle are pointedly avoiding engaging in the conversation between the Alpha and Luna.

"Don't Faye me! You fucking know this is bullshit. How many vampires did we kill just getting to them? If he knew they were there, and knew we were coming, do you think for one second, he left his little plantation active?"

"He couldn't possibly know we knew about both places. I was too careful." Jasper holds his hands up in defense.

"Yeah. You were. What about all the men you took with you when you scouted it?"

"They wouldn't betray us."

"Never said they would betray us, you idiot. I just said they weren't as careful as you."

"Hrmph."

"Don't you give me that sulky werewolf bullshit. You call this mission right now and tell those fucks to find another meat shield." Faye brandishes a finger at Jasper.

"You damn well know I can't do that. My momma asked me to watch over 'em."

"Which just proves my point that this is a bad idea!"

"Point taken. Unfortunately, we are still raiding the compound. Now stay here while I do some work." He steals a quick kiss before ducking back.

"I know you didn't just fucking tell me to stay." She punches him.

"I told you to protect the baby in your belly. Runnin' into a Goddamn vampire den is no way to do that."

"Who the fuck is going to protect you, asshole? These chumps?"

"I can take care of myself. I mean. I am Alpha, remember."

"And I'm Luna, remember."

"Which means you protect our pups, *remember!*"

Faye's eyes narrow, and she throws another punch. Jasper catches her fist and jerks her towards him into a heated kiss.

"I love you! You damn fool. Now, stay here, and protect our pup so I don't get distracted trying to protect you both. I can't lose either of you." Jasper's voice shifts from angry and demanding to a desperate plea.

"Fine," Faye mutters. "But the first sign of trouble, I'm savin' your ass. And the *only* reason I agree is so our pups don't have to go live with your mother."

Jasper laughs, knowing she's profoundly serious about that. He pulls her into another kiss. "I promise, our pups will never go live with my mother. We'll ship them to

Billy."

Faye slaps Jasper. "That's even worse. Have you seen how they spoil their pups?"

The entire truck erupts into laughter.

"Alright boys. Let's get this done before she changes her mind."

"You have one hour," Faye barks and points a finger at him, like a mother telling her kids to be home before sundown.

"Yes, ma'am."

The men strip down and shift into wolf form, before disappearing into the jungle and heading toward the compound.

Faye watches the horizon and then chuckles at the pup kicking up a storm in her belly. "I know, princess. Your daddy's an idiot. But he's our idiot, and he's doing this to protect us... Even though we don't need his protection." Faye instinctively rubs her belly in soothing circular motions. "He's really doing this to get into his mother's good graces. He's definitely trying to one-up Billy. I mean, heaven forbid we enjoy our private little compound in the jungle. No. Have to be the big bad alpha who protects all the people. Even when they're dumb."

Faye's worries Jasper has bitten off more than he can chew. He concealed his injuries from the soldiers he got in the recent fight that made them late to the meeting. Had Faye obeyed, Jasper and his men would be dead. She had to steal one of those fancy grenades from the soldiers to do it but has no regrets about that. She does regret not getting out of the truck and following Jasper now.

Faye grumbles. The pup won't settle down, mirroring her own worry for Jasper. The time ticks by slower than poured molasses.

The smallest sound from the jungle makes her jump and listen. No howling. Not even a peep over mind link. She doesn't dare ping Jasper for fear it would distract him. She glances at the clock. Only thirty-six minutes have passed. The pup is relentless in her tap dance, so Faye gets out of the truck and paces along the driver side.

The way the jungle goes silent at her presence brings her a small amount of pleasure. The pheromones from a pissed off pregnant Luna chases all the prey into silence; even the smallest insects keep their peace. Faye's head snaps up as soon as she smells the foul stench of the vampire. Her lip curls, and she shifts her weight into a defensive position, how Jasper taught her.

The vampire leaps from the shadows. Faye narrows her eyes and stalks to the door where the gear Jack gave her lays on the floorboard. She jerks the door open just as the vampire dashes into it. The resounding clang makes her chortle as she reaches into the Poppins bag of doom. Slamming the door shut, she grumbles at the person-sized dent in it.

"Do you fucking know how much this is going to cost? This is a fucking rental!"

The vampire, who's recovering from the collision, blinks in disbelief at the she-wolf. He hisses and starts to rush forward again.

"Of course, you don't speak English." She clicks the button on the fancy grenade and tosses it to him like they're playing catch.

He reflexively snatches it out of the air as Faye quickly ducks around the vehicle. All she hears is the surprised yelp, followed by sizzling flesh when the trap goes off. She counts to three, like Buck instructed, then saunters over to the pile of ash under the purple light.

"Hmm. These really are handy." She leans down and picks up the grenade, clicking the button to close it. Turning it in her hand, she sees the tiny ports at the bottom. "Huh. They're rechargeable. I guess I owe that soldier boy an apology."

She glances at her watch. Fifty-six minutes have passed. She hrmphs and climbs back into the vehicle.

"I'll bet you a peanut butter pickle sandwich your daddy is late."

Leaning her head back, she breathes slow and steady, trying to remain calm for the baby. Before she forgets, she reaches over and locks the door, just in case.

At fifty-nine minutes, Jasper breaks radio silence.

*Don't panic. We cleared the compound. Just cleaning up before we head back. ETA twenty minutes.*

*You sure you got 'em all?*

*Yup. Clean perimeter sweep.*

*Okay.*

With that, Faye settles in and waits. Her arms wrap protectively around the baby bump. Jasper does have a point about her needing to think more about protecting babies than fighting fights, but she'll be damned if she tells him that in front of his men.

When the men get back, only Hector puts his clothes back on. The other two warriors stay in wolf form while Jasper comes lumbering up in his massive Alpha wolf form. He shifts as she gets out of the truck. He coughs a little when he sees the ash pile and the dent but doesn't say a word about it.

"Hector, you are to take the Luna home. No detours, no pee breaks, no snacks, straight home. Do not pass go. Do not collect two hundred dollars. Then you are to send the Beta and every warrior with vampire experience we have.

Is that understood?”

“Yes, Alpha.”

Faye opens her mouth to protest, and Jasper pulls her into a kiss, pressing her against the dent in the truck so she can’t escape him.

“Listen to me, Faye. I love you. You’re the fiercest wolf I have ever seen, and you’re one hell of a warrior. But I need you and the pups safe. I need warriors who can shift and know how to fight vampires. I need you to be the leader our pack needs at home in case they attack us there. With our Luna leading the charge, our wolves will fight better. This is what a Luna does. So, I’m asking you as your Alpha, to go home and protect what’s ours.”

“How long have you been working on that speech?”

“The entire way back.”

“I can tell.” She kisses him with all the fervor of a wife sending her soldier to war. “You better not fucking get hurt.”

“Yes ma’am.” With a lopsided grin, Jasper pats her ass and helps her into the truck.

“If anything happens to her, I’ll find one of those head shrinkers to bring you back so I can kill you myself. Understood?”

“Yes, Alpha.”

Jasper watches as Faye and Hector drive away before he shifts into his wolf form again and the three of them take off running for the other compound.

The three wolves stop outside the perimeter of the compound the Night Rangers went to. Even though it’s early afternoon when they arrive, they’re cautious about any ghouls that may be lingering around. Silence meets their ears, and they pad into the compound. After a few steps, they all shift into lycan form and prepare for battle.

## BAD MOON RISING

"Turn the car around," Faye growls at Hector.

"I can't do that, Luna." His voice is the pillar of calm.

"I'm your Luna! I fucking command you!"

"Sorry, Luna. The Alpha's orders were no detours. No Snacks. No pee breaks. To take you straight home. Do not pass go. Do not collect two hundred dollars. Then to send the Beta with all warriors with vampire experience to him." He doesn't take his eyes off the road to even look at her in the mirror.

"That fucker used his abilities, didn't he?"

"Yes ma'am."

"What if I jump from the car?"

"Then I will chase you and bring you back, Luna."

Faye tries the door to discover Jasper knows all her tricks and flipped the child safety locks on while putting her in the back seat. "That fuck. You have to take me back.

He's hurting."

"If he's hurting, he's alive, and his orders still stand. The Beta will take care of it."

"I WANT TO TAKE CARE OF IT!"

Hector winces but doesn't comply. "I'm sorry, Luna Faye. But the Alpha's commands were explicit. No detours. No snacks. No pee breaks. Take you straight home. Do not pass go. Do not collect two hundred dollars. Then to send the Beta with all warriors with vampire experience to him."

Faye growls and whines but relents. If that damn fool repeats that damn Monopoly reference again, she might murder him. This also means he's telling the truth, and Jasper used his Alpha command on him. No matter how she tries, as long as Jasper lives, Hector will obey the command. In its own morbid way, his obedience tells her Jasper is still alive. Even if the pain he sends through the mate bond is excruciating.

The SUV rolls into the estate that looks like a treehouse in the jungle. Waiting on the ground is the Beta, pacing a track in the dirt. She's petite, and curvy, with dark wavy hair, and perfect olive skin.

As soon as Hector leaves the vehicle, she rushes him. "Where have you been? What took you so long? What the fuck is going on with the Alpha?"

"Beta Sophia, the Alpha is in Bogotá and requires you, along with all wolves with vampire experience. I brought the Luna back. Good luck." Hector pops open the back door of the SUV and bolts.

"You better run, you fucking prick," Faye snarls.

"Luna," Sophia says in a flat tone.

"Beta," she spits back. "Where are my children?"

"Resting. It's nap time. Now, I need to go to work and

save the Alpha."

It takes all of Faye's energy to not attack the Beta female who turns her back to her Luna as she walks away. Faye's strong façade crumples as she watches Sophia go. In her mind, Sophia has confirmed Jasper's preference of who he wants with him. Her lip quivers, but she storms into her home before anyone can see the Beta got under her skin.

Sophia and the pack's warriors set out at breakneck speed to get to Bogotá.

Faye takes the quiet moment after the warriors head out to hide in her massive soaker tub where she finally lets herself cry. She's convinced Jasper is going to leave her for Sophia. The unmated female has made it clear she thinks Faye is only good for making pups. Coupled with Jasper always sending for the Beta instead of her when he's in trouble, Faye is beginning to believe Sophia is right.

Faye curls into the empty tub and cries harder.

*Don't cry. Just a bad day at the office. I'll live. Love you. Now I need a nap. Talk to you after?*

*Okay.*

Knowing he's safe enough to nap and relieved he reached out to her, Faye is calm enough to face the world again.

******

When the Beta arrives with the warriors at the safe house, Jasper has slept, taken a shower, removed the remaining silver needles, and verified his injured warrior will live. He's pacing in what was Jack's office when Sophia walks in.

"What in the fuck did you say to my mate?"

"Nothing. I told her I needed to get to work. You sent for me." Sophia plays innocent and bats her eyelashes.

Jasper sighs in frustration and rubs a hand over his face. "This is the last fucking time I'll tell you this. Stop antagonizing my mate, your Luna." His voice rumbles deep as he puts the Alpha command into it.

Sophia's eyes widen, and her spine stiffens as she realizes he's commanding her. "Yes, Alpha," she murmurs and tilts her head to show submission.

"Good. Now that you are done fucking with my life, I need you and our best tracker to hunt the fucker that did this. I don't know how he did it, but he concealed his scent. So, I need that miracle nose of yours."

"Got anything of his?"

"Not directly, but there are remains of shredded gear you might be able to pick him up from at the compound."

"Got it." Sophia nods and leaves the office.

Jasper collapses in the chair and closes his eyes.

*You ready for that chat?*

Sophia storms out of the house to the other warriors. "Hector! You're with me!"

Hector falls in and the pair shift into wolf form to take off to the compound. The run only takes a few minutes from the safe house for the pair of wolves. As they slow down, Hector glances sideways at Sophia.

*What did you do to piss off the Alpha?*

*Nothing.*

*Are you sure it's nothing? Cause you stormed out of that office like it was something.*

*Keep your nose out of my business, Hermano.*

Hector shifts into human form and takes a seat on the ridge outside of the compound.

*What are you doing?*

"It's time we had a chat, Sophia. Shift so we can talk freely. Why do you keep antagonizing her?"

"She is unfit. And how did you know?"

"That you torture the Luna, and it pisses off her mate? Gee, I wonder."

"He deserves better."

"By better, you mean you?"

"Well, yes!"

"Sophia. I love you. You are no Luna. Do you know anything about Faye Baxter?"

"I know she's a foul-mouthed, uneducated, gringa."

"You think your language is any better?"

"Whose side are you on?"

"The Luna's. Do you know how she reacted when the Alpha got hurt?"

"She whined like a bitch and made you bring her home."

"No, Sophia. She tried to leap from an SUV going fast enough it would have killed her, or the pup, to get to him. The only reason I took her home is the Alpha Jasper used his command to guarantee Luna Faye safely got there. *She* wanted to fight by his side, even though she cannot shift."

"So she's too dumb to realize she can't fight and protect her pup while pregnant!"

"Sophia." Hector's voice is laced with disappointment.

"And she can't even speak Spanish."

"Oh, Sophia." Hector laughs. "She's fluent in Spanish and has been since the day she arrived."

"What?!" Sophia's jaw hangs open in shock.

"Hmm. Seems the Luna knows how to obtain information from people who think she's just a dumb gringa." Hector flashes a toothy grin.

"Still doesn't mean she's good for the pack."

"What is good for the Alpha is good for the pack. She's

learning and was not born a wolf.”

“Which is another reason she isn’t worthy.”

“Hermana, when did you become an elitist? You are the pack’s Beta. You should be doing everything to support both Alpha and Luna. If you cannot perform those duties, then you should step aside to allow a Beta that is worthy.”

“I earned this position fairly. It’s mine!”

“No, Sophia. You serve at the pleasure of the Alpha. How do you think he feels when you torture his mate?”

“I’m not torturing her. Just putting her in her place.”

“Her place is above you. You are lucky she’s not the kind of girl who runs to her mate to solve her problems. I’ll warn you once. Don’t cross the Luna. She’s far more vicious than the Alpha.”

“Whatever. You’re being dramatic.” Sophia shifts back into wolf form and storms off, ending the conversation.

Hector shakes his head and shifts to follow. She’ll learn, or she’ll get herself in trouble, and he’ll convince the Luna to help her.

The two wolves sniff around the remains of the trap left for Jasper, but find it only reeks of werewolf blood, silver, and humans.

Hector follows the human scents into the rubble that was a warehouse. Much to his dismay it only reeks of explosives and humans. He won’t find good leads in here.

Sophia, still angry at her brother, decides to take another building. Hers is still in decent order other than the human blood on the floor and the dents in the walls. She sniffs and sniffs, frustrated that nothing unusual hits her nose. Until she approaches one of the blood spatters. A waft of un-dead stench tickles her nose. Her ears perk up and her tail starts wagging. Sniffing harder, she circles the blood. The closer to the wall she gets, the stronger the scent is, strong being relative. She's certain not even Hector could detect this.

Sitting, she studies the walls to look for clues. Following the dent patterns in the concrete she can piece together a good deal of the fight.

Then she spots it.

A small hunk of metal with fabric drooping from it sticks out of the wall like it was launched there by a rocket. It's so high, it's hidden by the metal joists. She only spotted it because of the scent it emits.

She shifts into human form. "Gotchya!"

Sophia scrambles up to retrieve the hunk of metal and then lands with a thud. Turning it over and over in her hand unable to determine what she's holding, she frowns. This may not be enough to tell them where they need to go.

"Find something?" Hector appears in the doorway.

"Maybe? What is this?" She holds it up for him to see.

"That, dear sister, is part of the Yanks' armor. It looks like a piece of the collars they wore to protect them from vampire bites."

# THE VAMPIRE'S GUIDE TO HITCHHIKING

Marco's men arrive with means for him to clean himself and a fresh suit.

"Make sure she is taken to my personal quarters. I'll deal with the other three when I'm finished with her."

He takes his time cleaning himself up, still feeling the throbbing presence in his head. Whatever is happening to him, it clearly didn't come from her. Her kind doesn't possess people. He remains silent and focuses solely on today's events. This little hunter group proved more challenging than he had expected. Between the gumption and raw power of the first fighter and the surprise find in the woman, he's pleased with this capture.

"Once the hunters are loaded, take their gear, and stack it out in the yard. Take the little silver ball off the belt and set a spring mine in the center. Then scrub the place. Don't leave any traces that I was here."

"Yes, Sir."

Marco climbs into the SUV and follows his prizes back to his personal compound.

*Now, little one. Tell me what you think you are doing in my head.*

*Just hitchin' a ride.*

*I see. You're a parasite.*

*No, Sir. I'm a bona fide vampire.*

Marco chuckles and looks out the window. He marvels every time he can traverse the area during the day. Deveroux's fascination with technology has led to these amazing windows that block out the UV rays entirely. Today he cannot enjoy the view as he has a 'guest' that is young and arrogant to deal with.

*You are fond of the hunter.*

*She's pretty to look at. Ain't my type.*

Jackson tries to play it cool. Not wanting this vampire to get the idea that Murphy means anything to him.

*You can't lie to me, little parasite.*

*I ain't a parasite. I got a damn name.*

*Care to share said name?*

*You're the one that claims to be psychic. Why don't you tell me, Miss Cleo?*

*And deprive you of your ability to crow?*

*Well, aren't you smooth? Fine. I'm Jackson Pruitt, and damn proud of it.*

They roll into the compound and Marco exits without saying another word.

Jackson silently begins to sift through Marco's memories and secrets. He wants to know the hole in this man's wall. Before he plans to take control, he wants to make sure this vampire is worth his time.

When he jumped, he guessed Marco was powerful, but

that wasn't why he left the sweet redhead. He wanted Marco off of Murphy. For all his bad behavior, he's still sweet on the woman. Her memories flood his mind and all he wanted to do was make it right. He knows what it feels like to be fucked over just for being good at your job.

*Ah, young Jackson, you are a foolish child. Do you really think I cannot control you?*

Jackson frowns when Marco manifests in front of him, and the blank space of Marco's mind turns into a plush salon. Gaudy artwork hangs on the walls, and Persian rugs decorate the shiny wooden plank flooring.

Jackson casually strolls around the room, taking in the decor. He towers over Marco. The contrast of the Spanish vampire compared to the American bad boy would be comical if Marco were not looking at Jackson like a predator about to eat his prey.

"What's your plan for our girl?"

"My plan for *my* toy is none of your concern."

"Now, hear me out. We ain't gotta do this the hard way. I don't mean no harm. And that girl... She's been through a lot. You ain't gotta hurt her."

"Awe, how sweet. You have feelings for my toy. Oh, the ignorance of the young. You must be newly minted. After a hundred years, you lose that soft spot for humanity. She's merely for my amusement, nothing more."

"Our girl's pretty badass. Seems kind of a waste if you ask me."

"It's a good thing I didn't ask you then. You are too much of a simpleton to realize what you stumbled upon. Now me, on the other hand, I may just show you what *my* new toy brings to the table." Marco raises a hand, and the furious red energy sizzles and snaps along it. With a wicked grin plastered on his face, he jerks his hand into a crushing fist, sending Jackson to his knees.

"Fuck," Jackson groans, feeling like three elephants sat on him.

"You couldn't even tame her while she is dormant. What makes you think you had a chance against me? Time to scurry back under your rock, parasite."

Another quick motion and the floor gives way to a dark and dank abyss.

Jackson roars in anguish as he is dropped in like a sack of potatoes. All light vanishes as the hole closes above him, leaving him in the void of Marco's mind.

"Fuck!" He throws a punch to hit the proverbial wall.

"Is someone there?"

A man's voice, heavy and thick in Spanish, causes Jackson to go dead silent.

"Please. If you are there, tell me who you are. How did you get here? What are you doing here?"

Jackson isn't about to fall for this trick. Whatever that Spanish prick did to lock him in here, is now intending to torture him. In the few short hours of Jackson's life with Marco, he has learned the vampire is every bit the monster Lucien is. He needs to find a way out of this hell, and fast. While he knows he betrayed Lieutenant Murphy, he meant what he said. He would get her out of here.

"You are a monster," the man gasps.

Jackson bites his lip, grinning as he turns his attention to the man in the nothingness. He half expects his ability to see in the dark to not work, but as he focuses on the source of the voice, a dim light appears, like moonlight through a tiny window far above. "What the fuck?" Jackson sputters.

He takes in the young man cowering before him. His wide brown eyes, pale skin, and dirty brown hair are nothing compared to the well-groomed monster that locked him in here. He is covered in grime and his clothing makes him look like he escaped a renaissance fair. As the cowering copy of the vampire who threw him in this hole comes to his full height, Jackson feels like a giant. The man cannot be more than five foot seven.

"Please. You must end my suffering. This monster is not me. He has committed horrendous atrocities. Crimes against God and man alike! I've tried so many times to stop him, only to be locked in here."

"Whoa. Slow down there, Mister. Ain't no one killin' anyone here. All I wanna do is take over yer boy and have myself a good time without all the damn work. I'm not your grim reaper."

While Jackson speaks English, the human speaks Spanish, neither has issue understanding the other.

"Why don't you tell me who the fuck you are, and we'll go from there."

The human's face droops and he slumps back down on the 'floor'. "I am... Marco de Santi. Or what is left of him."

"You're telling me you are the asshole that threw me in here?"

"Yes," he frowns, "and no. I am merely a remnant, an echo of his lost humanity. He threw me in here hundreds of years ago. You are the first entity I have ever been able to communicate with."

"Hundreds of years ago? The fuck kind of shit is that? I ain't stayin' that long. You can just go back to your corner and mope. I'm gonna find my own way outta here."

"You don't understand! That monster has done terrible things! You must kill me. It's absolute torture watching him and being unable to stop him!"

"You can see what he's doing?" Jackson narrows his

gaze at the smaller man.

"Of course I can. I am him. He is me."

"But you can't stop him?" Jackson suspects this hindrance is bogus.

"I was stronger once when we were younger. Before my time with Erzsébet."

Jackson's head hurts, which he finds funny since he doesn't actually have a head. "What kind of name is *Erzsébet?*" He rubs his temples.

"Hungarian. She was a noble I was sold to as a boy."

"I don't need a history lesson. You were telling me you can see what you, or he, or fuck whoever, is doing, but you can't act."

"The monster is too strong. As I said, I was discarded centuries ago."

Guilt weighs heavy on Jackson. "Well, seein' as I got a girl to save, and a body to snatch, you're gonna tell me when he's not payin' attention. Then I'm gonna bust right through that gaping hole up there." Jackson motions to the tiny window of light flooding down on them.

"You will regret it. No one escapes here." The human Marco looks up at the window and then back to Jackson. His eyes blaze with disgust.

Jackson shifts uncomfortably, as if the smaller man is judging him. He brings his hand up and rubs the back of his neck, avoiding eye contact with Marco.

"I will help you, but you'll have to kill me."

"You keep saying that kill me part. Why the fuck do I have to kill you when you're already just a figment of his imagination?"

Marco steps forward and looks up at Jackson, holding his gaze. "I think, of all people, *you* would understand what a fragmented soul feels like."

Silence fills the air as Jackson weighs his options. "You sure this is the only way? I ain't got no beef with you."

"You would be giving me mercy. Trust me, this way will work. I guarantee you will escape."

"Fuck. Fine. Hopefully, you have a better plan than just me killin' you."

Marco says with a motion as he moves away from Jackson. "Come. I will show you what I mean."

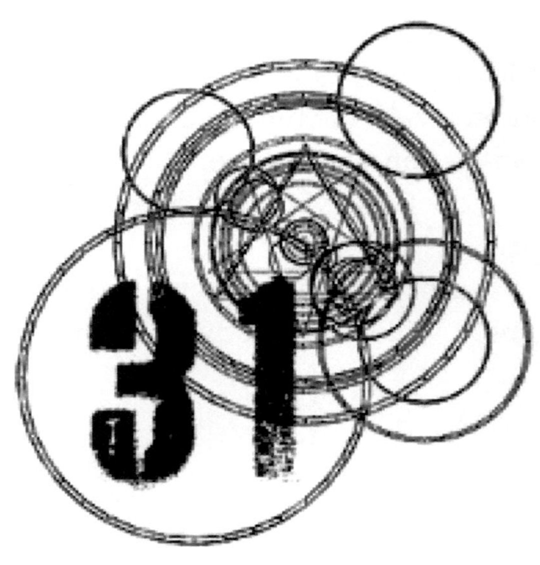



## SCOUT'S HONOR

Jack's eyes open to find himself in a motel room in Savannah. The sweet fragrance of his favorite stripper, Evie Fontaine, fills his nostrils. Confusion washes over him as the last thing he remembers was dancing with that vampire.

"Hey, Candyman," Evie coos.

"This isn't real. You're not real. Where the fuck am I?"

Evie pouts at him with her pretty blue eyes and begins crawling over him, wiggling her butt just like she did the last time they were together. "Awe! Don't be like that. We had such a fun time last night."

Jack's hands slide up her milky thighs. Her skin is soft and supple in his hands as he pets along her thighs. Her sweet scent fills the air around him. His hands grip her hips, and he rolls her over to pin her down.

She giggles and squirms underneath him. "Brute," she

teases.

"You are not fucking real! This isn't fucking real! I am in—." Jack's mouth cannot form the word to say where he is, and his eyes narrow at the giggling woman. To Jack's horror, the beautiful, long-legged stripper transforms into the petite vampire.

"Oh, soldier boy," the monster continues using Evie's voice. "You're in trouble."

Jack's eyes fly open to reveal a dark and dank cell. His hands are bound behind his back to a hard metal chair. There doesn't appear to be a door anywhere. The steady drip of water tells him they're deep underground.

"This would have been so much easier if you had accepted my offer. I must confess, I am thrilled you didn't. You have more promise than I gave you credit for." Marco chuckles and his eyes are full of delight, like a child just given a pony.

"I don't care what you do to me. I'm not going to tell you anything."

"Such bravado. I don't need you to tell me anything. I already know all I need to know from you."

"Then just kill me and get it over with."

"And deprive me of a perfect soldier?" Marco gasps with mockery. He begins the slow, predatory circle of his prey.

Jack opens his mouth to retort when Marco whispers into his ear from behind him. "You are going to be so much fun to break." Marco nips Jack's ear, sending a tsunami of pain crashing through Jack's body.

He screams hoarsely. His body trembles and he jerks against the restraints, only to feel the strong hands of Marco clamp on his head, holding it still.

Marco nips the other ear, quieting the pain. Releasing him, Marco steps back to allow Jack to collapse.

The restraints hold him in place, and he pants to catch his breath.

"That, my dear boy scout, was the stick. Are you sure you don't want the carrot?" As he speaks, he morphs back into Evie Fontaine. Her voice asks the question.

"Or do you prefer a different carrot?" Evie shifts into Tabby. She comes forward and caresses Jack's cheek. "You know, champ, you've always been the hottest of my boys."

The room transforms to the hotel in Houston where he kicked in the door. Twisting and warping until the two of them are sitting on Tabby's bed with her head on his shoulder.

"Please, just hold me for a while longer. I don't know what's happening to me."

Jack's head is foggy and heavy as his arm wraps tighter around his girl. The jealousy of her choosing Buck ebbs as she clings to him. Her bright green eyes stare up at him as she tenderly leans in and kisses him.

"Murphy," he breathes once they break the kiss. "You know I would do anything to protect you. Even this."

His hands pet Murphy's body as he draws her into a passionate kiss. Without warning, or hesitation, he snaps her neck. When the illusion doesn't break, he looks down at the limp woman and lays her gently back on the bed.

Stepping back, the slight niggle of doubt that this is an illusion worms his way into his consciousness. It only fuels his resolve and anger.

"Is this the best you can do, you pygmy motherfucker?" He roars to the ether. "I'm Major Jack Talbett, U.S. Army. Serial Number 85674291."

The door to the hotel room flies open. Buck and Trevor rush in, guns blazing.

"What the fuck, Jack! What have you done? Oh no. No.

Murphy!" Buck rushes to the dead woman on the bed, cradling her in his arms.

Trevor points his pistol at Jack. "On your knees."

Jack doesn't move a muscle. "I'm Major Jack Talbett, U.S. Army. Serial Number 85674291."

Buck springs from cradling Murphy's body to clock Jack square in the jaw. Following him down, he wails on him uncontrollably. "Why the fuck would you hurt her! I loved her!"

"I'm Major Jack Talbett, U.S. Army. Serial Number 85674291."

The room begins to dissolve like mist rolling off a lake, leaving Jack and Buck. Trevor and Murphy disappear with the hotel room.

"She chose me, you asshole! Not you! She's mine!" With each statement, Buck pounds Jack into the ground.

Jack grunts in pain, "I'm Major Jack Talbett, U.S. Army. Serial Number 85674291."

Buck dissipates, leaving Marco standing before Jack once more in the dank cell. "I knew I chose wisely when I decided to keep you."

"I'm Major Jack Talbett, U.S. Army. Serial Number 85674291."

Marco hisses at Jack, realizing he is using the mantra to bolster his defenses. "Fine. You don't want my gifts? Then you will feel my displeasure." He snaps his fingers and two vampires appear in the cell.

"You may not turn him. You may not kill him. But you may enjoy him." Like lightning, he grabs them by the throat and pulls them both into him, so they're face to face. "Now, repeat to me the rules so I know you understand where the line you cannot cross is."

They reply without hesitation.

"Good." He tosses them aside, looks down at Jack again, and sighs wistfully. "This would have gone so much easier for you, if you had just played along, little soldier."

Jack spits a bloody, phlegmy mess at Marco's feet. "I'm Major Jack Talbett, U.S. Army. Serial Number 85674291." He stares into Marco's eyes boldly, challenging him.

Marco laughs. "Oh, little soldier, I cannot wait for you to see the error of your ways. Now, if you will excuse me, Lieutenant Murphy has proved to be more pleasant company." Marco disappears from Jack's sight.

The two vampires look at each other and grin. In Spanish, "Want to see who breaks him first?"

"Oh, you know pleasure always wins."

"Fine, then you take pain this time if you know how to do it so well."

"Brother, don't sulk. It's unbecoming. Is the only way you can win is to steal pleasure from me?"

The first vampire scoffs and waves a dismissive hand. "Fine. Keep your pleasure. I will show you what a master of pain can do."

While the two vampires bicker like a cheesy vampire movie, Jack struggles to free himself. To his frustration, the restraints are secure.

"Oh brother, look at our little fish, flopping about. Perhaps we should give him a drink?"

Chuckling, "How droll you are, brother."

The two of them flank Jack and grin at each other before they sink their fangs into the soft flesh of his neck. Instantly, Jack's body is consumed with crushing pain and euphoric pleasure. Just when he thinks he cannot bear it any longer, he longs for it to continue. Every intimate moment of his life flashes before him. From his first kiss all the way to the last night with Evie.

Even his fantasies flood his mind. They're tossed amongst the horrifying failures of his life. Missions gone wrong. Squad mates lost. Enemies killed. Haunting torturous moments of his life, once compartmentalized, flood into the sweetest memories.

His brow sweats, his body trembles, and he grows hard as a rock. All cylinders fire at once, and his body can't decide which way to react. Should he scream in pain or blow his load? As much as he loathes this torture, his body longs for them to bite him again.

The two vampires pause to look at him like scientists in a lab, giving him a moment to recover. Each lick their lips at the taste of his blood.

"I'm Major Jack Talbett, U.S. Army. Serial Number 85674291," he stammers in his stoic fight to keep his mind.

The vampires grin at each other. "Marco is right. This one is going to be fun."

## WHEN IN ROME

Trevor's body aches all over. He hasn't felt this kind of pain since boot camp. Even growing up on the Southside of Chicago, he encountered nothing as rough as that damn vampire he and Jack ran into. He knew he was fucked as soon as he hit the wall.

Lying in bed, he listens for any sounds of movement. The room is quiet. Smells of incense and sage permeate the air, which confuses him.

*Why do vampires need sage?*

When he is confident he is alone, he opens his eyes. A quick inspection makes him chuckle. They took all his clothes but bothered to clean him up. He's not shy about his body and as he sets his bare feet on the concrete floor, he wriggles his toes at the coolness.

Rubbing his hand over his face, he sighs. He wants to leap off this bed and begin the assault for his escape.

Without gear, or hell, even clothes, that option will end in death.

He knows that fanged fuck who threw him into the wall already got all the information from biting him. They're all fucked. Unless, somehow, Tabby and Buck managed to kill the fucker. He doubts that as he looks around.

The room has no windows, and the decorations are antiquated, like someone raided a period movie. Pushing off the bed, he starts by rummaging through the nightstand closest to him. Opening every drawer, feeling for any hidden compartments, he makes no bones about searching the entire room for anything to help him. He tells himself he isn't going down without a fight.

The longer he looks, the less he believes he can escape. A new plan begins to form. He'll complete the mission by becoming a double agent. He'll let them turn him, then take them down from the inside. He'll become the monster to hunt the other monsters. Now, all he needs is a monster to turn him.

Padding quietly into the antechamber, he laughs at the buffet of delicious foods spread over the table. Everything from grapes to steak has been left. Decanters of orange juice, water, and what he thinks is sweet tea, sit nearby.

As much as he would like to remain the stoic soldier who doesn't cave, his body protests loudly. He grabs a pitcher of orange juice first, downing a good deal of it before he lets it clank against the table. Orange juice will help him the fastest. His hand still shakes when he snatches a roll out of the bowl closest to him. There's enough food to feed at least ten people.

"We weren't sure what you would like."

"Or how much you eat."

"It has been quite a long time since father let us interact

with a human."

Trevor stops, mid-bite to face the three voices behind him. His instincts are to fight, but the women, no girls, no monsters, are petite and beautiful. Their pale olive skin gives way to dark eyes and hair. All three look Eastern European.

Their eagerness reminds him of Murphy when she's going to cause trouble. What he wouldn't give for some of her sass right now. That girl knows how to rile the monsters up and distract them from the rest. The guilt of losing his teammates causes his chest to ache.

Sizing them up, he is sure he could snap one's neck, but the other two would get the jump on him. Then he makes the mistake of meeting the third one's gaze. Her pretty dark eyes remind him of a girl from his childhood.

"Don't," he begs. "Leave her out of this."

The vampire pouts and shimmers as she resumes her true visage. "But she is pretty, and you love her."

"We don't want to hurt you," the tallest of the three confesses.

"No. Father gave you to us and said we could do what we want with you once you answered all our questions."

"And if I don't answer shit?" Trevor's eyes narrow.

"Then father will be angry and hurt us."

"What the fuck kind of messed up shit is that?"

"Who's the girl? You are sad whenever you think of her."

"Stay the fuck out of my head."

"Don't be like that. We want to know you better. We want you to like us."

"So you can steal my memories and feed off me. Hard pass."

"Oh no. We are well fed. We don't need you. Though I do like the sounds you make when we bite you."

Trevor stares at the vampire smiling eagerly at him. Fuck, how old are these three? They don't look older than twelve, or thirteen now that he has gotten a good look at them. He's mortified at the idea they bit him.

He wants to deny it, but he feels the need to experience the euphoric waves of pleasure again. He closes his eyes to compose himself and flashes of the four of them in the bed burn behind his eyelids. "Don't fucking touch me again."

"But..." the quiver in their voices makes him want to cater to every whim.

"No. You want me to play with you? Then you gotta do something for me. 'Cause this shit ain't right. I'm a prisoner of war, not a plaything."

He dares to look at them again as they move a little away from him, talking in hushed tones amongst themselves.

*Jesus, they really are children.*

They face him again. "We'll try to do what you ask, within reason. Don't ask us to leave, or to give you weapons."

Trevor grins, thinking he is unhinged at even concocting this plan. Their willingness to negotiate enables him.

"Tell me what happened to my friends." He sits at the table, his body unwilling to remain standing, and digs into the food he put on his plate.

The three vampires linger before joining him at the table. The tallest, who he has learned is the leader, frowns. "Father took them. The pretty woman, along with the big one, are in his room."

"The big one?" Jack and Buck are typical broad-shouldered soldiers, where he has a narrow frame, good for hiding and taking sniper shots from uncomfortable places.

"Yes, he was with the woman. Father called them lovebirds." She clasps her hands together and bats her eyelashes.

"What about the other guy?"

The three look at each other, each pinching their lips together and looking toward the ground, none of them wanting to say.

"Is he dead?" Trevor murmurs.

"No," the quiet one pipes up. "But he is Father's."

"What do you mean?"

"Nothing you need to worry about. You belong to us. You will not suffer that fate."

Trevor grimaces at the thought of Jack being kept alive and tortured. If he is with that fanged fuck from the compound, then he isn't enjoying teenage girls and buffet dinners.

Trevor eats in silence, occasionally glancing at the three girls watching him. He isn't so blinded by the "kiss" that he thinks they care about him at all. They look at him like a pet, not an equal.

He is thankful for the table concealing his raging hard on. The mental anguish that he is turned on by these three adds to his resolve to play along, then kill everything with fangs when he has the power.

"Listen, girls. If we're gonna be friends, I need to know something."

"What?" the eager one who looked like his girl back home pipes up.

"How old are you, really?"

"Tsk. It is not polite to ask a lady her age," the leader teases him.

"Yeah. Well, good thing you ain't ladies. You look like little girls and I'm not a kid fucker."

All three vampires pout at his remark.

The quiet one replies, "We came with Father when he was a conquistador. Does that sate your human insecurity? I will have you know we were of marrying age when we were turned."

"Most thought of us as quite the prize."

"Don't men like young, pretty girls? You do think we're pretty, don't you?" The preen like birds on display.

Trevor laughs bitterly and nods. "You're all beautiful. Just gotta get my head on straight." Internally, he is screaming at how old these three are. They're far more powerful than he initially thought.

"How come your old man keeps you away from humans?"

They exchange a quick glance; a malicious smile forms on each of their lips.

The quiet one answers. "Humans are fragile, and Father doesn't deal with the fallout well."

Trevor swallows hard and works to push his fear deep down inside.

"Oh, do not fear us," the eager one whines as she hurries to his side. Her fingers gently pet the top of his hand.

Trevor loses all thoughts of fighting at her gentle touch. His brain fogs over and he is pained by the thought of upsetting her. His fingers reach up and brush her cheek, which makes her light up.

"Come. Let's enjoy each other's company." She tugs him from the chair.

The other girls follow, and Trevor willingly heads back to the bed. Any misgivings about laying with these three are gone. He pulls the eldest into a sultry kiss as they plop onto the bed. Soon, all three girls hover around him as he moans and writhes under their skillful touch.

"Oh, it is a dragon," the eager one coos as she licks his tattoo before sinking her fangs into him.

Trevor moans and arches like he is thrusting into her. The girls giggle as they intentionally make him believe they're fornicating.

"He is so delicious," the quiet one purrs. "We should keep him forever."

## THE GILDED CAGE

The first thing my brain registers is the dirty mildew smell. With a groan, I roll over and the scratchy edges of straw graze my skin. Pushing myself to a sitting position, I take in my new home. The only light source is too dim for comfort but is enough to reveal the cell I'm currently residing in. My eyes finish this sweep on the pale mass in the corner.

"Buck?" I whisper.

He doesn't respond. The vampires must have done a real number on him for him to look that pale.

Confusion washes over me. Vampires aren't known for taking captives. They turn their victims, kill their victims, or wipe their minds and flee. Live prisoners are nothing but trouble. If a vampire keeps a human, they ghoul them so the human is loyal. At least, that's what our consultant from Howell, Brigham, and Young told us.

The woozy feeling from losing too much blood causes me to lean back against the wall.

"Sergeant," I snap to wake Buck. When he doesn't answer me again, or move, I force myself to crawl toward him. My hands tremble as I get closer, and the lead weight of dread fills my stomach.

"Buck?" I mewl. I don't know what I'll do if he is dead. My heart races and tears well in my eyes.

"Buck." I call, needing him to answer.

"Stay the fuck away from me, Tabitha. Please." Buck's graveled voice begs me.

I pause at his words. Anger fills me as I finish moving to him, and I grab his shoulder, intent to roll him over to have it out with him. He doesn't get to dick around with my emotions, then outright reject me when we're trapped in a cell.

"I said stay the fuck away from me," Buck snarls and plants his hand in the middle of my stomach.

Instead of just pushing, he thrusts me off the ground and sends me colliding into the wall. Pain radiates through my body as I sink down.

My mind races to process what happened. Buck isn't that strong.

The pale skin.

The graveled voice.

"Oh, Buck," I mewl and cover my mouth. My mind races to find any solution that lets us both out of here alive.

He curls into himself more. "Just... Just... Leave me alone. It's better this way."

I have never seen Buck so broken. This hulking man never lets life bring him down. He loves blowing things up and having a good time. He loves his family and wants to make one of his own. He wants a shit-ton of kids on a big farm, running around and terrorizing the neighbors.

Tears cling to my lashes as I realize he has been turned, and I have failed him. If he is trying to keep me away, he hasn't fed.

I close my eyes and take deep breaths, forcing myself to calm down. I focus on slowing my heartbeat. Buck is struggling and being locked in here must be torture as I sing to the vampires like the fucking Hallelujah chorus.

"Buck, when is the last time you drank blood?" My heart breaks for him and for us, but I need to assess how bad he is to mitigate the situation if we have any chance of escaping.

"Fuck that noise. I ain't no monster."

"Buck, listen to me. You need to drink at least a little blood or you will become feral. Remember our training."

He finally sits up, hugging his knees to him and putting his back in the corner. His face is pinched with disgust. "Just whose fucking blood am I going to drink, Tabby? Yours?"

His angry question relieves me more than it hurts. Despite now being a monster, his humanity hasn't been completely stripped from him yet.

I remain across the cell to keep from agitating him. "Champ, you don't understand. If you don't take a little now, you're going to kill me later, whether you want to, or not."

He shakes his head frantically and mutters, "No. No. I won't do it. Not to you. Not ever."

I force myself to my feet and wait while my body strenuously objects to being vertical. Guilt and shame fill me as Trevor's angry confession about Buck trying to slit his wrist to feed me blood when he thought I was turned in Italy filters through my mind. This stupid, beautiful man is everything I wanted in a partner. He was willing to give his life up for me then. I'm willing to do it now.

My opportunity comes when he lowers his head to his knees and hugs himself tighter. Love compels me forward. I know I'll do anything for him, including sacrificing myself.

*We'll figure it out. He'll be okay. He just needs a little to calm down the beast inside.*

Another step forward and my mind goes back to the night in Charleston where he said he loved me.

"Buck, look at me."

He lifts his head, and his pupils are blown with the desire to feed. His fangs are elongated. His muscles jerk and twitch as his knuckles go white around his knees. He presses himself further back against the wall, trying to meld with it to escape me.

I'm unafraid as I gingerly force my way into straddling his lap. I may not have been able to save him from this fate, but I sure as shit can ease his suffering now, even if he kills me. I cradle his head and bring him forward, letting him rest against my chest.

His arms wrap around me, and he clings to me for dear life. His body shakes. "Tabitha," he moans. "I'm so fucking sorry."

"Shh. Big Fella. It's okay."

"No. It's not fucking okay. I love you so fucking much, and I threw you away."

I swallow hard not wanting to have this discussion right now. Even though I have been cold to him, I had forgiven him for being an idiot in New York. He thought he was doing the right thing. I run my fingers through his hair. "I love you too, Chester."

He pulls back to look up at me. His expression is so

serious. "Which is why you need to do what we both know you need to do. There must be something here you can use."

"Fuck that noise. I don't care if you are a vampire. We'll get out of here and go somewhere no one can find us. Just you and me. I *need* you, Buck. I can't go this alone." Tears roll down my cheeks. Selfishly I refuse to hold up my end of the bargain if one of us turned.

"I know it's going to be hard. But you're strong as fuck. You took down a were-bear for fuck's sake. You can do this."

I steel myself for what I do next. He's right. I'm fucking strong. Every hunter instinct in my body screams at me to stake his ass, but the lover in me prevails. I bring my wrist to his lips. "I <u>am</u> fucking strong. I can handle it. Now drink."

Buck tries to turn his head, but I thrust my arm up to catch his fang, forcing it to tear a jagged hole into my wrist. The scent of blood fills the air and Buck's expression change, his resolve gone. The beautiful, sweet man disappears as his beast takes control. He ravenously sinks his fangs into my wrist and sucks.

Buck's emotions are all over the place from love to rage, causing the pulsating waves of pleasure and pain crash over me faster than I can master, and I cry out. With my eyes closed, I pant between intense orgasm and crushing fear.

He jerks away from my wrist.

"Lick it closed," I gasp.

I open my eyes in time to see him awkwardly sticking his tongue out to barely touch my wrist, like he is grossed out by the prospect. It would be comical if I weren't about to pass out.

After closing the wound, he pulls me to his chest and wraps his massive arms around me. "I got you, baby girl. I got you." His voice is steady, and his body stopped shaking. "You need to rest. I'll be here when you wake. I promise."

I relax in his arms. Try as I might to keep from passing out, the siren's call of slumber beckons.

******

Buck pets along Tabby's back as she relaxes into slumber. He hates that she's right, and that she sacrifices herself to keep his sorry ass alive. He kisses her forehead. This isn't how this was supposed to go. He was going to make it right after the mission.

The ring sits in his go-bag. He was going to apologize and beg she take him back. If he had to grovel the rest of his life, he would just to have her. They were going to have the picket fence, the three kids, and a Goddamn golden retriever.

He lifts his gaze when he senses the oppressive presence of his sire. Staring directly at the beast pretending to be a man on the other side of the bars, he snarls. "She'll never be yours."

Laughter greets his words. "Oh, you foolish boy. Do you really think a chylde of mine could best me?"

"I don't need to best you. I just have to keep her away from you."

"Just how do you plan to do that, little Buck? You are locked in a cell."

"We've made it out of worse."

Mirth dances across Marco's face and he lets his fangs show in his grin before he   walks away. "Good luck with your escape plan. How long do you think she will last without food and water? Especially with how freely she feeds you."

Buck curls his arms around Tabby in a protective embrace. "Don't you worry about him, baby girl. I'll make it right... Somehow."

# LET LOOSE THE HOUNDS OF WAR

Five Days After The Raids

Jasper paces angrily in the office of the safe house. With no bodies, he can only imagine what has happened to the soldiers. He glares at his phone, trying not to call his mother.

*I should call her. If I call her, it'll be a full-on war. They're lost. She needs to know that. And then I admit I'm a failure... again. Fuck. Where are you, Sophia?*

His phone buzzes on the desk, Faye's calling. That's the last person he wants to talk to. He's confident she'll pick a fight. He feels her insecurities wreaking havoc on her emotions through the mate bond. Right now, he needs to focus on saving those damn soldiers and killing the vampire before he hurts anyone else.

He declines the call.

*I know you didn't just hang up on me, motherfucker!*

*Not now, Faye.*

*Yes, now, Jasper. Where the fuck are you? And why do I feel like a long-tailed cat in a room full of rocking chairs?*

Jasper stops pacing and palms his face. He forgot the mate bond works both ways. No wonder she's a ball of anxiety.

*I'm sorry, baby. Just waiting for the scouts to return so we can kill this fucker.*

*Uh-huh. How's Sophia?*

The blatant accusation hurts.

*Well, she and her fucking brother are the scouts I'm waiting for. So, I don't fucking know how she is. I told you nothing is happening there.*

*Oh, so you're willing to send her into danger, but not me.*

*IT'S HER FUCKING JOB, FAYE!*

*Right. Just like it's her fucking job to come when you call. It's her fucking job to heal you. What's my fucking job in all this?*

Jasper sighs. This is exactly why he didn't want to talk to Faye.

*Faye. Your job is to keep me sane. To make me a better man. To be the heart of our fucking pack. So maybe you could just get on board and give me a little fucking support.*

*Oh. So all I'm good for is being your cock warmer?*

*That isn't what I said.*

*Uh-huh.*

She cuts off the conversation.

Jasper looks to the ceiling, praying to the Goddess for patience. He *really* needs to find Sophia a mate that will give her pups and get Faye off his back.

Speak of the Devil, Sophia and her brother stroll in.

"What the fuck took you so fucking long?"

"I'm fine, thanks. You wanted confirmation, didn't you?"

Jasper's response is a low, threatening growl emanating from deep within his chest.

Hector rests a hand on Sophia's shoulder.

*He has obviously been talking with Faye. Your antagonizing the Luna has put this wedge between them.*

*That fucking wedge was already there. I just hammered it in.*

*Sophia.*

Instead of a disrespectful come back, Sophia tilts her head in submission, "I'm sorry Alpha. It was a long trip."

"I don't fucking need your apologies. I need your fucking intel. Quit fucking around and tell me what the fuck you found!"

Sophia grits her teeth as Hector grips her shoulder firmer.

"We located the compound and confirmed it's Marco de Santi."

Hector shifts his weight uncomfortably, "That is what took us so long. It was a full two days before we got visual confirmation."

"And neither of you were spotted?"

Sophia puffs up at Jasper's accusation. "I know how to do my job, Alpha. I have been a silent shadow in this jungle since you were a pup."

Jasper stares at Sophia, using all his restraint to keep from asserting his dominance on her. Despite his protests of not being interested, her defiance turns him on, much in the same way Faye does. It comes as no surprise to him the two women don't get along as they're identical. He rubs his hand over his face and pushes all thoughts of arousal out of his mind. He has a job to do.

"Great. What's the plan then?"

Hector speaks up but keeps his gaze averted and shifts his weight in discomfort at how familiar they are with each other. "If we push hard, we can be there by dawn."

"How hard?"

"We would have to leave now and move at full speed."

"Then, what are we standin' around chit-chatting for?" Jasper peels out of his clothes.

Hector Gibbs-smacks his sister when she ogles the Alpha shimmying out the window to shift into lycan form.

Jasper climbs to the roof of the safe house. It's far enough on the city's edge he won't attract too much attention. Looking down at the masses of his pack, he swells with pride. This vampire picked the wrong werewolf pack to fuck with.

He tilts back in all his seven-plus foot glory and howls at the moon, letting the war cry ring over his pack.

In response, hundreds of howls chorus him.

He leaps from the roof, shifting into his wolf form to land on four paws. Sprinting into action, he leads the tidal wave of wolves to war.

Sophia and Hector struggle to match his pace as they guide him.

Since they don't care about being seen or heard, the travel time to the compound is short. The night echoes with howls as the pack members coordinate attack positions. Flurries of commands rip through the wolves' minds, and they obey without slowing.

Breeching the compound's perimeter, the alarms barely have enough time to sound as the wolves blanket the grounds. Upon approaching the building, they leap into the air transforming to their lycan forms. Using the weight and momentum they blast through the outer walls in Kool-Aid man style. They hit the ground, roll, and pop back up to collide with the awaiting vampires. It's a hellstorm of claws and fangs. Snarling and growling fills the air as flesh tears into flesh.

Jasper lands and rips the heads off two vampires misfortunate enough to encounter the Alpha. He stands to his full height and inhales deeply, smelling the bloodline of the vampires. Immediately, he knows the scent of the master, Marco.

He stalks down hallways to the screams and hisses of vampires encountering his war-forged warriors as he hunts for his prey.

A poor cretin leaps in front of him, fangs bared and clawed hands out. Jasper doesn't slow as he palms the vampire's head into the concrete wall, crushing it. The creature might not die, but it will require time to recover. Another wolf will finish the job before then.

Jasper rips the door to the stairwell off its hinges and storms down into a dungeon. The putrid smell of death, decay, and mold irritates him. Marco's scent is strong here. Along with the sweet smell of that firecracker soldier.

Cell after cell is empty as Jasper passes by, his vision unaffected by the dim light. When he reaches the cell where Marco's scent is the strongest, confusion fills him. The bars have been bent open. The scent of a divine being, not human or vampire, invades his nostrils. With another sniff, burning flesh filters in.

He shifts into human form to cautiously step through the small opening. Approaching the body in the corner, he rolls it onto its back. He grunts in disappointment when he sees Marco de Santi fileted of his skin.

Marco's muscles are exposed, and his flesh burns as it

attempts to regenerate.

"What in the ever-livin' hell happened here?"

Marco hisses in pain and Jasper growls.

Instinctually, he shifts to lycan form and rips Marco's head from his body. Instantly, the muscled, skinless body that was attempting to regenerate turns to ash. Jasper stomps his foot on the ash pile, pissed at how anticlimactic this was. He wanted to duel to the death with this monster while defending his pack.

*Alpha, we need you. We have a problem.*

Hector's voice fills Jasper's mind, pulling him from his sulking. Without a second thought, Jasper leaves the cells.

*What is it?*

*Uh. It's hard to describe. You need to see this in person. I told the men to contain not attack.*

Sophia replies.

*What do you mean contain? We said no prisoners.*

*Uhm. Well, we're two men down and at a stand-off, if you will. Just hurry up.*

Jasper growls. The master is dead. The rest should be submitting. What could be strong enough to worry his beta like this? He speeds up, following Sophia and Hector's scents. Anxiety drives him faster as his wolves' scents begin to mingle with whatever escaped that dungeon. He's even more concerned that the soldiers are nowhere to be found. Whatever Marco imprisoned down there attacked him and is now terrorizing the compound.

# 35

## HELL HATH ONE FURY

One Hour Earlier

"Okay. You pull apart the bars. We find Jack and Trevor. We'll make a run for the wolves. They'll protect us, and we'll go home."

I repeat our plan for the millionth time, as I lean against the wall to keep awake. It's hard to tell how long we have been down here. Without any natural light to gauge time, it's all a big blur.

Marco was right about me growing weaker without food or water. He was wrong about Buck draining me dry. What little blood Buck does take seems to last quite some time. At least three cycles of the guards that pace these corridors. I chalk it up to whatever is going on with me, but I'm thankful for it. It gives me hope. Couple that with the wolf howls Buck heard recently, and I refuse to give up and close my eyes.

Buck nods and moves to the bars. Placing his massive hands at chest height, he begins to pull them apart. I smell flesh cooking as he grunts and struggles. Moving closer, I see smoke curling through his fingers gripping the bars.

"Buck! Stop!" I try to pull him back but am not strong enough.

His concern for me stops him. His hands are ruined from the silver coating the bars, and the bars are barely bent. He'll lose his hands before he can get the bars wide enough for either of us to escape.

Without hesitation, I offer him my wrist.

"No. I'll be fine." Buck turns his head away.

"No, you fucking won't. I need you at a hundred percent."

"It's just my hands."

"That you can fucking see the bone in now. I'm ordering you to drink, Sergeant." It's dirty to pull rank, but I don't know how else to convince him.

He frowns. "I'm not drinking anymore blood. The calvary's coming." Buck motions up, as if he is pointing to the werewolf howls.

"They're not here yet. And what makes you think Marco won't turn you against them?"

"Even more reason for me to have ruined hands, now isn't it." He wriggles his hands then winces in pain at his destroyed fingers.

Unamused, I play dirtier and scratch open one of the barely sealed bite wounds. The scent of blood will force his beast forward.

Buck's eyes widen, and he hisses at me like a cat before sinking his fangs in.

I whimper as I experience his ire at my actions. That's my punishment for forcing him to feed. I don't blame him.

I blame myself for failing to protect him.

He quickly licks over my wrist and then pulls me into a tight hug. "You have to stop doing that, Tabitha. What happens if I can't control myself?"

"Then you turn me and we're together forever?" I chuckle against his shoulder.

His laughter relieves the tension of how seriously fucked we are, and I nestle into his strong arms.

"Yeah. Then you have to call me Daddy." His chest still rumbling with mirth.

"You would like it too much."

"I am sure he would. Now, step back, little Buck." Marco says from right behind me.

Buck stiffens, and our gazes meet. The fury that blazes in his eyes doesn't match the action of him gently easing me from him and turning me to face Marco.

As I feared, he cannot resist Marco's commands. I purposely look at Marco's shoulder, not his face.

"Oh, little one, it doesn't matter what you do. All that matters is that you give me your power."

Fury fills me, and the heat in my core is like a volcano priming to erupt. Marco's fangs sink into my neck, and I moan with the pleasure forced upon me. My eyes flutter open to stare at Buck who's trembling with his own rage as he helplessly watches Marco feed from me.

Marco pulls me into his embrace and sucks harder. My heart beats slow. Black spots fill my eyes and time stops.

*I told you I'd get you out of this, darlin'.*

Jackson Pruitt steps out from behind Marco.

*You're doing such a bang-up job.*

My response is sarcastic.

*Actually, I'm doing quite the bang-up job. You see, darlin', Marco wanted to let go of you about one heartbeat ago. And I... Well... I needed you to die.*

*How does that help me?*

*'Cause I need that scary version of you to come out and play. As much as I hate doing this to you, it's the fastest way to wake you up. At least, that's what Marco thought before I killed him. And seein' as I'm not in your head to piss you off...*

*Asshole.*

Blackness clouds my vision and I feel weightless with the last of my life being drained by Marco. I don't have time to process the confusion caused by Jackson's response.

I go limp and open my eyes to find myself floating in space above an altar. The black sky glitters with stars. A woman stands before me, terrifying, majestic, and comforting all at once.

"Child of mine, you are in quite a predicament."

"Child?"

"Yes. Child. Do you not feel the wrath of vengeance in your veins?" She waves her hand dismissively.

"No. What I feel is annoyance that no one will fucking talk to me straight. Cut the bullshit. Who the fuck are you?"

Mirth crosses the woman's face. "You are definitely one of mine. You already know who I am, deep down."

"No. No I do—."

I pause, suddenly remembering Bobbi's cabin in Tennessee. The entire scene shifts there, only I'm looking at it from the outside. My body is asleep on the couch. The strange woman sits next to me, facing Jack.

Bobbi's voice fades in. "It is time, Jack Talbett, to ask your questions three."

Jack frowns and thinks for a minute before asking, "Can

I trust you?"

The strange woman speaks, but the words come from my sleeping mouth. "So long as you are worthy."

"Are you a danger to me and mine?"

"Only if you are judged unworthy."

"Will you follow my orders?"

I smirk in my sleep, then respond. "As much as I do already."

I roll my eyes, annoyed. "This is great but doesn't tell me shit. Who the fuck are you?"

"I am Tisiphone, the avenger of murder. The executioner of vengeance. I am the judge of what lies in the heart of man."

Bobbi snaps her attention in my direction. Can she see me standing in this corner like a peeping Tom?

Jack turns to see what she's looking at but shakes his head when he turns back to my sleeping form.

Bobbi speaks to me. "Finish your questions three, or you can never be."

Jack counts on his fingers verifying how many questions he asked, his brow furrowed in confusion.

I look at my sleeping self. "Okay. That's who the fuck you are. Who the fuck am I, then?"

"My daughter."

"Nope. Nuh-uh. I have a mother and father, and neither are you."

Silence reigns over the room for several beats before I realize I have not asked another question.

"Can I save Buck?" my voice is timid and I chew on my lower lip.

Tisiphone rises from the couch and comes to me, embracing me like a mother. "You already have, dear child. Now, all you have to do is open your heart to what was already there, and you will find the strength to finish what you have started."

She kisses my forehead, and I'm ripped back to the cell where this dirty fucking vampire has his fangs gum deep in my neck.

My eyes fly open, and the room blazes in blue fire. Unquenched righteous anger fills me and my skin itches as I burn to life, forcing the vampire to stumble back. When I turn my vengeful gaze upon him, Jackson Pruitt gives me a lopsided grin.

"Have I ever told you how beautiful you are with those wings?"

I blink in surprise as Jackson's entire life flashes before me, all his transgressions, all his good deeds. I see everything from the moment he was born until today. His time to weigh his existence had come and I'm the one who determines his fate.

"You have been judged and found worthy." My voice sounds foreign to my ears as I speak in tongues.

Reaching forward into the chest of the vampire, I pull the soul fragment of Jackson Pruitt out, freeing him from his prison. I fling the skin I ripped off of Marco's body to the ground, blessing him with my protection.

"You are now free, Jackson Pruitt. Do not squander my blessing."

I turn my back to him, leaving the flesh to form a body to house his soul.

My gaze falls on the fileted mass of Marco de Santi. Once again, visions of his entire life flash before my eyes. Everything from Marco's childhood as a slave, to the bloody massacres under Countess Báthory's guidance plays like a movie in my head. All the terror and fear he has reigned with for hundreds of years smother any hints of good deeds he may have done.

Him creating the drug, Kiss, purposely wanting to enslave and destroy the supernatural world reveals itself. The last vision I see is him turning Buck to torture me. This image is seared in my mind forever and is the straw that breaks the camel's back. The lack of humanity is evident in this beast.

"You have been judged and found unworthy."

He shrieks and collapses to the ground as his slowly regenerating flesh burns with my vengeful fire. As soon as it begins to regenerate it ignites and burns him all over again. I leave his screaming body on the floor as I turn to the person who matters the most to me.

I blink and nothing happens. I blink again and still, nothing. No flashes of memories. No resounding urge to judge him.

*You said I could save him!*

*You did, child. You kept him from becoming a monster.*

*No! Turn him back!*

"Fire wings, huh?" Buck grins at me as he pulls me from my ranting at Tisiphone. "So, what? You're some kind of Phoenix now?"

"Fury," I deadpan.

"Okay. Think you could do something about the bars, Miss Fury?" Buck holds his hands up in surrender, still grinning at me like a fool.

I smirk as I face the bars and part them like they're Play-Doh. It's addictive to be unstoppable. This is why supernatural creatures grow mad with power.

"Remind me not to piss in your Wheaties." Buck chuckles as we step through.

Once through, I whirl to face Buck and pull him into a brutal kiss.

His lips eagerly devour mine, and he slams me against the wall, pressing his body to pin me.

Breaking our kiss, "As much as I would love to fuck you stupid, we gotta find Jack and Trevor. You get Trevor. I'll get Jack."

"Shouldn't we stick together?"

"I don't know how long this new you is going to last." He waves his hand around in the air. "So, we should make the most of it. You use your superpowers and I'll use mine. Together, we'll bump back." He holds his fist up.

I laugh as Buck tries to make the best of this situation. He has a point. If we only rescue one because I lose my power, we'll never forgive ourselves. I bump his fist and quit arguing.

He pulls me into another crushing kiss. His voice is reverent when he speaks again.

"I love you." Then he leaves, heading further into the dungeon.

"I love you too, you big oaf," I murmur to the fading shadow of his back.

## DIVIDE & CONQUER

Buck stalks down the corridor. The dim lights from where he and Tabby had been kept are gone. Any soul in this area is suffering. He hears their hearts beating rapidly in fear as he passes.

The scent of blood is heavy in the air, and it's all Buck can do to keep from stopping and feeding. The beast within roars for the sanguine liquid and the power and wholeness it brings.

Still high on Murphy's blood, he resists the temptation, just barely. He didn't have the heart to tell her that her blood only made him lust for more. That sick fuck had intended to keep her as a fucking buffet by using him. If he could bring him back to life to kill him again, he would. But with Marco's death, all his power transferred to Buck. It won't matter much longer anyway.

Buck tilts his head in suspicion, staring at a dead-end

wall. To the human eye there's no door. Stepping closer, he puts his hand against the stone and is surprised to find his hand passes through.

He wishes he had his explosives to blow this fake wall away. Then again, he smells Jack on the other side and blowing it up would kill the man. With a frown, he tentatively steps through.

Normally, he would come in roaring like a lion. His size alone was enough to terrify anyone when he lived. Now, as a vampire, he is massive and oozes a menacing presence. One so large, the two vampires feeding on Jack stop to look at him.

Buck rushes forward without a word and punches the first vampire. The second one leaps on him, but Buck throws him against the wall like a cartoon. The walls shake, and the three collide in a blur of limbs and fangs.

Buck roars as he rips the head off the first brother. The other sinks his fangs into Buck's shoulder, causing Buck to hiss in pain. He pulls the vampire around like a cat who has latched on. They continue their waltz of death around the room until Buck finally snaps the vampire's neck, following it by ripping his head clean off.

Bloody and radiating with Murphy's fury blood, he pants as he scans the shadows for any remaining foes. All he finds is Jack.

Jack is hanging, restrained to a St. Andrew's Cross.

The blood covering Jack causes Buck to hesitate approaching him as the beast inside craves to be fed. Jack's heartbeat beats like a drum corps in Buck's ears. He looks away to keep from losing the hunger battle. Instead, he looks for the restraint keys to free his commander.

"I'm Major Jack Talbett, U.S. Army. Serial Number 85674291," Jack slurs.

The keys stick out of the ash pile of the first brother, and Buck snatches them up without caring he disturbed the ashes. He clenches his jaw and works to release his commander. Once he has Jack free of the cross, Buck hoists him over his shoulder. "I got you, Sir."

It takes all his resolve to not bite Jack with his heart beating so close. If Buck could cry, he would. He failed his team, and they have all suffered for it. He can only hope Murphy finds Trevor in time.

Upon exiting the cell, he sees the wolves rushing in. He tosses the keys at the first one and keeps stalking forward, hoping they don't attack him.

The wolves stare at the hulking man walking out of the dungeon with one of the soldiers over his shoulder. His scent confuses them and frightens them at the same time. They keep pace with him, but keep out of his reach, unsure.

******

I don't look back once I start out of the dungeon. It will only make me chase after Buck. Dread filled me as he walked away.

Why couldn't I judge him? I gave Jackson a second chance at life. Was Buck not worthy of a second chance? Tisiphone's bullshit doesn't help either. I don't accept that fate for Buck. If Jackson Pruitt gets another fucking chance, so does he.

A million questions about my abilities with no answers flood my mind. Everything is different now, and all I feel is rage and helplessness.

Every vampire I encounter as I rise from the dungeon cells becomes a pile of ash with a thought. My body burns, and my divine power radiates light like an angel of death as I stalk toward my prize.

The hallways up here are quiet. I have a vague memory of being here before I woke in the cell with Buck. These are bedrooms, I realize.

The first door I try is empty, but Marco's scent is everywhere. My scent is faint in this room as well. The briefest flashes of passion burn behind my eyelids. I growl and slam the door closed, disgusted he assaulted me and made me like it.

A young girl's shriek of anger snaps me from my maelstrom of emotions.

"He's mine! Mine!"

A girl flies out of a room no more than twenty feet from where I stand, shattering the closed door she came through.

"You thieving harlot! Father gave him to *me!* You cannot have him!"

I prowl forward, my curiosity piqued. Only Trevor could cause vampires to turn on themselves. I half expect to see him grinning in the room the door destroyer scurries back into. What I find is an ornately decorated room and three teenage girls snarling at each other.

"You get everything! I should get him. You had the last one." Two of the three girls get in each other's faces.

"That you murdered!" The tallest girl shoves the first girl.

"Father said to share him." The third tries to wedge between the two.

"Stop being stupid. Only one of us can turn him."

"Then it should be me. He likes me most. I look like his girl." The third girl preens.

"The one he was supposed to kill?" The other two say in

unison, rolling their eyes in annoyance.

"But he didn't! He kissed me!" She stomps her foot.

Screaming ensues from the other two in their jealous rage.

I cross my arms and lean against the door. They might kill each other for me, making my job easier. Then I see Trevor.

The walls crack on impact. Beautiful decorations are shredded to pieces. Furniture buckles under them. I ignore all of it as I keep my attention on Trevor.

His heart is barely beating, and he is bleeding. The vengeful fire blazes anew with his state. I look at the three who finally notice my presence. Their squabble ends as they spread out encircling me.

I push off the door and stand to my full height. My wings flare out in flickering flames of death, causing radiant light to fill the room.

"Sorry, girls. He's all mine. You have been judged unworthy."

With the flick of my hand, they shriek in horror as they turn to stone from the inside, leaving three beautiful statues in place. Their vanity immortalized.

I rush to Trevor's side and whimper as his life flashes before me. His misdeeds as a boy, the defining moment that made him the man he is today, regret, guilt, and all that is Trevor lays before me. Tears fill my eyes as this means he's at death's door.

"You have been judged and found worthy." My voice is foreign again.

I touch his forehead, and he heals enough to stabilize. With little effort, I pull him up over my shoulder. I'm eager to meet back up with Buck before he does something stupid.

Passing between the statues, I'm greeted by a small group of werewolves. Their snarls and positioning tell me they won't let me walk out of the room with Trevor.

My body pulses with the divine power as two of them leap on me. I turn my back to them, crouching to lay Trevor on the ground. When the wolves collide with my wings, they're flung away. I try not to kill them, but the force with which they hit the walls renders them unconscious.

I stand and face the remaining wolves with my hands out. "We are on the same team."

They respond with confused snarls.

Even to my ears, I'm speaking in tongues. As my frustration builds, my wings strengthen and burn brighter.

The wolves spread out, but don't attack. The way their eyes gloss over alerts me to them mind-linking. The room falls silent as we stand off. I teeter on the balls of my feet, uncaring that I'm naked in front of them.

They keep their lycan form, distrusting of me. Throwing two of their kind against the walls didn't help. As I look from one to the next, I don't get flashes of their lives, thankfully. The massive beasts part and in struts a perfect specimen of werewolf.

He has to duck to enter the doorway, but his presence fills the room much like I did minutes earlier. Coming to his full height he is over seven feet tall. His gray fur is speckled with blood and his eyes pierce mine in judgment.

I lift my chin in defiance and square my shoulders, showing no fear.

In the blink of an eye, he shifts from the massive gray beast to the handsome Jasper Coeh. He holds his hands up and speaks gently, "We're all on the same side, right

Lieutenant Murphy?"

I laugh at this big bad scary werewolf Alpha talking to me like he would a toddler and relax.

*We're safe. We're going to go home.*

"We are. Tell your people to stand down."

Another of them shifts into human form and she barks at Jasper in Spanish. "She fucking threw two of ours against the wall! She's not human. What the fuck is she? You're just going to trust her?"

I open my mouth for something witty in retort when Jasper growls at her. The noise is low and menacing, and the aura he radiates makes the entire room bare their necks in submission. "Drag their sorry asses out of here. Lieutenant, I'm taking your friend there," he motions to Trevor, "so I appreciate you not harmin' anymore of my wolves."

I nod.

His eyes glass over for a brief second. He then cautiously steps forward to pick up Trevor.

My eyes never leave him as I follow him carrying my teammate.

The other wolves gather up their fallen brothers, and the entire entourage makes its way out of the compound. I hope they haven't encountered Buck and killed him. If I ask, it alerts them to him being a vampire.

# HOME IS WHERE THE HEART IS

It's still dark when we reach the surface. The sky has turned the slight hue of gray blue to hint the sun will rise soon. Some wolves ready the area for the helicopters while others tend to Jack and Trevor.

My eyes dart from one person to the next, looking for Buck. My heart hammers in my chest, and I struggle to remain calm, thinking they may have killed him. Tears cling to my lashes, and my lip quivers. After all this, I'll never forgive myself if he was murdered while rescuing Jack.

A blur of movement catches my eye near the garage. A quick scan to see no one else noticed, and I move carefully to follow it. If it's not Buck, then it's a vampire trying to escape, and we can't have that. The grass is soft under my bare feet as I follow the blur. I stop when it stops and turns into Buck, looking at me.

Relief washes over me, and I glance over my shoulder again to make sure no one is following before I hurry to catch up to him.

The power wanes when I reach him. My wings dissipate into the ether, and I no longer feel like a volcano waiting to erupt. "Where are we headin', Champ?"

Buck gives me a big goofy smile. "Somewhere a little more private." He takes my hand as we continue to walk.

As tired and weak as I suddenly feel, I'm not saying a damn word. My fingers lace into his and I lean against his arm.

We pass through the trees until we reach a clearing with a fallen tree. Buck guides us to sit on the trunk and pulls me in close.

"You know I love you, right?"

"Yeah? I love you, too."

A genuine smile creeps over his lips. "Took you long enough to realize it."

"No. Nuh-uh. I knew I loved you the first time we fucked."

Buck laughs. "Whatever. You know you're going to be okay, right?"

"We both are." I narrow my eyes at him. My pulse quickens and I cling to him tighter, as if he is trying to get away from me, even though he hasn't moved a muscle.

"We both know I can't stay like this. This is no way to live. I'm not a monster."

"No, you're not. Which is why we're going to figure it out together."

Buck's sweet smile fades into a somber look. He reaches down and brushes a blood-crusted lock of hair back from my eyes. "Tabby, we both know there's no coming back from this. This is a one-way ticket and mine's already been punched.”

“No! No! I can bring you back.” I push away from him to face him again. Blinking in rapid succession to try and trigger seeing his life.

“At what cost?”

“I did it in the cell for Jackson! I’ll do it for you.”

Buck winces and shakes his head no. “I’m not sure what you did back in that cell, but I definitely don’t want to experience that torture from you.”

I realize once I freed Jackson Pruitt and put him under my blessing, no one could see him until he is safe. “No. Buck. Listen. I *can* do things. Even bring people back from the dead. I saved Trevor. Please. We have to try.”

“This is my choice. I don’t want to put you through all that pain and torture. If it fails, it’ll just make me more of a monster and will crush you. I’ll be damned if I let that happen.” He juts out his jaw and snorts, like a donkey digging in.

“It won’t fail,” I say with such conviction I even believe myself. “I can’t lose you, Buck.”

“Tabby, we both know that in war you lose those closest to you. At least this time you have a chance to say goodbye. Just... Enjoy the sunrise with me, please?”

I can’t stop the tears that flow and shake my head. I try to call on the power inside again. But there’s no rage. No furious righteousness. Nothing. When I look at Buck, it’s just his big, beautiful smile looking back at me.

*This isn’t freedom! He’s going to die! Why can’t I save him?*

*You did save him. You gave him the chance to atone. He is choosing the path of death. Would you keep him to satisfy your own selfish needs?*

*He wasn’t fucking guilty! He is a victim. Help me save*

*him. He's all I have!*

Silence greets my mind, and I sob against Buck. His strong arms enclose me and pull close.

To my surprise, his heart's beating. His arms around me are warm, chasing off the morning chill. I realize he is putting all his power into the illusion of being alive one last time.

"Take care of my brothers, will ya? Don't let 'em join the Night Rangers. Try not to kill Carla." He gives me a boyish grin.

I puff up a little. "I might just have to judge her ass."

"Oh, Tabby." He's chuckling as he brushes the same unruly curl back from my face. "You're so fucking beautiful. This isn't what I wanted for us."

"So, stay and make it up to me," I plead.

"I would if I could, Tabitha. But you know me. I have to go out on my own terms." His voice grows timid. "I truly am sorry about New York."

"Fuck New York," I whine. "Please don't leave me alone. Please."

"You *will* be okay. And I'll always be with you, Tabby. You're my girl."

He kisses me to silence further protests.

As the sun rises over the horizon, panic fills me. There's no place to hide him. Not even the shade of the surrounding jungle would protect him. He's too young a vampire, even if he did want to try. His chosen path is shattering my heart.

"You really are a damn stubborn idiot, you know that?"

"Yeah, but I'm *your* damn stubborn idiot."

He tenderly kisses me again and cups my cheek, brushing his thumb over it. The sun hits the clearing, and his body begins turning to ash.

"Goodbye, Tabitha."

His eyes never leave mine as he becomes a cloud of ash and is blown away by the breeze.

I drop to my knees and sob. The wailing sounds fill the clearing. It's the ugly crying as I try to cling to any bit of him left. The sun covers me like a cruel blanket.

"Darlin'," Jackson calls gently. "What are you doin' out here? You alright?"

I look up to see him standing cautiously at the edge of the clearing, dressed in what must be scavenged clothing from the ashed vampires. He sets his small satchel down as he gingerly approaches.

"I'm fine." I hiccup as the tears continue flowing.

"Uh, you don't look fine, darlin'. You want a hug?" He opens his arms in invitation. He looks awkward and cautious, like he's afraid I might burn him alive.

I laugh bitterly at how delicate he's being with me. He's terrible at this. I shake my head no and wipe the tears off my cheek, along with the snot bubbles.

He fishes out a handkerchief from his bag and hands it to me. The fine silken cloth is gaudy with its embroidered gold M in the corner. I further wipe my face and blow my nose before I offer it back.

"All yours, honey. I'm good. You sure you don't want a hug?"

I sigh. I do want a hug, but not from him. "You should get out of here before Jasper picks up your scent."

"About that. Don't know what you did to me, but I literally shook my dick at him, and he didn't even so much as blink."

I snort in laughter, imagining that scene.

"See, now you're thinkin' about my dick." Jackson gives me a smooth smile.

I roll my eyes and take a jagged breath as the tears threaten to flow again.

"Whoa. Hey. I was just jokin'." He braves the small distance between us and pulls me into an awkward embrace. The fear radiating off him is making me nauseous.

I chuckle and hug him in return.

"As fun as this has been, I'm gonna head North. You wanna tag along?"

"No," I say as I ease back. "I have a ride." The brush cracks as someone approaches.

"And that's my cue to exit, stage right." He shoots me a finger gun, snatches up his bag, and pauses at the tree line. "By the way. Never did get a chance to say thank you. Maybe when you come to see my dick, I'll thank you properly." He winks and vanishes.

Seconds later, Jasper enters the clearing, wearing a pair of boxers. He gently lays a hand on my shoulder.

"I'm sorry he's gone." His voice is gentle, and I wonder how he knows. "I hate to rush ya, but the choppers are gonna be here any minute. And as pretty as you are, my wife would kill me if she saw you like this." He offers a small bundle of clothes.

"Thanks," I mutter. As I unfold the dress, I laugh and make a show of putting on the child-sized garment that barely covers my ass. If he was trying to make me decent, he failed miserably.

"Well, at least your tits are covered." He scoops me up and winks. "Hold on tight."

Then he takes off at a dead run, much faster than I would be in my current state. I must look like I'm about to pass out if he feels the need to carry me.

I stare at the clearing until the jungle swallows it from

sight. The dull roar of the helicopters drowns out all other sounds as we approach.

Jasper and his wolves hand the three of us off to the medics for our free ride home.

As soon as we are off the ground and truly safe, I give up trying to be the strong one, joining Jack and Trevor in blissful unconsciousness.

# WITH FRIENDS LIKE THESE

October 2006 - Night Ranger Base

The initial sessions with Doc Ford were not so bad. They started as standard grief counseling and psyche evals. Doctor Ford appeared sympathetic. She brought comfort in my grief over Buck and gave me great advice for dealing with Trevor and Jack.

The mission forever changed the three of us. Jack and Trevor don't know Buck was turned, just that he didn't survive.

The two of them have been much slower in their physical recovery than me. Every day for the past twelve months, I have visited them. We talk together, eat together, and I go to physical therapy for moral support. Even after a year, none of us are cleared for anything, including desk duty.

I've seen this before. Anyone kept this long in medical is retired.

The downside of the Night Rangers is you can't make a lifelong career out of it. Unless you're Armstrong that is. I'm still not sure how he does it. Human minds and bodies were never meant to manage the trauma caused by supernaturals. In our group sessions, we talk about what we'll do with our lives after we get out.

Jack plans to go back to Savannah and live a quiet life.

Trevor wants to find his baby's mamma. I doubt he'll succeed, as she was put into wit-sec over ten years ago, but I wish him luck. He's struggling with survivor's guilt.

We all are.

I didn't think it was weird they never asked me what I'll do when I get retired. At least not for the first six months of sessions. Then I started paying attention.

Doc Ford handles Jack and Trevor differently. She encourages them to let go of their military training and to relax. She talks about job ideas that fits their skills and gives them medication to help cope with the night terrors. Jack specifically. He endured more torture than Trevor and me. We catch him muttering his tag number when he gets stressed.

But with me, the questions are not about integrating back into civilian life. Each session, she pushes harder and harder to learn about my abilities.

I don't know what to tell her. Sure, I know I'm a fury, descended from Tisiphone, the Fury of Vengeance. I also know that her prodding doesn't trigger the rage, like Jackson or Marco did.

I have not once seen my wings since Bogotá. I know I have the powers. They bubble just beneath the surface, ever watching, but I don't know how to activate them, or how to control them. It's all instinct and necessity.

So, here we are, twelve months later, and all I want to do is punch Doc Ford with her clipboard until she quits clicking that fucking pen and asking me asinine questions.

"Lieutenant," her voice draws me from my irritated fog.

"Doctor."

"Do you think today is the day you will show me how your abilities work?"

"Is today the day I become a circus monkey?" I teeter with a singsong to my voice, like a circus monkey.

"We have gone over this before. Without knowing what your abilities truly are, we cannot make a proper assessment."

"By we, we mean you. I'm still Murphy. Still the girl who makes the runes and does the support thing for the team. I would think after twelve months of nothing, you would realize it was divine intervention that helped us."

"Well, if divinity is willing to intervene on your behalf once, it has done it more... so. Case in point, defeating a were-bear in a boxing match."

"Oh, for fuck's sake! I got lucky." I throw my hands in the air.

"I would disagree. Now that you are aware of your divine powers, it stands to reason that you manifested them to defeat the creature."

"Yeah. Against a creature. Are you telling me you're a creature, Doc?"

"So," she leans forward with enthusiasm, "is that what needs to happen? We need to produce something you are threatened by before we see a manifestation of your abilities?"

"You're the doc. I'm not a freak show."

"You are claiming you have not tried to manifest your

abilities at all since your last mission?”

“Nope.” I pop the P for emphasis as I smoothly lie to her.

Doctor Ford clicks her pen as she lets the fallacy hang between us. Her schoolmarm look suggests she’s not buying what I’m selling.

I’m not as smooth as I thought.

“Okay, fine.” I dramatically sigh, “I tried to see my wings.”

“Did they manifest?”

“No,” I mutter. My eyes cast to the hem of my shirt as I fidget with it. Sadness threatens to send me into a blubbering mess as I’m reminded of failing to manifest my powers to save Buck.

“What method did you attempt?”

“Fuck, I don’t know, Doc. I clicked my heels three times and thought about home.”

“Does not have active control over abilities.” She notes it on her paperwork.

“I wouldn’t say I don’t have control.” I get defensive.

“Then you do have control?”

“Well, no. Yes. Wait. Fuck.” She has me so frustrated I want to cram that clipboard down her throat again.

“It’s a simple question, Lieutenant. Do you, or do you not, have active control of your abilities.”

Standing in his office, General Armstrong watches the live feed. Tabitha’s after-action report told him everything he needs to know about her and what happened in Bogotá. Impressed the team completed the mission, he also lost three good Rangers. Four, if they cannot gain insight to Lieutenant Murphy’s abilities.

He has yet to determine what to do with her.

He ordered Ford to pressure her to see how she reacts. His concern for waking the fury abilities is low. Often the

Furies are misunderstood. They're the judges, juries, and executioners of monsters, not the average man.

His bigger concerns are the lingering effects of the trauma from the past two years. Will she be able to function among humans undetected? Can she withstand the vampire's siren song? What happens when a teammate is sent to their judgment, and she is the one standing as their grim reaper?

He is forming a plan to use her against the others in the program. He can weed out those who have fallen prey to the powerful call of supernatural abilities.

She could be useful for bolstering the troops as well. He can only imagine how fearsome she looks in battle. Not to mention, having a Fury under his thumb is always a positive.

As the two women continue to talk in circles, he observes Tabitha's agitation grow until she finally shoots to her feet and snarls at Doctor Ford.

"Fuck you, and these sessions. I'm not a Goddamn circus monkey. It's not a fucking parlor trick I can just turn on and off. Now, if you're done being a raging cunt, I'll be in my bunk."

The General laughs as she storms out. Her fire amuses him to no end. It reminds him of his daughter, who's also no end of trouble. Pressing the intercom button he says, "Please have Lieutenant Murphy report to my office." He takes his seat behind his desk and opens the Night Rangers file for Lieutenant Murphy.

Her military record sits above this file as he reads over it. He remembers the day he recruited her. How excited and eager she had been to prove herself. Her father was skeptical and while Armstrong had been eyeing one of her brothers, when she walked into the room and asked him how a General got such insane tattoos, he knew she was the right Murphy to recruit.

Armstrong has been the father figure she hasn't gotten from her actual father. The girl lost her mother as a teen while her father was leading ground troops in Desert Storm. Her family fractured after that, taking lines of hating her father to defending him. Her two brothers barely tolerate the man, while she forever seeks his approval.

The request for her transfer sits in the file. Major Talbett had delivered it when they left New York, but Armstrong sat on it on purpose. He was well aware of the relationship between Lieutenant Murphy and Sergeant Buckminster and allowed it because of the team's exemplary performance. Such fraternization will be prohibited in the future.

Guilt weighs on his heart as he looks at the records before him. He knew she was not ready after Italy. Holding her back would have revealed his fondness for her and showed favoritism. The rest of the Night Rangers could never see that.

So, he pushed her out to the wolves, and she proved to be the bigger predator. Now, he'll have to play the villain to keep her from becoming a monster they must hunt.

Any hopes and dreams she had of living a normal life are gone. Having a family would be impossible. She can no longer live freely among the humans to prevent them from knowing about her abilities. He rubs his hand over his face in frustration at what a shitty hand this is for her.

Suppressing her memories would do far more harm than good. Should Lieutenant Murphy prove the threat Ford thinks she is, he'll use that option, but only as a last resort.

"You wanted to see me, Sir?" Tabitha appears in the doorway and hesitates, like a child sent to the principal's office.

"Yes, Lieutenant. Close the door and have a seat." He motions to the chair without looking up.

## WHO NEEDS ENEMIES

I look suspicious at General Armstrong's ambivalence but obey. My gaze flickers down to the files on his desk and frown. By the image paper-clipped to the corner of each file, I know they're my files. I knew this discussion was coming at some point, especially after rage-quitting Ford's last session.

Armstrong looks tired and frustrated. The silence grows longer. That heebie-jeebies feeling I always get from him is tamped down today, like he turned it off on purpose. I break the staring contest first and fidget in my seat.

"How are you doing, Tabitha?"

"Informal first, check. I'm peachy keen, Sir." I give him the standard bullshit answer with a fake smile.

He chuckles. "We both know that's a load of shit, Lieutenant. Be honest with me."

"What do you want me to say, Sir? I've spent the last

year of my life being poked and prodded by that psychopath you call a doctor only to realize she's getting my best friends ready to re-enter society, but not me."

"You always have been quite astute. You are correct. You are not being retired."

"Why the fuck not?" I then add, "Sir."

He laughs and sits up, resuming command posture. "Lieutenant Murphy, unfortunately, you cannot be retired to civilian life because of your awakened abilities. The military has strict protocols regarding the discovery of a supernatural in our ranks. You have been exposed to too many situations and cannot guarantee the safety of those who are unaware."

"Are you fucking kidding me? I'm not safe around civilians?"

"Well, it's fairly simple. You have not shown us you can control and master your abilities. What conclusion are we supposed to draw?"

I grit my teeth as Doctor Ford parrots out of General Armstrong's mouth. My eyes widen at the sudden surge of power welling. I close my eyes and take a few deep breaths to calm down, though I feel it still lingering.

Something about Armstrong is making me want to judge him.

When I open my eyes again, he is staring at me intently. I never want to play poker with this man. He knows how to take bland to a whole new level.

"What about Jack and Trevor? They can't do this anymore. Please tell me they're out."

His expression softens, and he nods. "They're human, Tabitha. It has always been given that they would be discharged on medical disability. I had hoped for a few more years from Shadow Squad. I'm relieved that we only lost one of you."

I tear up at the mention of Buck despite my best efforts to refrain from doing so. Clenching my jaw, I wipe my tears away on my sleeve.

Armstrong sits like a statue, letting me be a torrent of emotional fuckery alone. I clear my throat and force myself to calm down for a second time.

"I'm human too." I sulk.

"No, Lieutenant, you are meta-human. You have never been human. We altered your medical records to allow your team to comfortably integrate with you. We assumed you were a Half Divine un-awakened."

"But I'm not a Half Divine. I'm a Fury."

"You are a descendant of a Fury, making you Half Divine. There's more divinity out there than the Hebrew God. Furies are divine in the Greek and Roman Pantheons."

I rub my temples. This cannot be happening to me. "You're going to keep me prisoner here forever?" Panic fills my voice.

"No. You are not a prisoner. You are a soldier. Your life will not change regarding your freedom. You will be granted leave like normal, to allow you to live your life as best as you can, but you will always be a Night Ranger. When you can no longer work in the field, you will be assigned a desk job."

"You cannot fucking keep me in the military. I'll just put in my papers and not re-up!"

"Who do you think is in charge of your paperwork? If it's not approved, you would be considered AWOL."

"You can't do this to me. It's not fair. I've given you everything!"

"I agree it isn't fair, Tabitha. But what happens when

you lose your temper with someone at the grocery store?"

"I wouldn't fucking hurt anyone!"

"Are you absolutely certain of that? According to Ford, you don't even know how your abilities work."

"Oh, for fuck's sake. Sir, I would *never,* and I mean never, hurt a person because they irritated me. It doesn't work like that."

He crosses his arms, "So you're telling me that if you found... Say a stranger in the grocery store, who's an at large serial murderer that hadn't been caught by the police yet, and you judged him unworthy, you would not strike?"

I freeze. I don't know what would happen. The more Armstrong talks, the more fearful I become that I'm out of control. I had no idea what it was when I fought Gunther.

His tone softens, "That reaction is why I want you to stay. Tabitha, we can help you grow and learn how to control your abilities. You can still save the world. You can protect Jack and Trevor properly. You can honor Buck's memory. If there was any way to let you go live in peace, I would do it. You have my word."

I sink in defeat into the chair as my whole life crumbles before me. "Yes, Sir," I murmur.

"If we are to follow Doctor Ford's recommendations, you would be working in her division. She is here to help you and isn't the enemy, Lieutenant. I expect you to find a way to, at minimum, humor her requests so we all better understand your capabilities. Without that knowledge, it makes it impossible for me to defend letting you into the field." He pauses and frowns. "We both know your talents would be wasted behind a desk."

"Yes, Sir."

"Good. Now, I know it feels like all your plans have been

thrown into disarray, but you still have leave. You will be using it to go to Sergeant Buckminster's funeral."

"Yes, Sir," I reply again, choosing not to fight and lose any potential privileges. He is choosing the carrot over the stick, but there's no getting out of my life as a Night Ranger.

He rifles through the stack of reports next to my personnel file to retrieve my after-action report for Bogotá.

"One last thing, Lieutenant." He flips it open and begins to read, "The enemy, Marco de Santi, triggered the awakening of my latent supernatural abilities by draining me to the point of death." He tosses the pages down and leans back to stare at me.

"Explain to me, Lieutenant, how a creature that old and powerful, makes that amateur of a mistake."

I swallow hard, not wanting to mention Jackson Pruitt. I had carefully crafted my entries to allow all the oddities Jack and Trevor likely reported to be chalked up to being a Fury.

Armstrong's penetrating gaze holds mine in silence for more minutes than I care to count before I finally break. "Jackson Pruitt, Sir."

His expression turns from concerned grandfather figure to menacing warmonger in no time flat. He sits up and clasps his hands in front of him on the desk. "You are saying you failed the mission in New Orleans?"

His question confirms the off-the-books murder of a U.S. citizen came from our very own General. "No, Sir. We succeeded in New Orleans."

"Then how did Jackson Pruitt cause Marco de Santi to make a mistake? Why did you lie on your after-action report of New Orleans?"

"I didn't lie, Sir. At the time of the report, we believed we had eliminated him. It was not until after, that he made his presence known in my head."

"How does a vampire get into one's head without one knowing it?"

I grin as Jackson doesn't even know. When his life flashed before my eyes, I gained the truth of my hitchhiker. "He is a mind mage, Sir."

"Is? Lieutenant, are you telling me he is still alive?"

"Yes, Sir."

The range of emotions that wash over Armstrong's face before he pulls the poker face veil down is comical to me. "Is he still a threat to humanity?"

"No, Sir. I guaranteed he would not be. He was judged worthy of a second chance. He was critical to completing the mission in Bogotá. Were it not for him, you would have lost the entire team."

Armstrong sighs. "You know you have brought an extremely hard life to that man. It would have been far kinder to let him die in Bogotá."

"No. It would not. I saw his life and judged. There is no mistake." My voice takes the tongue-speaking tone.

Armstrong's expression hardens. "Be that as it may, that man is a human turned vampire, killed, reborn by wolf, killed again, to be reborn as human."

"Not human, mage."

"There are an untold number of entities out there that are going to cause him extreme duress for the rest of his life."

"Which is why I woke his mage abilities."

"You added fuel to the fire. Yet another reason it's paramount to keep you with us, so we better understand the choices you make."

"No offense, Sir. Jackson Pruitt was a kid in love with a girl. He was sent to his death more than once by her father, only to lose her to the werewolf. He made a lot of bad choices under the influence of Lucien Deveroux. He, of his own volition, chose to fight with us, at great detriment to him. I made the call in the field to give him the fighting chance no one else would. So, whoever ordered you to execute him, is the monster you should be looking at. Not the kid who just wants a picket fence, a pretty girl, and to make fat babies."

He leans back in his chair, assessing me with his critical gaze. He nods.

"I will take it under advisement, Lieutenant. Hand in a corrected report before you leave for the funeral. There will be repercussions if you omit important details such as this again."

"Yes, Sir."

He starts cleaning up his desk.

I don't move, as he has not dismissed me.

When he looks up to see me still sitting there. "Don't you have a funeral to get to? Dismissed."

# ALAS, POOR YORICK

The apartment I shared with the rest of Shadow Squad feels empty and cold as I return to it.

Trevor has already packed and moved his boxes into the moving truck. We haven't spoken to each other outside of therapy in months. The glares he gives me when he thinks I don't notice tells me he blames me for something.

Jack told me to let it go. Trevor will work it out, but I don't buy that. Trevor's hurting, and his mind is all screwed up. He calls for those vampires in his sleep. I turned them to stone. I didn't ash them. Could they be taunting him still?

Jack's things are partially packed. He takes his time and plans to finish after we return. That man projects he is a fucking machine, but I see the pain in his eyes. He won't talk about Marco, or what happened in that cell, other than to say, he didn't give in.

The tension between us is high because I refuse to talk about Buck with him. I just can't do it. I can't bring myself to talk about Buck at all. Even thinking about him right now brings me to tears again.

I walk away from Jack's doorway to my room. All of Buck's things are boxed and sit in my room to prevent them from being shipped to his father and that ungrateful bitch of a stepmother. I promised Buck I would take care of his brothers, and I'll be damned if his things are taken from them.

"You plannin' on packin' when we get back?" Jack's voice comes from the doorway. I hadn't heard him enter.

"Ain't packin', Champ."

"I see. Well, if you're not going to pack. You might as well help me." He jerks his head towards his room.

I nod and follow him across the living room.

A glance at my watch shows me we have a few hours before we have to get dressed and catch the flight on the other side of base.

I silently tape boxes together and gently put his things inside. The time ticks by, and Jack's stoic silence comforts me. When the last box is taped shut, I come around the bed and, without warning, pull him into a hug.

His arms wrap around me. We don't need words to fill the air. His body relaxes, and we just stand there, hugging each other. I'm still not ready to tell him the truth about Buck. Whatever tension was between us, eases with this small gesture.

We part with a nod, and I return to my room to put my dress uniform on. I don't bother with make-up. It will run when I cry, anyway. I can't lock my emotions away like Jack does, and this funeral is like watching Buck turn to ash all over again.

The three of us ride together to the plane and it's a short flight to Arlington. No word is spoken. Whenever I catch Trevor's gaze, he is staring daggers at me. I'm thankful Jack is between us. Jack must notice it too, as I see him nudge Trevor more than once.

The lack of people at the funeral breaks my heart. It's the three of us, Nate, Buck's middle brother, and the veterans that show up at every fallen soldier's funeral to prevent that soldier from being shipped off without a friendly face. I feel the rage well inside that his father isn't here, and that cunt of a stepmother probably prevented Daniel from coming.

Buck is a Goddamn hero, and no one cares he is gone.

My fists clench and everything is too hot. I want to scream and yell at everyone around me and turn them all to stone so they can forever honor him. Tears burn down my cheeks as the chaplain says his kind words. I look to the sky; thankful I'm wearing sunglasses far too large for my face.

Buck's arms slide around me as the breeze blows through the cemetery. The sun shines in the sunset. When I look back down at the casket, Jack's warm hand rests on my shoulder in silent support.

Nate's trying to hold it together, but tears cling to his lashes.

The three-volley salute begins. As the shots ring out, I am hollow and lost. How could Buck ever think I could do this? How could I have been so stupid as to not fight for him in New York? If I had only been honest, this wouldn't have happened. They would have sent him to another team. We would still be together. Everything is my fault, and there's nothing I can do about it now.

The honor guard fold the flag and present it to Nate,

who clenches his jaw in the effort to remain a strong soldier. The boyish features he had that night in Charleston are gone. When he squares his shoulders, he's the spitting image of Buck.

After the service, Trevor walks away without a word. He slams the door closed in the vehicle that brought us here.

Jack and I exchange a glance. He shakes his head before gently pushing me to Nate and heading to the vehicle himself.

Facing Nate, I'm afraid of what he might say. Without a word, he pulls me into the tightest hug I have ever had. His strong arms lock around me, and he buries his face against my neck. His shoulders shake from the sobs he's trying to hide. Though he's not as tall as Buck, I still have to lift on my toes to hold onto him. I rub his back as he works through his emotions.

"He loved you," he rasps.

"I know," I croak.

"He wrote to me and asked me to take care of you if anything happened to him."

I have to laugh at Buck asking this of his twenty-year-old brother.

"Don't laugh. I intend to," he huffs.

"Oh, Champ," I sigh and ease out of our embrace. "I don't need you to take care of me. You got your whole life to live. You're gonna find your own girl and then you'll be done for." I stop him before he can protest. "You keep in touch. If you need *anything* call me. You promise?"

He sniffles and sulks. "Guess that means no comfort sex?"

I laugh harder. "You really are Buck's brother. No. No comfort sex."

He gives me a lopsided smile, and it breaks my heart all

over again. "Not even a comfort blow job?"

I palm his face and push him away, laughing through tears. "No! Jesus, you're just like Buck."

"Only with a bigger dick."

"Why isn't Daniel here?" I change the subject and kill the mood.

"Carla," he says. "That bitch wouldn't let him leave when I went to pick him up."

"You won't have to worry about that cunt much longer. I need you to sign these." I pull out the custody papers for his brother Daniel.

"What are these?" He looks them over and then stares at me in shock. "You're serious? Do you really think my old man will sign these?"

"I do, and he will. Or I'll get Child Protective Services involved. I would take Danny into my home in a heartbeat. But he's *your* brother."

Nate nods once and holds his hand out for the pen. After he signs, I take the papers and pen back. "Where's he going to live? He can't live with me on base. I'm in the barracks."

"You're being upgraded to a family apartment. He'll move in with you until he turns eighteen. Then you two can decide from there."

"You've really thought of everything."

"You're my family. Of course I did." I flash him a grin and give him another hug before we part ways.

When I slide into the back seat of the truck, Jack and Trevor are sitting in silence with their arms crossed. Whatever took place between them didn't go well.

I tuck the papers into my jacket pocket and lean my head against the window to let the coolness rush against my hot cheeks. "Goodbye, you big oaf," I whisper.

## CLEANING HOUSE

Halloween 2006

Back at the base, Trevor drives off without saying goodbye. I help Jack load his truck, and we decide to spend one last night in the apartment together.

At six o'clock, he bangs on my door.

"You're fucking retired. Go back to sleep!" I shout at the door.

His laugh is muffled. "You got thirty minutes, before I'm leavin'."

"Forty-five."

"Twenty."

"One Hour!"

"Fine. Forty-five."

I laugh and get up. I wasn't asleep, anyway. For all my special abilities, nightmares are still a thing.

Armstrong filled me with doubt about doing the right thing for Jackson Pruitt, and every possible horrible ending for him taunts me in my nightmares. I hope he's happy wherever he is and staying out of trouble.

I throw a few days' worth of clothes into a bag with my toiletries and pull my hair into a messy bun without combing it. It feels like old times, like we are getting ready for the next mission. I grab a jacket and make sure I have all the legal paperwork for Danny.

Fifteen minutes after our negotiation, I'm greeted with a cup of coffee in a to-go mug and Jack's grin. We make a final sweep to make sure we have everything before we load into his truck.

"You came in this thing? You're braver than I thought."

Jack grins at the Star Wars reference and pats the beat-up old truck's dash lovingly.

We are stopped at the gate and show our IDs. Jack gets his ID back immediately and is thanked for his service. I, on the other hand, drum my fingers for a good five minutes before they come back with mine. I roll my eyes and thank the young man on guard duty. It's not his fault Armstrong's a dick.

"Ma'am. I'm instructed to remind you that if you are not back on base in five days—."

"Yeah. Yeah. I got it. Gloom and doom await. Thanks."

Jack chortles as we pull through the gate. It only takes him an hour before he turns the radio down.

"Is this where you tell me, since I'm a captive audience, I need to listen to your sage Veteran advice?" I quip.

"Nah. I was just bored, so I was gonna chat. But if you want me to lecture you, I'm sure I could find something to talk about." He grins deviously at me.

I punch him in the shoulder.

His playful expression fades. "I do want to ask you one thing."

Here it comes. He wants to know about Buck. I steel myself for it and tamp down the urge to unlock the door to tuck and roll.

"So, you gonna tell me what really happened to Buck?"

"He died," I whine. "End of story."

"Murphy, we both know there's a hell of a lot more to this story than that."

I look out the window and frown, struggling to find any kind of Night Ranger security clearance protocol bullshit to save me from the truth. When nothing comes to the surface, I sigh. "He was turned," I whisper as if saying it aloud would somehow trigger cosmic doom.

Jack drums his fingers along the steering wheel and gives a small shake of his head. "'Bout what I assumed. Sucks to hear it confirmed. How are you holding up?"

I don't look at Jack. I'm not holding up, and the last thing I want is him to comfort me. I want to feel miserable and lonely. "I'm fine."

Jack laughs hard enough the truck fishtails as if he's going to run us off the road. "I don't think that word means what you think it means, Murphy. But, in all seriousness. You will be fine. Until then, as your ex-CO I order you to not be fine."

I huff. "Yeah, good thing you aren't my CO anymore. Can't court martial me now for telling you to fuck off."

He snorts and drums his fingers again. "Is he still out there?"

"No," I reply without hesitation. "He carried you to safety while I got Trevor out. We spent his last moments watching the sunrise."

"You two always were good for each other. I'm glad he

got to see one last sunrise with you."

For the rest of the trip to Savannah, we avoid the heart wrenching topics. Jack talks non-stop about a stripper named Evie Fontaine. Boy, the stories he tells. Good thing I'm not in the Navy or I would be blushing.

We stop at a rundown building that is Jack's apartment just before lunch and unload. I shake my head at the accommodations and hope it's just temporary.

We make a pit stop at Denny's, his favorite, and enjoy some terrible diner food before we hit the road for Charleston. This stretch of the trip is significantly more somber. Neither of us want to break the peace we have with Buck by talking about what we're going to do.

When we pull into the driveway of his father's home, Jack puts it in park but doesn't kill the engine. "How do we want to play this?"

"I got this."

"Okay, so do you want backup or not?" he holds his hands up showing his confusion in my answer.

I cut him a look and shake my head. "You're the get-away car."

"You know this thing doesn't go that fast on a dime, right?"

"Keep your panties on. I'm going to go in there and have them sign the papers. Tell the kid to pack whatever shit he wants to take with him, and then we're coming out."

"You sure you don't want backup? You know what? I should go with you." He starts to reach for the key.

"You kill that engine, and you will regret it, Sir." I point at him.

He slowly looks at me. "Am I going in, or not?"

"Fine. Whatever." I throw my hands up and get out of the truck.

"You know that's a non-answer, right?" Jack grumbles as he hops out of the truck, leaving the engine running.

We walk up the steps, and I pull out a carton of Newports and a carton of Marlboro Reds before I knock on the door.

"When the hell did you pick up those?" Jack stage whispers.

"When we gassed up."

The door flies open and standing before us is Buck's youngest brother, Daniel.

"Hey, champ," I smile. Taking in his state, I struggle to not crush the cigarettes in my hand.

He sports a black eye and a cut along his jaw.

Before he can respond, I push the door open. "Where are they?"

Daniel stumbles back. Jack is hot on my tail as I storm into the room where his parents are. Carla's on the couch, flipping channels while Buck's father snores in a recliner, the beer in his hand threatening to topple over.

"Danny, go pack your things. Anything you want. If you need help, Jack will help you."

"Whoa. As in Major Jack Talbett?"

As angry as I am, I chuckle at the hero worship in Danny's voice.

Jack grins and nods, motioning the kid up the stairs.

"Remember, they're human." Jack looks pointedly at me before following Danny up.

Once the two of them are upstairs, I face Buck's parents. "Wake up," I growl as I kick the footrest of the recliner.

"What the fuck are you doing here?" Carla shouts.

I throw the Newports at her. "Sit down. Shut the fuck up and pretend like you fucking have a brain cell." There's a scratch in my voice as rage threatens to bubble to the surface. I never take my gaze off of Buck's father.

"I thought I told you that you weren't welcome here." His speech slurs a little from being drunk.

"I don't give a fuck what you said, asshole. I'm here for Danny." I fish out the papers and brandish them at him. "You're going to sign these fucking papers, releasing him to Nate. Or we're going to have a problem."

"I ain't signing shit. Carla get my shotgun."

Jack's voice cuts across the room, "Ma'am I suggest you sit back down and not escalate this situation."

I had not noticed when they came back down.

"Who the fuck are you?" Carla shouts again.

"I told you to shut the fuck up," I raise my arm and Jack grabs my wrist.

"No," is all he says.

I inhale sharply. "Fine." I cut Carla a look. "You're fucking lucky he's here. Now, you, asshole. Sign the fucking papers, or I'm calling the cops for abusing Danny. I'm sure an ER trip will land your ass in jail. Once you sign, you don't have to ever see me again."

I lean down and let the burning rage shine in my eyes. His father takes a swing at me, and I grab his wrist. I don't break it, but I squeeze his closed fist causing the popping sound to warn him I could.

"Don't test me, fuckhead. I'm doing what Buck asked me to do before he fucking died protecting humanity."

I stare at him long and hard while he processes. He takes the pen and papers and, with a shaky hand, signs every place I point to. I snatch the papers back before he can do anything to them. Without a word, I storm out. If I stay, I'm going to kill them both.

Jack catches up with me and laughs as we approach the truck. "I don't think I've ever seen anyone stay in the truck."

"What?" I laugh and look at him.

He motions to where Danny sits in the center of the seat in the cab.

I shrug. "He's a good kid, him, and Nate. Buck loved them very much. Besides, *Major Jack Talbett* told him to stay." My rage subsides and sadness fills me again even though I'm smiling.

"C'mon. I need a drink," Jack pulls me into a light hug before we get into the truck.

"So, I'm movin' in with you, right?" Danny looks at me with hope in his eyes, definitely a Buckminster with that look.

"No, champ. I live on base, and you can't live there. You're going to live with Nate."

"Nate lives on base too."

"Different base. Different clearance."

"But I want to live with you."

Jack and I chuckle.

"Kid. You're adorable. You're too young for me, and your damn brother would haunt me from his grave if I messed around with you. You're going to go live with your brother and finish high school. Then, whatever you want to do, do it. I'll be there if you need me. I promised Buck."

"I had to at least try," he mutters.

Jack laughs hard again. "You're definitely Buck's brother."

# WHEN THINGS GO BUMP IN THE NIGHT

We roll into Savannah just after sundown. The MPs won't be here until the morning to pick up Daniel. Jack takes a shower and dolls up in his best non-uniform clothes. He tells the kid to clean up as well. Jack and I didn't need to have the conversation about checking out the kid; he just closes the door to handle it discreetly.

I'm flipping through solitaire for the third time when they come out of the bedroom. Danny is dressed just like Jack, even styling his hair the same. While Jack usually keeps his hair high and tight, it has grown out a bit. The look suits him, giving him the boyish charm all the girls love.

"Well, shit. I'm underdressed." I grin.

"Oh, where we're goin', there's no such thing."

"Ha ha. You think he can handle that?" I motion to Danny.

"You want to leave him here, so he gets himself into trouble? Instead of us getting him into trouble?"

"Hey! Why do you think I'm going to get in trouble?"

"You're right. He's going with us." I reply. "So, Candyman. What's the occasion?"

"Why did she call you, Candyman?"

"You'll see." He winks.

The three of us pile back into his pickup for the short ride to the strip joint.

The Shooting Star is packed tonight for a costume contest. Not to mention, strippers are everywhere. When we pile out of the truck, Danny's eyes go as wide as saucers.

"Keep your cool, champ, and no one will say a thing with us around."

"This is so fucking cool," he whispers as he heads in the door.

I'm grinning, but it's breaking my heart that this isn't Buck walking in with us. It feels hollow and empty. I'll be damned if I'm going to ruin this kid's first night in a strip club, so I put on the happy face and act like I'm having the time of my life.

We take up residence in our usual spot, chasing off some pervert who was sitting alone. I wave for a round of shots and the topless server nods.

Danny's eyes are glued to her as her tits bounce with each step.

Jack's nervous and keeps rubbing his hands on his thighs. I cock my head to the side, and he's looking everywhere but here. Then it dawns on me that he's looking for Evie Fontaine. Now I'm curious to see the woman that makes Jack Talbett nervous.

I'm not watching the girls, but I know when Evie

Fontaine takes the stage. Jack lights up like a Roman Candle with hearts in his eyes. The clank of shot glasses pulls my attention away and I motion for the server to lean down. "Extra fifty if you teach the kid how to do a body shot."

She grins and snatches Danny's shot up before he can and settles into his lap, nestling the shot glass between her ample breasts.

He looks at me nervously, then back to her.

"Sugah, ya put yer lips around it and suck it up," she coos.

I snort my shot when he absolutely dives into her breasts. Buck would be laughing his ass off at Danny who comes up grinning, covered in Tequila. I pay the nice server and look up to the stage. The whole room erupts into a combination of cheers and jeers as Jack Talbett climbs it.

"Awe, fuck," I mutter and bounce up to rescue him before the bouncers reach him. I pause when the woman, a long-legged, all-American Georgia Peach holds up her hand, effectively halting the attack.

She pulls Jack into the dance with her, stripping him out of his clothes. His shirt hits the floor, and she stops moving, staring at him. I Put a Spell on You blasts over the speakers. The other strippers shake their wares for all they're worth.

Jack's smile is infectious as he drops to one knee, drawing collective gasps from audience and strippers alike. He pulls his tags over his head and pops the chain open to slide a ring off.

"When the fuck did he get a ring?" I mutter.

"Evelyn Fontaine. Would you do me the honor of makin' me the luckiest son of a bitch here and be my wife." Jack's voice booms over the blaring music.

The music cuts off, and everyone goes silent, now staring at the couple on the stage. Before long, Evie's high-pitched squeal cuts through the room.

"Yes! Yes! Oh God! Yes!" She tackles him, nearly toppling them off the stage as she peppers him with kisses.

The room roars in excitement. Music resumes, and the bouncers assist them off the stage so the others can get back to work.

Jack's smile is permanently plastered on his face as he guides Evie to the table.

While I was watching the stage with everyone else, Danny downed all our shots and ordered more.

I wish I could be as happy as Jack looks, but seeing his happiness only makes my heart ache more.

"Who's the kid, Candyman?" Evie's voice giggles over the music.

"I'm not a kid! I did a body shot!" Danny replies in his drunken courage.

We erupt into laughter.

"Oh, sugar. Hey Diamond! Come show my new friend a good time!"

Diamond, a tall and curvy Black woman with electric pink braids, comes sauntering over. "You payin', Evie?"

"Nope! He is!" She points to Jack.

Diamond trails a finger along Jack's jaw when he nods in agreement. "C'mon, darlin'. Let's get to know each other."

Danny's eyes widen, and he quickly bolts out of the chair, not even bothering to check with me.

I fade into the background, enjoying the happiness around me. Evie doesn't leave Jack's lap once. The two of them drink and pop pills like candy.

When Danny finally returns, I pay Diamond for her time and tap Jack on the shoulder.

"Come on, lovebirds. Time to pumpkin."

Jack scoops up Evie and follows obediently. I fish his keys out of his pocket, and he hops into the bed with Evie while Danny climbs into the passenger seat.

I drop them off at his apartment and see them inside safely.

"You ain't stayin'?" he asks. He doesn't really care. He's high as a kite and removing what little clothing Evie still has on.

"Hell no, I'm not stayin' in your one-bedroom apartment while you fuck her brains out. You two have fun. We'll see you in the morning."

"But we could share!" Evie pouts between sucking Jack's face.

I palm my face and pull the apartment door closed. The last thing I want to do tonight is watch two people in love fuck their brains out.

Danny's snoring lightly in the passenger seat when I climb back in. I smile softly at the boy and take us to the motel we usually use when on leave here in Savannah.

"Just you tonight, Miss Murphy?"

"Yeah, Jules. Just me." I pay the man and drive around to the motel room. "C'mon, slugger. A few more feet and you can crash for the night."

"She has diamonds everywhere," he slurs.

"I bet she does."

"And they're chocolate," he grins. "Not pink," he pops the K.

I stare at him, trying to decipher what the fuck he's talking about. Then I shake my head and help him into bed. It's better if I don't know.

"I'm in love," he coos.

I snort. Before I can come back with something witty, he's snoring into his pillow. I get the trashcan from the bathroom and set it next to him. That boy is going to be hurting in the morning.

I flop onto the bed and stare at the ceiling, unable to sleep. The tightness in my chest from pretending to enjoy myself all night is rough. The steady snores are ratcheting me to eleven as all I'm reliving the moment where I nearly cursed his stepmother.

If Jack hadn't been there to stop me, I would have done exactly what Armstrong was afraid of.

"Maybe I should be locked up?"

I realize I'm being dramatic, but it puts working with Ford into a whole new light. I may not understand how my powers work, but I could at least use help controlling when I use them.

How arrogant I have been to think I could be the master of abilities I didn't even know I had until a year ago. Buck sacrificed everything for me. I can't let him down now. The Night Rangers is all I have left of him. So, you know what?

"Fuck it".

I'm going to bump back.

<h1 style="text-align:center">EPILOGUE</h1>

Mardi Gras 2010 - New Orleans

Jackson Pruitt takes his time coming home. With all of Marco's memories in his head, he rewards himself with Marco's fortune. Without identification and a means of travel, he had to plan his way out of Bogotá. True to Lieutenant Murphy's word, he didn't run into a single bit of trouble once until he came back to this God forsaken city, New Orleans.

Shelle-Belle is here. His blood, sweat, and tears went into this bike. He isn't parting with her for anything. He's even willing to risk being found by the Devil, herself, to get this bike.

Mardi Gras is the perfect time to sneak into the city. Every underworld creature is partaking in the merriment without consequence or hiding from the irritating humans partying to excess. He quietly strolls to the bike's storage unit. When he purchased the unit, he paid for ten years up front and took great care not to share its location with anyone.

The sun beats down on the pavement as he rolls the orange door up to reveal the garage bay sized unit. Not only is Shelle-Belle parked in the center, but there's a workbench with tools to take care of her.

Jackson reaches up and pulls his now shoulder-length hair back into a ponytail at the base of his neck. After the few years as a vampire, he forgot how fast his hair grows. The girls seem to like it, so he's left it longer. His skin is tan, leaving him looking like a golden God.

He rubs his hand along his stubbled chin and smiles at

the bike. He's not too proud to admit his boy crush on Shelley Baxter led to the name of his true love before him.

"How ya doin', darlin'? Miss me?" He coos to the bike as he strolls into the garage. Peeling out of his jacket, he gets to work making her run like she's new. He hasn't touched her in years, and women get finicky about things like that.

Shelle-Belle sputters to life after a few tries, and he nods, getting the tools he needs.

When he turns back to the bike, his heart begins to race and fear washes over him. The sheltered garage is as dark as night with shadows blocking any hints of sunlight. This is never a good sign. It can only mean one person. "Louise," he says in his sweet baritone voice, sounding as calm as could be. His heart hammers in his chest.

The urge to fight or flee is strong, and Jackson silently prays whatever invisibility cloak Lieutenant Murphy gave him is still in place. He grips the wrench in hand like a weapon.

Louise saunters toward Jackson, relishing in the thundering heartbeat from his chest. There are so many questions she wants to ask. She had been convinced he was turned to ash by the hunters during hurricane Katrina. When she is close enough to touch him, she leans up and inhales deeply at his neck.

Jackson stands still, unable to even crack a joke about being back. He silently prays she doesn't turn him again. He had forgotten just how much he liked sunshine.

"Très intéressant," she purrs to him in French. She eases back to look up at him, and he closes his eyes.

Laughter is all he hears before he feels the warmth of the sunshine again. Her oppressive shadows are gone when he cracks an eye open. "Come on, Shelle-Belle, we need to get you running, pronto."

Two Days Later - The Triple Six: Savannah, Georgia

Jackson's bike rumbles smoothly as he pulls into the bar where it all began. He remembers the night he got his colors. He had just turned eighteen and stole Shelley's first kiss out back. Now, the building's all new. Guilt fills him for causing the original building to burn down.

Fear keeps him on his bike for a good five minutes before he kicks off and comes strolling in like it's just another Thursday. He stops just inside the door to let his eyes adjust and to take in the new decor.

The bar's still has a honky-tonk feel with that feminine touch. The crack of pool balls echoes in time with the digital chimes of the dart boards. A jukebox sits in the middle of the room, flashing as it plays rock 'n roll music.

His gaze shifts to the bar where he watches Shelley clean glasses behind it. Her beauty still takes his breath away.

Swallowing hard, he takes up residence at a barstool near the door. Just in case shit goes sideways. Another nervous glance, and no one seems to pay him any attention.

There's a drunk in the corner that's obviously a Coeh. He can't remember which one, nor does he really care. He's not there for them. The man looks sound asleep.

"What can I... What the fuck?" Shelley yelps and throws herself back against the wall of bottles behind the bar. "H..h...how are you alive?"

Jackson holds his hands up to show he means no harm. "It's a long story, darlin'. One I ain't gonna bore you with. Not why I'm here. I just came to make amends. What I did to you and yours was wrong. I'm sorry."

Shelley's back stiffens, and she regains her courage. "You said your peace. Now get out of here."

Jackson droops as he had hoped she would forgive him, and they might try to be friends. He misses Lieutenant Murphy. She's the only one in the whole wide world that ever actually gave two-shits about him. Why she thought he should live is beyond him. But he nods, not putting up a fuss.

"Yes, ma'am."

He pushes up off the barstool and forces himself to walk out without saying another word. He wants to tell her he's not the monster she thinks he is.

He knew that was too easy when standing between him and his bike is the massive motherfucker that ripped his head off.

"What the fuck do you want, Coeh?"

Billy Coeh squares his shoulders and crosses his arms. His voice is laced with the growl he can't contain. "Mehzebeen wants a word."

Jackson stiffens. "You tell her I'm leavin' town, and ain't comin' back."

Three other wolves circle around Jackson.

"Let me rephrase. You are going to see Mehzebeen."

"Well, shit."

# BIOGRAPHY

J.R. Froemling was born in Indiana and currently resides in Illinois with her husband (Mr. F). She has a Bachelor of Science in Information Technology, a Master of Arts in English and Creative Writing, and is currently working towards a Master of Science in Marketing.

She got her love of writing in the early 2000s when writing fanfiction for a Star Wars community online. For several years she facilitated the online writing community before branching out to author her own stories.

Want to find out more about J. R. Froemling?

jrfwriting.com